Redemption Has No Limits

By K. L. Ciprianna

Zoe Life
Christian Communications

Copyright © (2019)

Published by:
Zoë Life Christian Communications
P.O. Box 871066
Canton, MI 48187 USA
www.zoelifebooks.com

All rights reserved. No part of this book may be reproduced or transmitted in any form or by any means including, but not limited to, electronic or mechanical, photocopying, recording, or by any information storage and retrieval system without written permission from the publisher, except for the inclusion of brief quotations in review.

All Scripture quotations, unless otherwise indicated, are taken from the *King James Version* (KJV) of the Holy Bible.

Author: By K. L. Ciprianna
Cover Designer: Zoë Life Creative Team
Editor: Zoë Life Editorial Team

2019 1st Edition

Publisher's Cataloging-in-Publication Data

Redemption Has No Limits

Summary: When someone prays, something happens greater than our imaginations.

13 Digit ISBN: 978-0-9995405-7-2, Paper Back, Perfect Bind

Category: Christian Thriller

For current information visit Zoë Life Christian Communications' website visit www.zoelifebooks.com.

Printed in the United States of America

#v2 10-31-2019

Acknowledgments and Credits

First of all, I want to thank my Lord, Jesus Christ and all leaders and ministers who inspired me to write this story. Second, I want to credit my Italian/Sicilian family (you know who you are) and the beauty of this unique culture inspired me to describe Amy's and Will's features as one who looks like my dad's side of the family. My silly brother Chris, who emulates Will in ways as humorous and teasing in the story. I added a few more touches to Will's character. My other brother, Tony, as Byran, is loner and resourceful. My awesome mother who I love dearly and inspired me to never give up and taught me to be strong in life and to never give in.

Thank you to attributing the models: Joe and Eliya to put a face to the characters shown on the front and back of the novel.

Redemption Has No Limits

By K. L. Ciprianna

Table of Contents

Chapter 1	9
Chapter 2	21
Chapter 3	27
Chapter 4	35
Chapter 5	45
Chapter 6	55
Chapter 7	71
Chapter 8	83
Chapter 9	91
Chapter 10	99
Chapter 11	107
Chapter 12	117
Chapter 13	125
Chapter 14	143
Chapter 15	155
Chapter 16	169
Chapter 17	173
Chapter 18	181
Chapter 19	191
Chapter 20	199
Chapter 21	215
Chapter 22	229
Chapter 23	239
Chapter 24	253
Chapter 25	263
Chapter 26	273
Epilogue	279

Chapter 1

A loud clang came from the prison cell door.

"Well!" Officer Johnson exclaimed. "We finally got him, and justice is served! Oooh boy! They will have so much fun with him in this place. He has murdered his family and other people as well. Prisoners don't like teens being touched, especially young children!"

Officer Johnson taunted the prisoner as he spoke to Officer Clayton. "Good old Andrew Bryan Conners, how does it feel to be helpless and stuck in here for life? Because that is what it's going to be, you evil thing!" Both men taunted the prisoner more as they laughed at him.

"This man has been nothing but trouble for the law ever since he was a boy, and his family was a bunch of low lives," Officer Johnson continued. "Everyone knows about his loser family—the dad was a drunk and the mother a druggie. Lord knows, what happened behind closed doors. Evil does beget evil."

Bryan could not speak, but he was boiling with rage as his knuckles went white.

"How dare they talk of my family like that?" He thought in anger. *"Yes, my family needed to pay for what they had done. A memory played in his mind—his was father dragging him by his feet. His head was bumping against the rocks as he

was dragged into the back yard. He felt blood dripping from his ear. He heard his father say, 'After I get done with you, I bet you won't talk any mo' stuff.'" All he remembered after that was seeing a bat held over his head, and then darkness. The scream that came out of his mouth was the last sound he ever uttered.

He shook his head, and his thoughts returned to the police standing around him with clubs. *"They just want to taunt and humiliate me!"* Bryan was so scarred, physically and emotionally from the abuse he went through, he was left mute and hadn't spoken a word in years.

His face was beaten and bruised. The local justice system had made sure he'd had a quick trial. He was a dangerous individual, so no time was wasted with him going through a long, drawn-out hearing. Justice had been served. The community in Bryan's hometown wanted this psychopath off the streets for good, and quickly. Some said he was cursed because he survived several stabbings and gunshots. Bryan paced his cell and vowed he would kill those men who taunted him so ruthlessly. He tried to figure a way to get out, but it was no use. It was a maximum-security prison. He had spent his teen years in and out of the juvenile system and in state hospitals.

He sat down and breathed heavily. He thought about his mask. His beloved mask. It hid all the ugliness inside him—it hid the shame, the dirt, and the humiliation in his life. He knew he would never see his mask as long as he was in this place. People would see everything—they already knew everything. He was all over the news, all the local and state stations of Harding, Indiana. He must be cursed, he must be evil, a demon, or the devil himself. That was what the news said about him as he overheard it on the television that echoed down.

All he wanted to do was kill and hurt people. He hated people and all they had done to him. He wished he had never

Chapter 1

been born. Rage boiled up inside of him, and he slammed his fist into the wall. Halloween was the best time of the year to kill people because of the darkness the holiday represented, just like the darkness in Bryan's heart that had been building up since he was a youth.

Halloween was the season he chose to do his deeds of darkness. This was the time he wanted the people and society *to pay* for all they had done to him. Bryan was a big, broad, muscular man who was a force to be reckoned with. He was able to easily catch up to his victims with one step. His fist did not even hurt as he punched and mangled his victims. He was used to not feeling anything, including pain. His strength was incredible. He was used to lifting them before he plunged the knife in them or choked them. He hated they had normal happy lives, and jealousy welled up inside of him. *Was there anything at all that represented love in life? If love existed, he had never felt it. So, there must not be love, but misery and more misery and hate!*

Supper came and went, and no meal was delivered to his cell because no one wanted to take it to him, so he sat there starving. His cell was damp and cold, and he wrapped the thin blanket around him. He fell into a fitful sleep in flurried thoughts of hatred and vows of revenge.

"Psst, wake up!" Bryan stirred and wondered who was trying to wake him. It was the middle of the night, and three night shift officers came into his cell. He did not know their names.

"Well, well, well, who do we have here?" One of them said. "You evil S.O.B! You killed my baby cousin!" They came with batons in hand, threatening to beat him. The blows and kicks came over and over again. He did not see their faces because they had covered them with ski masks. Yet, he knew they were guards because he saw the uniforms they wore. He could well take all three, but they had him already on the floor. He covered his face as they beat him unconscious and left him lying in a pool of his own blood, vomit, and excrement the rest of the night.

The night shift guards said in their report that Bryan had been making all kinds of noise in his cell, banging on the bars. He had attacked one of the guards that came to quiet him down. So they had come in and beaten him to restore order so he would not kill the officers who came to check on him or the other prisoners in the cell with him. The chief officer turned a blind eye, and more lies were told against him. Bryan was put in solitary confinement, where he would not be able to see or talk to anyone for many months.

Cold meals were delivered, but always under the door, never face to face with any human being. His cell was damp, cold, and away from everyone else. All viewed him as evil. No one wanted to be locked up with him. Anyone who did see his face said his eyes were evil. He hid his face every time someone looked in on him through the door. He felt naked without his mask. How dare they look at him without his mask? The covering made him feel alive and powerful. The pasty-colored mask with well-set lips fit him perfectly as he had pasty skin himself. He always seemed to become one with that mask as if it was his own face. Well-set eye holes were cut out, giving the mask an eerie dead-like appearance and soft black real hair jutted out all over the mask in a tousled way. Oh, how he felt secure in that mask! That precious mask! He was never one for being in the fresh sunshine; all his life had always been inside some juvenile jail cell, in some local mental hospital, or being seen and examined by doctors who never seemed to help in any way.

Bryan thought perhaps he had just been born this way—a freak of nature. A misfit who would never amount to anything. His Dad would always say those words about him to his face. His mother wished she never had him. Those words were the standard regular conversation pieces at the dinner table, like daggers or knives that stabbed deep in his

Chapter 1

little heart. Ironically, that would become the very knives he killed people with, as though it somehow relieved the pain inside.

The beatings his Dad would give him, for inhumane reasons, were so bad, he sometimes could not sit down at the table during a meal or at school. Just for being him, or for any mistake like forgetting to do a chore a certain way, out came the belt.

He remembered one time, how his Dad had humiliated him by beating him with a belt in the car after school so all his classmates could see. The next day was the worst ever as his classmates taunted him. "Ha, you still get whippings?" Bryan could say nothing; he just ran and hid his face in humiliation and shame. Charlotte, a pretty girl he liked, had even laughed at him when she saw the belt incident from the bus.

As an adult, Bryan no longer felt physical pain when he was beaten. He was so hardened to it and did not care who he hurt in revenge for everything he had been through in his life. Killing was the only way to survive and not getting hurt again…ever. He did not need love, and love did not need him. He did not believe in love.

He showered and ate his cold breakfast. It was now winter. He saw the snow begin falling through a window high above his head. The empty branches scraped the window. The first time he had seen this cell was when the leaves were budding, so he must have been in solitary confinement for almost a year. For a moment, he wondered what was going on out there in the world…how the victim's families were suffering. '*Well, good for them*,'' he thought. "*Even if I was on the other side, what would I even do with my useless life? All I know is stalking and killing.*"

He played with his food. On the plate were watery eggs, greasy bacon, and hard toast. Hungry, but not hungry. He wondered how he was still alive after he was shot and stabbed by his victims and so-called protectors of society called "police."

Redemption Has No Limits

Bryan viewed the police as enemies. All they wanted to do was shoot at him and beat him. *I guess that's what they do. I must do what I have to do too.*

In solitary confinement, Bryan could not do any more than think about many things. It was impossible to break out of prison because he was surrounded by several foot-thick concrete all around and very thick doors that prevented anyone from smashing or pulling them off the hinges. So, Bryan waited and waited more.

One morning, Bryan heard voices that were coming his way. They were faint, but for sure coming his way. The door opened, and ten guards stood in his cell with batons and guns ready. In stepped a man in a black trench coat.

"Hello, I am Dr. Smith. I want to observe you, Conners." The doctor extended his hand, but Bryan refused to acknowledge him. "I understand you have had a long history with some mental issues, and I want to help," the doctor continued. Bryan said nothing.

The man had black hair, a pale complexion, and beady prying eyes that seemed to look through him. Bryan turned his face away. He did not want to be seen as some deranged mental patient, but the man seemed to want to put the label on him. Other doctors tried to label him and judge him in the last hospitals and prisons to which he had been assigned. Bryan knew exactly who he was and what he wanted to do. He just wanted to kill and make society pay for what they had done to him. *For what his parents had done to him. They had no right!*

"He won't talk," one officer said.

"I will make him come out of his shell—you and everyone will see," Dr. Smith said. "I am known throughout the world for my methods and medicine. I am well informed about Bryan's case. Eventually, he will be able to trust me. Even if no one else can or will take a crack at getting to what is underneath it all, I can. I have my Doctorate degree and have also been well educated in international psychiatry studies."

Chapter 1

"Well, Dr. Smith, I guess if anyone can take this case, you can do so," said one of the officers.

Bryan felt rage like they were treating him like a scientific specimen. *Dammit I am human being, not a lab rat! He thought.*

"Well, Conners," Dr. Smith said. "Until we meet again." He extended his hand and Bryan ignored it. "Have a nice day." Bryan gritted his teeth in anger.

A few months passed, and there was no sign of the shrink or anyone else. Bryan was relieved. He just wanted to be alone. He had gotten used to this dingy lonely cell, and having no one else to talk to was okay with him. He did not talk anyway, so any conversation with another human was a waste of his time. The only communication he heard was the scrapping of the budding branches on the window sill high above him. He had been there a year already, and the branches told the story that it was springtime.

One time, he was awakened in the middle of the night to the sound of the smashing of batons and footsteps through his cell door as many officers crashed into his cell. He was beaten all over again, and many needles were plunged into him by officers in ski masks.

"Make sure he is sedated really good! In fact, over-sedate this monster!" Said one of the officers. Bryan felt his head spinning and blacked out. He could not resist the effects of the needles.

After several days, Bryan awoke in a different place. It was a heavily-padded room filled with all kinds of instruments. He was in a straitjacket and heavily chained. Electrodes were attached to his muscular bare chest. There was no way he could break free. Wardens with batons stood nearby to give any punishing blows that were needed, to keep him properly restrained.

"Good morning," Dr. Smith said as he entered the door. Bryan gritted his teeth in anger. "You will be here now,

Redemption Has No Limits

Conners, in my care for the long term. The Chief officers and I struck up a deal. I take you off their hands for rehabilitation and to clear the space for another inmate who now has your cell. You have mental problems and I need to help you, Conners."

Bryan cursed the doctor within himself. *"If only I could talk, I would let you know how I really feel!"* Bryan's eyes flashed rage as he struggled hard against his heavy chains and harnesses. He was used to breaking out of things, but the beatings and tranquilizers from a few days ago seemed to weaken him, and he could only struggle.

"Whoa! Don't do it," said the doctor. "You will only hurt yourself if you resist me. As I said, I can help you if you let me." Bryan turned his head away. A big needle was inserted into his arm before Bryan could react, and a nurse came in to assist with shock treatments. A device was forced into Bryan's mouth, and the electrodes were turned on as a cap went over his head. One shock after another was administered, and Bryan fell limp and blacked out.

Most of the time in the months ahead, Bryan lay in a heavily sedated state and was always chained up like an animal. His mind fried from the repeated shock treatments, and there was also talk of a lobotomy. The doctor would always come in and pick his brain and delve into his past and ask why he did what he did. Pills were always ground up in his food to keep him from experiencing rage or anger.

Bryan wondered if this was how they treated people in concentration camps and how they even survived. Bryan was considered evil, even by this doctor, and he knew if he ever got out of this, he would kill this doctor who had interrupted his peaceful life in solitary confinement! He wondered why this shrink was so interested in him—even obsessed with him!

His thoughts angered him. Insidious voices that tormented him as they became louder inside his head.

Chapter 1

Perhaps he was crazy; perhaps he was the devil. He'd been hearing things, concerning killing others, in his head since he was a child,.

"Today is the day we are going to do your lobotomy. It is needed because I don't see an improvement," said Dr. Smith. Bryan struggled and fought with all his might and turned the gurney upside down and crashed to the ground. Blows from the wardens were delivered as he was beaten again. "No! Don't beat him so hard. I must do the procedure!" Dr. Smith warned. He scrambled to prepare the procedure as a nurse took a large needle and quickly plunged it into him, knocking Bryan out. He was quickly placed back on the gurney and chained tightly.

After the lobotomy procedure, Bryan was in a fog most of the time, strapped to a stationary gurney that would not move. Every time he would be awake enough to move, he was sedated again. He was still able to feed himself, but he was chained up by heavy chains with armed wardens standing by, so he could not move much. He could still hear the angry voices in his head; in fact, they seemed clearer and more amplified due to the procedure. Nothing seemed to help him. He did not want to be helped, and weeks had gone by. The doctor tried therapy after therapy, and often in the most humiliating and shaming ways. Bryan did not even feel human, but more like a specimen or lab rat. Perhaps he thought he somehow deserved all that was happening to him.

Dr. Smith would pick his brain continually daily with questions about his family, and others like how he felt about the people he killed, and if he felt anything at all about one thing or the other. The questions came in droves daily, like a torture device of words, and he could not break free.

Dr. Smith finally said one day, "I have tried everything to break you. You will remain in my care the rest of your life, and I will do more procedures as I see fit. Bryan, you won't talk to me. I can't help you if you won't talk to me. Please talk to me."

Bryan suddenly stood up, eyes flashing with rage, grabbed a piece of paper and pen nearby and wrote: "*Let me go!*"

Dr. Smith beamed. "Ooooh so now we have a breakthrough! Bryan, that's good. Thank you for responding to me. So from now on, you can write to me if you want to talk." The doctor was pleased and feeling smug as he walked out the padded door and clicked the deadbolt into place. Bryan remained chained in captivity. He felt sad and dejected, but would not let the doctor see him in a weak state, which was more than humiliating.

The next day the doctor brought something of value to Bryan—his beloved mask! How he missed that mask! The token, of course, did not come without a price as the doctor grilled him with more questions about it. Bryan refused to respond or acknowledge him and only paid attention to his precious mask. That mask was his everything! That mask was heaven to him! The mask brought him security and was his safe place. The mask was his god! Everything else could go away, and it would just be him and his beloved mask! He held it to his chest.

"You love that mask, don't you, Bryan?" Dr. Smith asked. After a few moments, the doctor said, "Okay, I must take the mask back." Bryan roughly shoved the doctor's hand out of the way.

The nurse nearby said, "Oh, just let him keep it at least for the night." One of the wardens also urged the doctor to let him keep it. So, without much protest, the doctor did, stating it may be therapeutic for Bryan to keep it.

Bryan slept soundly like a baby that night for the first time in a very long time, holding his beloved mask close to his heart as if it could comfort him. He dreamed of a happier time when life briefly seemed normal. But the memories of the children tormenting him, and the humiliating beatings his Dad gave him, came back in his dreams. Remembering

Chapter 1

all the killings, remembering everything in his life that was bad, and all the tormenting fingers pointing at him from people like teachers, peers, and family, he awoke in a sweat.

Chapter 2

"What are you talking about?" Dr. Smith asked, as handcuffs were placed on him.

"You're under arrest for conspiring, deceiving, kidnapping and moving an inmate without permission. Also, bribing cops with a payment to do your dirty work, so you can mess up someone's mind even more then they are?" The officer asked.

The director of the state hospital, Dr. Shaffer said, "what is going on?"

The officer responded, "Dr. Smith has appeared to have kidnapped an inmate that was in our prison and had no orders from anyone to move the inmate to receive treatment."

The director said, "Dr. Smith, you are barred for the rest of your life from practicing medicine of any kind and therefore relieved of your duties."

The police officer said, "Did you have any idea this was going on?"

Dr. Shaffer responded, "No, this was all done under my nose, after hours! I was not aware that any of this was going on!" The nurses and staff were then questioned, and they were also put under arrest for assisting Dr. Smith. Punishments would be delivered, sentences given, and licenses revoked. Bryan would never see the doctor again. Dr. Smith would later commit suicide in a lonely prison cell of overwhelmed by humiliation.

Redemption Has No Limits

Bryan overheard the conversation as he waited to be delivered back to prison. He still had his beloved mask and made sure he would never lose it again. He safely stuffed it under his clothes. He heard something about a bribe and something about money. This so-called Dr. Smith had only wanted to make himself more well known in all his arrogance. He cared nothing about Bryan, and only the fact that Bryan was well known as a serial killer led Dr. Smith to help himself to his own accolades. *"I guess evil comes in all forms and even in white coats and I won't have to kill him,"* Bryan thought. He hated that doctor and wanted him dead! He balled up his fists, they were whiter than the rest of him. Bryan was heavily chained up and tranquilized again to ensure a safe travel for all the police. The stocks hurt his feet and he could not move, as he was transported back to the prison again.

He came to and once again in his solitary cell he saw the familiar branches that greeted him with a wave "hello." The trees were in full bloom. It was summer, and he wondered what the warm summer sun would feel like. It had been years since he had been outside enjoying any fresh air and he knew he would never feel it again, being locked away for life and all.

He would probably burn in the sun, he had such white skin. But he had his beloved mask and took great care to make sure no one would ever find it or take it away from him again! The mask's, well positioned, gray lips had angled down slightly on one side, giving it a clown-like appearance, but it was his. It belonged to him and it comforted him! It almost looked like him! His own lips were full, well set and ruddy,. His eyes were blue and set with full arched eye brows. His hair was straight and blackish brown, mimicking the mask. The coveralls they gave him were black, because they had run out of the usual orange color.

He awoke to the sound of voices coming towards him down the hall. *"Oh no! This time I will really have to kill*

Chapter 2

someone!" He said to himself. He braced for the attack while yet in chains. All the previous incidents made him more like a lion ready to kill anyone who was trying to harm him.

Instead, to his surprise, before the door opened, the chief officer said, "I have something to tell you. You're being summoned to court immediately." Police officers filled his cell once again, only they did not come with the intention of beating him.

The hearing was set for August 30th, near the end of summer. Bryan was presented with a state appointed lawyer who argued, "Your honor you can see how Dr. Smith messed up his mind, the defendant cannot even answer for himself." The other lawyer argued that he was that way before Dr. Smith got a hold to him.

The case took hours of arguing back and forth and finally so much evidence was presented that the judge ruled, "Due to a technicality in the evidence, I therefore have no choice but to release Andrew Bryan Conners back into society." The courtroom was filled with gasps and howls of anger! "Whaaaat? No way!" Sharp curses filled the air! Everything that presented itself as professional courtroom etiquette went out the door, as the crowd erupted into a protest frenzy!

The Judge ignored the protests and said, "It's over and I have the final say. All the paperwork is clear and regarding this case this court is permanently adjourned."

A heavily chained Bryan, was hauled off the stand and taken away abruptly. In all his rage and anger, the evil Andrew Bryan Conners, the demon, the devil and mass murderer, and every other label society gave him, did not know what to say. He was still suffering the effects of all the shock treatments and the lobotomy that somehow began to change his perspective. He still hated people and wanted them all dead, but to suffer was just not his character and he was the one who wanted others to suffer for what they did and not him. He thought of the precious piece tucked under his clothes his precious mask! He had that and that's all that mattered to him! Like a precious, priceless gem he kept it safe and tucked away.

The next thing he knew, he was being transferred back to Harding, Indiana that evening—back to his home town and parents' old home. Still heavily chained, Bryan had a mixture of emotions. *"I don't believe this! I am a killer and I will kill again!"* He grinned with an evil laughter inside himself. Something else was nagging at him. *"How can I begin again?"* A voice he never heard before. *"They hate me there! Everyone hates you! You can't go back! They will hunt you down!"* The shocks and lobotomy brought other voices in. *"What where they? All I know is to kill! What's become of my old house? How could I even be with people? There is no one there for you anymore! I'm a monster!"* The voices tormented him.

The paddy wagon, transferring him back to his town slowed down on the side of the road almost to Harding and the police officer said, "So long sucker—have a nice life! Walk the rest of the way!" The officer kicked him abruptly out of the wagon on the side of the road, where he rolled down the hill until he stopped in a ditch. He was covered with mud and filth, but he was free and with his beloved mask! What was wrong with him? Voices of reason and voices of "why?"

Perhaps the procedures had done some damage because he never cared before, so why would he care now about people, their feelings or anything?? All he knew was hate, violence and death.

He was thrown out of the paddy wagon that evening. Dirty, bruised and still in chains. He walked along a brook. The moon guiding him home. He knew the way, the brook was all too familiar to him as he would stalk at night. He played in the brook as a child alone, because he had no friends growing up.

He found some heavy rocks and smashed the chains that connected the handcuffs to his hands and feet, over and

Chapter 2

over until the chains broke, so he could walk better.

The voices, in his head, tormented him more and more as he got closer to his old home. For most of the night he had walked and splashed in the brook to get the mud off him.

Thankfully, it was only late August and the coldness of fall had not set in yet. He began to hunger, and he found a garden near dawn. It was still dark, so he could eat to his content before anyone would be up. He feasted on vegetables and cantaloupe and took some with him. So, he would have more for later. Finally, his old neighborhood loomed ahead, and the first streaks of dawn appeared in the sky. He had walked all night. He was somewhat excited to see what had become of his house. There it stood at the end of the block. Old, abandoned, spray painted (that angered him), and tore up—but it was home to him!

He found the key, he had hidden in the structure. His parents were also careful to make duplicates and hid them years ago in the cracks of the house's exterior. He quickly went inside before anyone could see him.

He first went into the basement and cut off the remaining metal left from the handcuffs on his wrist and ankles with a steal cutter that was in the basement. Then he quickly went upstairs and looked around, thankfully no one was up in the surrounding houses and the bushes blocked anyone from seeing him. His parents' bed was still in their bedroom along with all their belongings and the belongings of both of his siblings. He fell asleep soundly and slept like he had not slept in a long time. He was home, in his home, and with his beloved mask. That's all that mattered.

He slept for many hours, and when he awoke he was very careful not to be seen because he knew he would be on everyone's hit list of hatred and they would hunt him down like prey had they known he was back living in his home.

Suddenly he wondered was he afraid? Fear? He had never known fear before—fear of people, what was wrong with him? He delighted in making people fear him. The looks on their faces as they breathed their last breath before he ended them. He was the one in control—he was the one. This new emotion angered him so much, he punched a hole in the wall! "*I am not afraid of anything! I am fear itself!*"

He did not understand this new thing that he was feeling. Perhaps it was the thought of not being able to break out of prison this time and, fearing again, being subjected to another doctor's tormenting scientific experiments was more than he could bare…he punched another hole in the wall.

Angrily, he did not understand any of it. Why had he not been able to resist all these things people, yes people, were throwing at him and not being able to destroy, overtake and overpower them as he had done in the past as a mass murderer. He had been humiliated. His mind was messed up more than ever, and beaten repeatedly? The voices turned to a maddening roar, tormenting, taunting him as he ripped the door off the hinges in his parents' bedroom in a rage. "*There, now it's better,*" he said to himself. The voices seemed to quiet. He remained hidden, only going out at night for food when everyone was asleep. He would not kill yet—it was not fall. Or would he?

Chapter 3

"Lord, I am so grateful that you have blessed me with such a special granddaughter. She loves me and more importantly she loves You! Father, she is so special and her heart is so pure, but even more importantly she sees your great grace and potential in everyone. Father, I have a special request, You know I will be coming home to be with you soon. I thank you for bringing into her life a match made in heaven for her. Someone who will love her beyond words." In Jesus' name, Amen and Amen.

Amy stood at the entrance of grandmother's door and watched her pray. She wondered what she was praying about, but didn't want to interrupt her, so she just waited until she heard her grandmother say amen. She then moved quickly to her side and helped her to stand. Her grandmother smiled at her and said, did you hear what I was praying.

Not really, grandmother.

Good, said her grandmother, smiling. Can you get me some water?"

"Sure Grandma," Amy Angelo said and poured her grandmother some ice water.

"You know, you are, and always have been my favorite, and only granddaughter. Your brother is far away from us. He is also very unpredictable. You have been here to care for and visit me in this nursing home since my illness. Your mother would have been proud of you. I know life has not always been easy for you, growing up. Your mom did the best she could with the what she had. I helped her whenever I could because I had a little more. I called you here today to talk to you about something."

"Sure, what is it?" Amy said.

"Can you go over there to the dresser's bottom drawer and open it." Amy did as her Grandma requested. "There is an envelope at the bottom of the drawer near the back. Do you see it?"

"Yes," Amy said.

"I want you to open and read it," said Grandma. Amy opened it, read it and gasped. It was her grandmother's "Last Will and Testament," that clearly stated she had over $50 million and she was bequeathing it to Amy.

"G-Grandma, I could never take all your money!" Amy said.

"Now dear one, what would I do with it? I am dying and want you to be taken care of. I have no more heirs to give it to and your brother, William, cannot have it because he lives a reckless life. He would not be responsible or to be wise with the spending so, it's all yours and please don't tell anyone. My father made a fortune once the economy came back after the depression. I took what he made and invested it, gaining even more. Of course, I also took a few trips and enjoyed myself, but all that is futile, and money could never buy happiness and peace. I know you have a job as a creative arts director at your church, but this is for you and your future and I wanted to leave this world knowing you will be okay. You will never be in want again."

"T-Thank you," said Amy, her large dark eyes filling up with tears and gratitude as she hugged her Grandma. The women visited into the evening hours. Amy loved her Grandmother and they were very close, and she could not bear the fact of losing her. Grandma was all she had. She left

Chapter 3

when she saw grandma was drifting off to sleep. She drove home a new millionaire. The first thing she would do is fix up her home and perhaps buy that piece of property at the end of the block that so needed repair and of course save the money for a rainy day.

Amy was used to living frugally, her Mom taught her that. Growing up dirt poor, they had to stretch money and food for the family. She remembered all the things she went through with both of her parents gone and her brother far away pursuing his marketing career. She was a fighter and could make it in any situation. Holidays were very hard growing up without a father in the picture.

Her father had died when she was very young, and she hardly knew him and her mother worked multiple jobs all the time and she spent most of her time with her grandmother. Now her Grandma was ill, and she did not know how much longer she would be alive, so she cherished each day and each moment with her.

Amy was in her late 20s, with dark brown beautiful eyes and olive, warm honey skin, dark brown wavy-curly hair and full lips. She could have easily passed for Italian, Greek or Mexican. She had an exotic look and was not necessarily slim, but curvy and had the thicker legs of a dancer. She took after her dad of Italian-Sicilian descent. The men at church, either wanted to date her or avoided her.

Amy thought "maybe I am never meant to be married and I am okay with that." Her passion and focus were the arts. She loved directing and putting together dances at her church and using the arts to reach the community. She was a designer and made clothes for plays and for the dancers as the church budget allowed her to purchase fabric and create things when they had productions. She loved where she worked, and everyone was so nice.

The church was a prominent part of the community.

They put on monthly food giveaways and would help the poor during the holidays. What was nice is that everything was within walking distance. The church was about a half a mile away. Amy could walk to work in the morning and did not have to be there until 9:00 a.m. Shed worked till 3:00 pm. Her boss, Pastor Mark, would even let her take off Fridays if she wanted to. Amy's work also included training the dancers and actors for productions that would be performed at different local places during the holidays.

It was now early September and Amy had to come up with a song and dance. She also needed to put together a skit for the Christmas play. Amy never tired, because it was her passion that drove her, and she loved all she did for the church and community. The church paid her a salary and she lived off that. It was a modest salary and she was content with it. She was taught money can never buy happiness and she was very happy, even before her Grandma told her the news of her inheritance.

She got the job through a friend of the family that saw potential in her. In high school, Amy would put together plays and productions and she was interviewed by her pastor, then hired right out of high school and they paid for her certification in the arts. She never wanted to work anywhere else, so she stayed put. She loved being a part of this community and belonging. She also was aware of the dark past that seemed to cast a shadow over this community—the murders of ten years ago and subsequent years.

Instead of isolating people, these horrible events brought the community closer together. She wondered whatever happened to him—the masked murderer. Some said he was a legend or a demon and kept coming back to life after being shot and stabbed! She knew evil was real and how serial killers hear voices to kill, how they start with animals then turn to eventually kill people. She watched this documentary one time about it. She did not want to find out or run into him!

Chapter 3

She was glad she was safe, and he was locked away forever! It was all over the news and she was glad the community was once again safe!

She took great comfort in her faith. She had peace and was not afraid to die. She had almost died as a child from a very high fever and measles. She knew the peace that death brings. Even though she was very sick she was at peace. There must be more on the other side, but she was not ready to die. She shook off the morbid thoughts as she finished the work day. She walked home, and the first chills of early fall filled the air. It was yet too early for the leaves to turn, but they would eventually, and fall was her favorite time of the year. Her colorful personality matched the colors of fall. Everyone loved Amy and she was one of those people who would give her last dollar to them.

She made her way inside her house and made some coffee. "Dance practice Wednesday," she thought, and she planned her schedule for the week. Just then the phone rang.

"Miss Angelo we regretfully are calling to tell you your Grandma passed away in her sleep this afternoon," the voice coldly stated.

Amy began to cry. "O-Okay, I will be right over." She drove over to the nursing home and spoke with the doctors and nurses. Grandma had already arranged her own funeral, so everything was already taken care of. "She must have known," thought Amy through tears. How she would miss her beloved Grandma. With no other family present, her church came to support her during this time. Her Grandma died Monday, and the funeral was set for Friday. Amy canceled dance practice and took time off work to grieve. She had only seen her Grandma a week earlier when she heard of the news about her inheritance.

A luncheon preceded the funeral, which was short, sweet and modest, as her Grandmother wanted it. Her Grandmother's favorite song, "Amazing Grace" was sung at her funeral as the casket was lowered into the ground.

Redemption Has No Limits

Amy's pastor conducted the funeral. "Ashes to ashes and dust to dust. We go, but our spirit lives on forever and there is hope in eternal life for those who trust God." Final prayers and remarks were made, and the funeral closed. Amy's Grandmother would go to her church with Amy when she could, but her later years made her frail and bedridden.

A small group stood around, but then filtered out one by one. "Amy call us if you need anything. We will be here for you if you need anything, including a hug and please know we are praying for you," and other well wishes echoed through the air.

Amy was then alone. She stood for what seemed like hours, she thought about many of the good times with her Grandmother, her thoughts took her down memory lane. She took comfort in those thoughts and smiled. "Grandma was no longer suffering, but young and free again!" Her thoughts were startled by a twig snapping and a rustle in the bushes. "Hello? Is someone there?" Amy said and turned around. Amy thought she was hearing things and shook her head "Nothing, must be the wind." It was a cool, breezy day and she headed home.

The weekend was spent going up to the nursing home and clearing out her Grandma's belongings and keepsakes she kept along with the other valuables that belonged to her Grandma. Amy kept her Grandma's wedding ring. It was so beautiful and an antique and perhaps she may wear it one day to her own wedding to honor her Grandmother. Amy also kept her china tea cup collection. She was very thankful for her church and friends who were so supportive during this time as cards from the community came in.

Amy needed some rest, so she headed home and ordered pizza. "No cooking tonight," she said to herself. She put on some relaxing music and tried to make sense of things, but she never felt lonely because of her heart for the arts and serving the community.

Chapter 3

She soon fell off to some much-needed sleep and dreamed of a masked man chasing her. His pale skin, clown like face and black coveralls coming towards her, threatening with a large knife as she walked home in the night. She sprouted wings and took off flying. She landed, but wherever she landed he was there waiting. "Aaagh," she screamed. She woke up in a sweat. "What in the world?" She thought. "Must be a pizza dream," she said to herself. She made herself some hot herbal tea and eventually went back to sleep.

It was Monday again and now it was mid-September. Amy could not help but think of the dream she had. It seemed so real and haunted her as she worked. "Was it? Could it be? The killer everyone had spoken of?" Others refused to speak of him referring to his name as profanity, nothing more. "What if he really did come back? Would he kill again?" Her thoughts bothered her as to why she had the dream.

"Amy, would you like some coffee?" Mary the secretary said.

"Sure, thank you."

"Are you okay?" Mary asked.

"Just some crazy dream," Amy said.

"What kind of dream?" Mary asked.

Amy told her the dream. Mary said "Oh no, there is no way he is coming back! They locked him up and threw away the key. Besides the community would not stand for it. He is not fit for society. He is mad and evil."

"Well perhaps," said Amy. "Thanks for the coffee by the way."

"Your welcome," Mary said.

Amy walked home singing one of her favorite songs out loud, "*We are a vapor, You are forever, reining on high.*" She had to sing to get the song inside her and dance out the words. So, she rehearsed the song's lyrics aloud as she walked. "An artist's work is never finished, she laughed out loud, there is always something new to practice," she thought to herself. She and her dance team would practice this song for the Christmas pageant. It was settled that this was the song for Wednesday night practice.

Upon walking home Amy got the feeling she was being watched. She turned around. "Nope, nothing there, Amy stop spooking yourself!" She sharply rebuked herself inside. "It was only a dream!"

Chapter 4

He was in the graveyard the day Amy's grandmother's funeral was going on. He was far away from everyone and hidden. He thought perhaps he would find peace in visiting those of his family he killed. He was lost in his own tormenting thoughts of the voices, then he saw people. His eyes flashed red at their blood. He wanted them dead. He thought of how many more he would put here as a result of his next killing spree. Autumn was fast approaching, and he was thirsty for more blood. In a flurry of his evil thoughts and those heinous voices whispering to him prompting him to kill, he saw her, Amy.

He crept closer in the bushes nearby only to hear the voices that tormented him to act, but he could not. It was not yet fall or even night. It was daytime, and everyone would see him, and he only acted at night. He stood there for what seemed like hours. He watched the funeral as they sang songs, and the final message given. He seen the people go to their cars and depart to their homes and then it was only her. Her long dark curly hair flowed down her back like a waterfall and she was in an aqua dress. Her olive skin glowed against the aqua colored dress. Her eyes were like doe eyes, dark and large with perfectly arched brows. She was not slender, but was curvy and well built. He thought it odd she would wear that color to a funeral. He watched her as she stood alone. When he accidentally stepped on a twig, her dark head whipped around and he looked into her eyes. She was beautiful. He quickly sunk back into the bushes not to be seen. The bushes were thick and provided the needed covering.

He dared not make another sound and quietly sneaked away along the tall bushes that lined the road. In all his tormenting voices in his mind the voices wanted him to kill her. "Kill her! Kill her," they said. His black coveralls blended well with the shadows even in thick bushes and the white mask blended as well. His food supply was dwindling and soon it would be too cold to go to any gardens at night to get food. Being in the north, gardens were not year-round.

That night he broke into a family's home a few doors down. Fortunately for them, they were on vacation and were not home, so he took whatever food they had in their pantry. He went back into the woods, killed, butchered, and gutted a deer, and preserved it as his grandfather taught him. He had food to last for a while. He enjoyed killing the deer as the sight of blood made his heart race. He wondered what would happen if she saw him? "This is crazy!" He thought to himself "Why am I even thinking such things?" He first seen her at the funeral and overheard it was her Grandma's death in the conversations that followed. This woman seemed to glow with something unusual. Her eyes were dark, but they were filled with a light he'd never seen.

He was used to killing all the sleazy people that slept together and that was infuriating to him and disgusting, just like his family he killed; but she was very different. *"Why not kill her? They ALL bleed the same?"* Came the voices. *"She is no different,"* and on and on the voices taunted. *"No there was something different about this one,"* he fought and argued inside himself.

Chapter 4

He watched her walk home from work from in the bushes and heard her sing. Her face seemed to fill with an unearthly light every time she would sing. First, he saw it at the funeral, then on the street as she walked home. He knew she worked down the street at that church, because he would watch her pass down the street from inside his house. One day he ventured out to follow her from inside the bushes only to hear her sing. "*What was that song?*" He thought and never heard it before, or anything spiritual. His parents taught him that's "*this*" was all there is to life and mocked anything churchy and those hypocrite Christians. "*There is no God!*" The voices taunted. "*You're going to hell forever! You belong to us! No one wants you! God don't even want you.*"

He knew the community officials knew he was out again, and they kept it quiet because they did not want to alarm the community that was already scarred, because of the heinous crimes he committed. Police did police business and kept it secret. He would overhear the police talking about him as he stalked around at night. There were simply too many people after him and wanted him dead and the police also had a group of vigilantes to keep watch as well.

He thought to himself he must be cursed and why would he not die when he was shot or stabbed at the hands of police, his old doctor, or victims before he overpowered them and took their lives. For some reason he had developed a rule for killing, it was, he would only kill in the fall, no time any earlier. The voices seemed to urge him to act. He would punch and destroy things in his home out of rage and frustration, late at night pacing the floor in torment. Sleep was scarce because of the tormenting voices.

What was it that drove him? Was it hatred? Because it could not be possibly love, because he did not believe in love, God, heaven, or hell for that matter. Yet he knew he belonged to something evil and sinister, because it controlled him and possessed him and there was no getting away. His lust for blood grew as Halloween approached. It owned him, and he felt it was him. It would always own him, and it would always be him. There was no escaping the wickedness inside of him that seemed to possess him. His thoughts flashed to a movie he had seen when he was young about a girl that was possessed by the devil, but she found freedom in the end and the priest died. Maybe that's how people seen how he looked when they looked into his eyes with the mask on, or no mask on, like when he was in prison.

He believed his mask would cover up the evil within. His wild evil looking eyes as people would say, "How he has the devil in him and nothing inside but demons; no soul and no sense of right or wrong." Others would make fun of him saying and taunting him with things like, "Boogey man, freak of nature" and many other horrible things people said to him.

He hated people for judging him, for all the labels they put on him, and all he wanted to do was teach them a lesson and kill them for making him feel less than human! *"They ALL had to pay!"* He screamed inside himself. No amount of lobotomies, psychology, or shock treatments would ever change how he felt towards people. The day that this woman turned to look at him was the day he did not forget- even during all his torment. He remembered her eyes. He made up his mind he was going find out more about her, no matter what stood in his way!

"Cut. Let's take it from the top," Amy said. "Now you guys must come in with the scarves and then the flags. It is imperative you flow with the music. Let it get inside of you." The dancers sighed as they repeated the moves. Amy had a good dance team of five women and the other team had four children. They always came to the practices and were reliable. They put up with her spirit of excellence and she would buy them gifts for Christmas as a token to say, "Thank you," Amy thought to herself.

Chapter 4

"Make sure when the music changes pitch you all turn right, then left, then the twirl part. Remember, flow with the rhythm." It was Wednesday evening and 7 p.m. dance practice was well under way. They would practice till 9 p.m. depending on the need to tweak things. "The children will come in last and wave the smaller scarves in front of you all, at the end," Amy said. They ran through the song about five times with just the ladies doing their part, then Amy had to work with the children and their parts in the dance. "Remember we must do our best because there may be people who don't normally come to church, and we must be professionals about this." Amy was always patient and understanding with her teams. Her team understood her and her expectations as they practiced. Amy had her dancers' outfit on with the white dress chiffon overlay and red pants. She made all the dancers' garments and things they used, but they saved the more expensive garments for special occasions. She always found the best deals for fabric, and the church would give her a budget to work with. She was able often find fabric at a $1 a yard and make something beautiful out of it.

She and her team practiced, and she also would stay in case there was something her dancers were not clear on, or to just talk about life. She was easy to talk to and open to suggestions. She would also work with dancers who were not sure of when to come in, or their moves. Some dances required a lot of moves and some not so much. Any drama was a no...no on her team. "We are all equal and there will not be jealousy or competition on who does anything better," was her motto and she stood by it and her dancers loved what she stood for. She knew a leader must also be humble and teachable as well. "We will meet again next Wednesday," Amy said.

"Okay, have a great night," all her dancers told her. They all hugged good night. "What a loving team," Amy thought.

Redemption Has No Limits

It was already dark as they made their exit out of the church and into their cars. Amy walked home in the dark in her outfit. She was happy with how practice went, and the women and children would be well ready for the Christmas pageant. He watched and heard the dancers chatter and the songs they practiced inside the church. Some dancers were older than Amy was and some younger, but he was not watching them, he was watching her. He stood in the bushes watching and waiting and hearing everything that went on through the stained-glass window. She strolled home humming the song from dance practice.

The next play practice would be tomorrow evening at 7:00 p.m. Amy had a lot on her plate, but she loved what she did. Friday, she had plans to do some slight remodeling on her house, and possibly go down the county commissioner's office to see if she would be able to purchase that broken-down home down the street. She wondered if they would sell it to her for pennies on the dollar. It might generate some income, or she may be able to turn it into some outreach place for the church. There were many possibilities of what to do with that home. Amy was lost in her thoughts when she heard footsteps. Slow, but steady she heard them and began to walk faster. Her steps crunching some of the leaves that begun to fall and she thought she heard those footsteps crunching the leaves too, but when she looked behind her, it was nothing. "The wind again," she thought to herself. The bushes and trees lined the sidewalk of her path home, so it was hard to see anything.

Amy quickly hurried home and secured the door behind her. She could not help but wonder why she has been spooked lately. "Was it that dream?" She knew October was coming soon and she knew of things that happened during that time in her town.

He followed far behind her to make sure she would not see him. He was tormented because he was so used to

Chapter 4

stalking and following people to their homes and cars, but for some reason, he could not kill her. He willed himself to do it to "obey" the voices inside, but he could not. Something was stopping him. He followed her right up to her house and stalked around her house. She was in the kitchen enjoying a sandwich and a cup of coffee listening to some quiet peaceful music.

All the doors and windows were securely locked, and her house had an alarm on it, so he could not enter in to do what he was used to doing-terrorizing people and killing them. He enjoyed their fear and it made him feel invincible and he took great pleasure in their fear. He realized he could not get anywhere as he made his way back down the street to his house for another restless night of torment.

Amy soon went to bed as she always did around 11:00 p.m. The caffeine from the coffee never affected her so she was able to sleep. She dreamed again. She was in an unknown place watching this man get beaten in a prison - like place, over and over again. She could not see his face. Then the dream changed again, and this same man was being tortured by devices that were used to treat insane people, like shock treatments and lobotomies. She watched as this man went through all these ordeals at the hands of this corrupt doctor. The man came out of it, stood up off the table, saw her and began coming after her. She ran and ran but he always caught up to her. She ran through the darkened streets of her neighborhood, his breath and footsteps hot behind her, but when he was about to grab her, she woke up screaming and her heart racing.

"Oh my gosh, that dream was so real!" Amy muttered to herself. She quieted and calmed herself with some peaceful music and reading a devotional, Psalm 91:5, *"Do not be afraid of the terrors by night nor the arrow that flies by day."* "Wow! That really applies to this," she said. She eventually fell back into a fitful sleep.

"Amy, you look so tired," said Mary, the secretary.

"I am. Just another crazy dream," Amy said.

Mary inquired, "Don't tell me your dreaming about that psycho again."

"Well, I don't know who it was, just some guy coming after me and I could not see his face," said Amy.

Mary replied, "We all dream some crazy things. Sometimes God gets our attention that way."

"I guess," said Amy.

"Coffee?" Mary asked.

"Sure," said Amy. Mary was an older lady near 60 and she was like a mother figure to Amy, always caring and looking out for her. Amy loved working with her.

Amy willed herself to stay focused on what she had to do at work. Next Friday the church was having a special worship prayer night, bonfire, and hayride where contemporary bands would come in and it would go late; and she had to make sure she made the fliers and invited the community and other churches. The church held about 100 people; it was one of those middle of the road churches that was not the flashy type and had been in the community forever. It had some land out in the back of it that reached into the woods and they would have fall festivals. A nice crowd would be there Friday, because this was a yearly mid fall kickoff event. Everyone loved music and the bands that would come in. It would be a very moving time. The church was always trying to help people forget about the past and enjoy the fall season. Amy was looking forward to it. "First, play practice tonight, then fun time Friday." Amy was still planning to take Friday a week before next Friday's bonfire off, to inquire about that house down the street. She was eager to see what was on the inside of it and was sure it needed an overhaul inside and most definitely on the outside. She certainly had enough money to buy many houses if she chose to, but for some reason, she had her eye on that one and Amy was not very materialistic, but always wanted to help others like her Grandmother.

Chapter 4

"Places, places everyone," said Amy. "Okay, you stand here, and you stand there. Remember those who are playing angels must lift their hands at the cue from the song. Mary and Joseph come in at this part of the song. The children playing the animals stand here and there on both sides of the stall." Amy yawned and slowly made her way through the play practice, trying to push the dream out of her head that bothered her. It's almost 9:00 p.m. "So, let's run through it one more time and we will come back to rehearse next Thursday same time." He was out in the bushes listening and waiting. He had gotten used to following her at night and he would watch her walk through the windows of his home on her way to work and back home.

Everyone said their goodbyes after practice and made their way home. Amy made sure the doors of the church were locked. She walked home in the darkness and the streetlights scantly lit up the sidewalk. She walked on pondering the dream and then remembered the devotional and stayed focused on that. There was no reason to fear anything because she was protected. She heard a rustle in the bushes about ten feet away and looked behind and said "Good, no one is following me." She walked on and again she heard it. She looked back again and there was indeed someone standing there watching her. Tall and imposing he stood there. But did she imagine it? "No!" He was a ways away, but he was real. She walked faster and quickly got into her home and locked the door. She thought maybe she saw a flash of silver in his hand.

It was very close now to October and weird things happened in this town. Amy explained it away in her head that maybe people are putting up their Halloween decorations and that meant sometimes things that look like people or figures would be standing there, and sometimes they would string figures over the sidewalks too. "Maybe that's it. Geez calm down! Nothing has happened in this town lately and

Redemption Has No Limits

the psycho killer is locked up forever. That is what the news said," Amy comforted herself. Nevertheless, Amy slept with the lights on that night. She always felt safe in her home and loved by the community. He thought for sure she had seen him, and he wanted to make sure she had not. He did not want to make a scene, so he stayed far behind and he knew when to reveal himself and when not to.

He slinked around like a cat to her home and watched her for a while, but then left. She was smart not to leave anything unlocked, and the alarm on, and this was a type of alarm he could not cut through or shut off, because everything was controlled from the inside of her home. He knew she had a generator inside. He had seen it from inside one of her rooms and he could not cut the power off. Her home was like a fortress he thought.

He tortured himself looking for ideas about ways to get inside her home, but it was useless. He would have to wait until another time to get to her. What was it about her? He had seen beautiful women before, but he could not forget about her honey olive complexion and wondered what it would be like to cut it. She seemed matchless to any others he had seen. That day at the cemetery was drilled into his mind, even amid all the crazy thoughts to kill. Her eyes were an unmatched purity, innocence and light, he never saw in anyone else's eyes. He had never been on a date, with, or intimate with any woman before, and the thought was disgusting to him, but this was different. He could not forget about her and it was driving him crazier by the minute.

Chapter 5

"Are you crazy?" The county commissioner said to Amy.

"No, I am not. That property is an eyesore and I want to help. I know I am young, but I can afford to fix it up."

"Do you not know the history of that place?" Asked the commissioner.

"Yes," said Amy, "but he is gone forever and locked up. The news said they threw away the key and there would never be a chance for parole. I know some bad things happened, but there is always a place for redemption. All things can be made new, and perhaps if that home is fixed up, perhaps the community can heal even more," Amy said.

"Well taken, and I sure hope so! That man was a monster," replied the commissioner. He motioned to his secretary, "Print me off the papers for transfer and redo the deed to that property and I will deliver it at the right time."

"Sure thing," she said. "How much are you willing to part with it for?" Amy asked.

"I want it out of our hair," said the commissioner. "I will give it to you for $1 on the conditions you fix it up to current code."

"Okay," said Amy smiling brightly at him, "deal is done!"

"Here is the original key," said the commissioner, and he handed her the key to the house. They shook hands and the commissioner said, "Good luck. A whole lot has to be done there to erase the memory."

Amy said, "it's worth redeeming and I won't disappoint." Excited, Amy went out the door to her newfound fortune of a second home and she was eager to begin. She called a construction company that day to begin working on the house the following Monday, with the instructions to make sure they put everything that was still in the house in the basement.

Amy was curious about the remaining possessions that were left in the house. On her way home, she walked up to the house and looked up at it. Did she just see a shadow in one of the bedrooms? The glass was broken, and the curtains fluttered against the windowpane in the breeze, so it probably was nothing, she shrugged.

It was near noon when Amy entered the house." Wow!" There is a whole lot to be done in here," she said. She moved through the house from room to room visualizing how she wanted it to look. She could find deeply discounted furniture at the wholesale place up the road and make it warm and inviting, she thought to herself, but first she had to fix-up and remodel the entire place, she casually thought. The walls were spray painted with profanities, cursing the man who murdered in this house and his family. Beer cans and wine bottles were everywhere suggesting, maybe some teens dared have fun in previous years or pranksters or druggies that just wanted a good scare.

Anything could have happened here, and Amy hoped to end it all and erase the past. "Now that this home has a new owner, they may stay away," Amy thought to herself.

Bryan was very careful not to show himself to her. He hid and ducked in the bushes as she went through his house. "What was she possibly doing in his house?" He thought. "*This only means one thing, that she bought it!*" The thought angered him, and he vowed to act. "This was HIS house and no one

Chapter 5

else's! It would never be anyone else's," and then the voices in his head said, "*You need to kill her right now!*" Bryan shook his head violently and refused. Responding to the voice, "*it was not time yet.*"

A construction crew of ten men began work on the house early Monday morning. Bryan quickly made his way deep into the woods earlier that morning and he knew they would be there all day and everyday until the house was complete.

Amy said to the crew, "please remodel the home similar to the old structure. Keep the paint the same on the inside and the wallpaper I will pick out." The crew did as she requested, and remodeling was well underway. Walls and floors were torn out, wires were re-wired, pipes were redone and cracks in the foundation fixed. The construction took about a week. The crew was amazingly fast and did good work. The house was redone on the outside and repainted and new appliances delivered.

The city inspector came by with the commissioner and they inspected the home, and determined it was move in ready. They gave Amy, the green light, and now she owned a second home.

The inspector told Amy, "It looks great! However, I hope you realize what you are getting into, this home has such a violent past."

Amy said, "He cannot harm me. He is gone for good."

"I hope you are right," the inspector said.

A lot of people asked her, over the week, why she would buy such a property and she gave them the same story as she gave the commissioner. "She was trying to help the community forget the past the best way she could to help them." Amy spent about $50,000 fixing up the place. Almost the price of some home's in the neighborhood, but it would be worth it in the end she thought. She could easily afford it, but kept the promise to her Grandmother to not tell anyone about her wealth.

Redemption Has No Limits

Bryan had no place to lay his head during that week his house was remodeled. He could not risk going back and forth, to his house and having her, or anybody else, see him yet. He slept deep in the woods under a makeshift shelter of branches and leaves.

The thoughts of someone buying his house, infuriated him. He was tormented by those thoughts. For them to get rid of all his family's possessions and memories that remained was maddening to him. He gritted his teeth in rage! He killed and gutted some rabbits and cooked them over an open fire he made with a lighter he found during his walk to the woods and preserved the meat in salt he stole from the pantry of another home the night before. He broke in while the family was away for the night. *"What was this? They are not home again?"* He thought. He kept breaking in homes where people were gone or on vacation. Either he was not so lucky, or they were lucky, because otherwise I could have killed them, he thought!

Either way, he needed food to survive, because he knew no one would give him any handouts and he would not show his unmasked face to anyone, because he was evil and he was sure he looked evil. He had the skills to survive, but that would not come in handy when it became very cold outside. So, he had to think of something else. He was angry because, actually, he was always angry, he thought to himself, as he thought about her, Amy. It seemed like she just pushed him out of his own home, and made him sleep in the woods, it was all her fault and she would pay for it!

Amy was so excited for the upcoming event on Friday, at her church, she could barely contain herself! "Mary, I wonder if this year, I will meet Mr. Right?" She asked. "I mean, I'm not really looking for anyone and I am pretty content with my life as it is."

"Amy you are beautiful inside and out and there are many men who would love to date you. You are still young so don't rush it," Mary said.

Chapter 5

"Trust me. I am not," replied Amy. "I heard sometimes it's faith and sometimes its fate."

Mary concluded, "Your right."

Amy breezed through the week and all her evening dance and play practices with ease, keenly forgetting the nightmares she had in previous weeks and looked forward to relaxing with friends and making new ones. Bryan did not follow her that week because of the house being remodeled, he stayed well out of sight.

It was 3:00 p.m. on Friday and Amy was finally off work. "It is finally the weekend," she said. "I will see you tonight Mary."

Mary said, "No, I think I'm going to stay home tonight, I am feeling somewhat under the weather."

"Okay, feel better," said Amy, and she headed out of the door. Amy strolled home and the sun was shining. "Such a beautiful fall day," she said to herself. "No rain in sight."

Amy enjoyed walking to and from work because it kept her in shape and saved on gas. So, she walked during the warmer months and drove in the wintertime to her job. She made it home in half the time. "Let me just get a quick bite to eat and something to drink," she said to herself. Amy fixed a light snack of some cheese and crackers and popped open a can of soda. There would be food there at the hayride and bonfire. The event would start at 6:00 p.m. and go until midnight. It would be a late night for her, "but, oh well, it was the weekend and that's what weekends are for - fun and socializing."

Amy hopped in the shower and washed her hair and blew dried it. She did not want to catch what Mary had with the weather changing she needed to stay well, because her schedule was full. Fall always brought the usual flu and cold sickness and Amy had no time for that, so she popped some vitamin C for extra protection just in case the flu virus tried to come after her, she was always cautious, she thought to herself as she took the chewable pill.

Redemption Has No Limits

"I think I will wear this pretty orange fuzzy sweater," Amy said to herself. "It will be warm and cozy for the evening by the fire." She donned on her favorite jeans and took a jacket, just in case, and put on her favorite artsy fire - colored jeweled cross necklace. She also made up her face with shades of oranges, bronzes, and golds. She then put on lipstick, lined her eyes and put mascara on her long lashes. She smiled when she looked in the mirror and thought to herself, "this make up goes so well with my clothing. The whole outfit made her skin glow with its olive hues. She put the final touch of bronze blush on her cheeks. "Go get 'em girl," she thought smiling. Maybe tonight, is the night, I will meet that special someone, but if not, oh well," she said to herself. She happily bounded out the door to the church.

That morning Bryan came back to the edge of the woods and saw his home was done being remodeled. All the construction trucks were gone and the men who he thought violated his home were gone. He clenched his fists in anger and carefully walked along the bushes to his home. He pulled out the key from his jumpsuit, hoping that they had not changed the locks, and slipped his way inside his house. The house was indeed warmer then the drafty boarded up place he called home.

He walked from room to room getting more and more enraged. Wanting so bad to punch in the walls. *"Where is our stuff?!"* He thought to himself. He rasped and breathed heavily in rage, so much so that his mask puffed in and out as he breathed against it. He stomped through the house with heavy footsteps. He would get her for violating his home, he thought enraged. *"Tonight, would be the night!"* He vowed. His heart was blackened by the evil inside of him and he thought of ways to torture her before he killed her. Somehow, he would get her and kill her. He made his way down to the basement and realized she did not dispose of his things after all. He calmed down, but very little, as the voices still urged him onward to act.

Chapter 5

It would be dark soon and he put on his mask and plotted to somehow find her. Somewhere people were having happy lives and he hated it. This was his hell, if hell existed, and certainly heaven did not, because all he had was hell in his life - no good ever came to him. He slammed his fist down on the floor. He was careful not to damage anything in the house, because he felt if he damaged something right after it was fixed would cause alarm and decrease his chances of getting her and carrying his out plan to kill her. The walls had been repaired and new dry wall was hung and painted, but nothing was put on them yet, the floors and fixtures where also new.

It was now the end of September and he was going to go into October fighting. That was him and that was what he did. After all, he was a demon - the evil one. People had spoken this all of his life and so therefore, he must be all that people have said.

Amy arrived at the church about 6:00 p.m. and was greeted by Matt, the church janitor.

"Hi Amy," he said.

"Hello Matt," she replied.

"It's going to be a good time tonight."

"Yes, it's good to see you here, you look great," said Matt.

"Thanks!" Amy answered. They talked for a little longer, then parted ways. He looked at her with his blond curly hair and she knew he found her attractive in the way he looked at her with his blue eyes, but she was just not interested. He had a goofy look about him that she found unsettling. Amy had, had several boyfriends, but never gave herself to them. She was saving herself for the right one in marriage. Even though it was considered old fashioned, Amy had her wits about her, and she held her ground. There was so much use and abuse and Amy wanted no part of it or wind up pregnant.

"Hello Sheila and Pam. It's so good to see you here," said Amy.

"We are having so much fun." The two ladies were some of the most faithful dancers on her team and the women talked future projects and the upcoming events. Amy felt hungry.

"Let's go get some grub," she said.

"Sounds good," commented the ladies. There where picnic tables in the back of the church and the bonfire was burning bright in the field the church owned. Chili dogs, nachos, and chips were served with many other fall treats including candy corn, smores and caramel apples. There was a machine for hot chocolate and flavored coffees. Amy nibbled at the treats on her plate and walked among the crowd and conversed with everyone. She was like a social butterfly in these types of situations and everyone knew her as a prominent figure as the church arts director. Several guys came up to her at once and began to talk about the new house she bought as she warmed herself by the fire.

"So, I hear you brought that piece of junk at the end of the block," Ted said. "Why?" Amy told them the same story she told the commissioner the day she purchased the house. Tom leaned into her. He wanted to get closer to her on purpose because he liked her, and he wanted to smell her sweet perfume, but he never had the courage to ask her out. She backed away and knew what he was up to. He was good looking with black hair and hazel eyes, but there was something sinister about him. Doug stood as a bystander listening to the conversations the men had with Amy. The three burly men went on and on about Bryan Conners and him being a monster. They would kill him if they could and Amy felt uncomfortable and unsettled with all this attention directed towards her and there was a deeper unsettling that she was beginning to feel inside as the night wore on, but she could not put her finger on it.

"Hayride anyone? Hop on! Hop on! This is your chance!" Mr. Otis the local area farmer cried out.

Chapter 5

"See you later guys!" Amy said, waving to the guys and scrambling with the crowd onto the wagon. She quickly got out of that uncomfortable situation and breathed a sigh of relief. The hayride went through the field with a "bumpety bump." They laughed, sang and told jokes as they rode and had hay fights. Amy looked up and observed the stunning beautiful harvest moon as it gently made its way through the thin clouds. It was eerie to look at, yet beautiful.

She remembered seeing this type of moon in her dream of being chased by that maniac who's face she did not know or see. She also thought of the other dream of the masked man, but shook it off and chose to enjoy her night of fun. Coincidence maybe? Still, she felt unsettled inside.

Chapter 6

The hayride made its way back to the church and Pastor Mark said, "Okay it's time to Praise the Lord!" Everyone scrambled off the hayride and into the church. Volunteers helped clean up and put away the tables and the food. Then they made their way into the worship concert. Soon there was no one in the field. Bryan warmed himself by the dying fire. His mask took an eerie appearance by the glowing embers. The eye holes of his mask were black and he stood tall, strong, and imposing.

He had seen her. She was here!! Tonight, would be his chance to finish her off for good, for coming into his territory, once and for all. The house would be his again and only his! He crept up slowly beside the church. The music was loud and booming, and several bands would take the stage. The voices inside his head were now screaming at a crescendo loud enough to make his head explode and were shouting at him and punishing him because he did not obey. They punished and taunted him in his thoughts. He could not take it as he banged his head against the brick church wall. He was well hidden in the bushes and yet could hear everything inside. He saw all the men that were talking to her and clenched his fists. His thoughts screamed. *"What was wrong with him? Why did that anger him? He never cared before. People talked* with each other all the time. *He never cared before, so why now?"* He watched and saw all the earlier events of the night from the woods edge and stood there for hours and waited for the time he would do the deed. Over a period of time, for some odd reason, the voices inside him quieted as the music went slower. He heard melodious tongues and listened to the singers sing "you have made me clean, nothing is too dirty for you, your sweet sacrifice, this blood that ran down."

"*BLOOD? What and why are they singing about blood? I am used to seeing a lot of blood in my kills*," he thought. He listened more. He was beginning to feel some weird, warm, syrupy way inside. His thoughts strangely quieted at the melodious sounds of the songs. Still he was determined to kill her, but he was not being driven, but wanted to listen to more of what they sang about. This "blood" song perked his ears up. He never heard a song like that before. There was another song about Heaven's beauty, but the "blood" song perked his ears up. He had his knife in his coveralls ready to go for her. "*I guess if they can sing about blood, I can spill it,*" he thought. The music stopped, and the pastor gave a short sermon and bid everyone good night. Everyone filed out of the church and went home. Bryan remained firmly planted against the church, in the bushes.

"Amy are you sure you don't need a ride home, its nearly midnight?" said Pastor Mark.

"No," said Amy. "I need to walk off all those goodies we had tonight."

Pastor said, "Okay, please be safe."

"I will," Amy said. Bryan made his way quickly and quietly to the other end of the street, near his house. He would take her life there, well hidden by the trees and bushes. Amy walked along the sidewalk singing a song from the concert and was looking forward to a warm bed and pleasant sleep. She put her purse on her opposite shoulder across her body and started home, she had some money and her devotional

Chapter 6

tucked in it.

Amy neared the area to where her new house stood, stopped and marveled how pretty the remodeled home looked in the moonlight. He waited until she got close enough. It was his time! Just then, larger than life, he stepped out of the shadows. His tormented eyes looked wild and crazily, insane in the moonlight, his clown-like mask and his hands were white as snow in stark contrast against his black coveralls.

"Lord Jesus save me," she cried! Before she could run, there was a big strong hand over her mouth from behind and something that looked like a huge knife. He held her firmly in his strong clutches from behind. In a flash she recalled how similar the dreams she had been having to this moment. But it was futile to struggle, he was too strong, she blacked out.

The next day she woke in a familiar place. The basement of the house she had bought! Was she dreaming again? No! It was not a dream! He was sitting right there watching her! She tried to get up and realized she was tied to the bed. His bed! "Oh my gosh," she thought. "What is he going to do? The news said he was locked away for life!" A million thoughts assailed her mind now on what she could do to break free. His eyes were wide, wild and crazy. "Okay, how do I communicate with him, if at all?"

He was watching her the whole time through the night. He tried to kill her but could not. It puzzled him as to why, he could not kill her. He just stared at her. She almost found it laughable that he stared and stared at her for what seemed like hours. In her nervousness, she managed to say something, "A-A-Are you Andrew Bryan Conners?" He just cocked his head and did not say anything, but stared. "Uhmmm, okay, now what? She thought, and fought back nervous laughter, bit her tongue hard, as she was used to laughing at little things or facial expressions. "Is he going to kill me later? What is the hold up and why has he delayed in doing so?"

Redemption Has No Limits

She tried to be very careful to not set him off, because she knew people that were unstable could snap at the drop of a hat. His knife was on the nightstand and he rearranged the basement area to look more like a room. "He must have another key to the house," she thought.

"S-S-Sir, I am sorry I disturbed your home. No one told me y-y-you would come back ever, and I wanted to help the community by…" Bryan stood up and grabbed his knife and began slashing the mattress violently. "Whoa!" I am not here to hurt you, your things, or your house!" Bryan stormed out of the room and slammed the door. She was left alone in the basement for many hours and day turned into night. Bryan came back and sat down and stared at her more. Amy's stomach growled. The last thing she had were the goodies at the party the night before. Bryan must have heard her stomach growl as he left for a while and returned with a few apples. "It must have been those apple trees near the field," she thought. She realized maybe he had been watching her the whole time and he may have been at the event last night. How did he know she was there? She could not put her finger on how long he had been stalking her, but it must have been weeks. He sat down across from her and watched her eat. "Thank you, sir," Amy said.

"I am going to have to use the bathroom over there. Can you please untie me?" Amy realized she had been holding it all day into the night and dared not set him off. He took his knife and cut the cords that bound her in one swipe. She quickly made her way over to the bathroom and closed the door and made sure she did her business quickly, because she did not know when she opened the door what he would do.

As soon as she finished her business and came out, he grabbed her and held her against the wall by the wrists, pressing himself hard against her in a threatening way, and would not let her go. His masked face was so close he could kiss her, but only stared deep in her eyes. She tried to

Chapter 6

maintain her composure and reached for the faith and peace deep within her soul, and it reassured her that all would be okay somehow, and she would find a way to get out of this nightmare that became a reality with this masked individual.

She read somewhere he was not one to rape his subjects, but when someone is insane there is a first for everything and he was unpredictable. He tied her back up on the bed. The thought to ask him to release her was unthinkable. "He could snap at anything," she thought. Amy was not one to cower in shame and she knew who she was, but she did not know how to react with this individual people said was the devil. She knew of something greater then evil, and this was the time her faith would be put to the test. Amy searched on the inside of herself and prayed on what to do. "Sing melodies of comfort," came the gentle nudging. "This will help." So, Amy began to quietly hum as he stared at her. His wild eyes shifted back and forth, and as she looked at them from time to time, they were not black, but blue and very human - crazy - but human, not demon's eyes at all. "People are so quick to put labels on others. No matter how wicked and crazy some were, people should not look at the wrongs others may have done. Not one of us are perfect," she thought.

"Do you talk?" She asked Bryan? He just looked at her. "Sad!" she thought. "He must have really had a hard life," and wondered at the depth of blows of life itself that made him that way. All it took was a look into those eyes that told the tale. Did she see sadness and pain masked by anger perhaps? This was a cold-blooded killer who did not think twice about killing someone and leaving them for dead. She understood her own hard life growing up and thought perhaps his life was not much better. Perhaps he was abused growing up and took all his pain out on people. She guessed him to be about 10 years older than her or so. But she still could not figure out what he wanted to do with her. She had this discerning gift to see right through people into their pain and hurt, and she knew somehow the things he had gone through, and he was crying out somehow.

"Bryan. You know it's getting colder outside, and I-I-I don't mind if you reside here it is your house. I just wanted to make sure it would be warmer for you if I fixed it up," Amy said. She thought maybe bargaining with him, and hoping somehow, he would release her. His eyes flashed rage and Amy knew she better not talk about that anymore. Bryan got up and left the room. She eventually fell asleep with fits of nonsense dreams she could not piece together—a belt striking something over and over—harsh words towards a child being whipped—a woman she did not know and a drunken, pale man.

Amy slept, and he came back in and watched her. She moaned in her fitful sleep and he watched her eyes dart back as she slept. Her dark curly hair fell gently across the pillow in rivets. He resisted to touch her hair. It was like swirling waves that lay in all directions across the pillow. Her skin was smooth and olive colored, in contrast to his pasty white skin and glowed in the dim light. Her full lips were full and opened slightly as she slept.

He did not understand why he was not able to kill her. He did not understand what it was about her that was different. Was it the way she looked? He had never met anyone like this who seemed to look right through him into his soul, if he even had one. That night he could have easily plunged the knife into her, but something stopped him. An invisible force threw his hand back and he could not bring it back down to plunge the knife into her stomach from behind. He tried again but his arm remained immobilized, so all he could do was drag her back to the house before she revived from blacking out.

His plot and plan to kill had failed! This was the first time ever in his rotten history of being a serial killer, something like this had happened. He also realized the voices

Chapter 6

he heard were silent ever since that happened, or no longer shouting inside his head since she had been with him in his house. Was she some kind of good luck charm? She must have been, being all, he ever had in life was everything bad. He peered closer to her face, almost within an inch. He just had to get a better look. It was near dawn and she stirred. He jerked back quickly and fell off the chair startling the woman.

"Wha..Wha...What?" Amy said. He quickly sat back up on the chair before she knew he fell off the chair.

He cursed and chastised himself within, "*You clumsy, stupid idiot!*" Her eyes fully opened, and she sheepishly waved "Hello." He tilted his head to her. It was Sunday and she would be missed at church, and people would wonder where she was at. She shuddered at the thought of it. Then work Monday. How would this go with Pastor Mark, or would she ever see her Pastor and friends again? If she survived through this, she was quite sure she would be the talk of the town. Her boss was quite easy going, but her not showing up to work Monday without calling was another problem. She began to search for a way out of this. Bryan left the room for a while.

She prayed within - and understanding came to her about all the dreams. She realized she had been dreaming about him all along and God was showing her the future, and Bryan's horrible abusive past. "No one should ever have to go through that," she thought. She realized what the belt was hitting. It was Bryan. She felt his humiliation and everything he went through. She was quite certain he was teased at school. She wondered if he ever had any girlfriends. "Was she too going crazy?" This person who she did not know personally, who tried to kill her, his soul somehow became an open book. Or was she feeling God's heart toward him? Her pastor once said "No one is beyond redemption. There is hope for all."

She tugged at the ropes of the bed and could not get free. If she did, he may come back and kill her. No one ever escaped Andrew Bryan Conners…no one! So, she realized she better play her cards right and pray to get through this storm alive. When Bryan came back into the room, she was somewhat embarrassed because she knew some things about him he never disclosed to her. But she also knew and he carefully guarded that inside information like a precious treasure. She avoided his eyes as much as possible, because she knew humiliating things that were hidden behind those mad eyes. She just hummed and took comfort in her own song.

Bryan listened to her hum. He sort of liked it and it seemed to relax him. He thought it odd. Still no voices in his head. He too, seemed to be sleeping a little better, as he drifted off in the other room the next night. Amy woke up early the next day—the cords around her wrists were off! She quickly made her escape in a full blast sprint, but only to crash into him at the top of the stairs. His masked face hot with fury on her face. He again raised his knife to her throat and hauled her downstairs and tied her back up. Once again, he could not kill her. He had raised his knife, but could not deal the deadly blow of slicing. He just did not get it.

"Bryan, please sir, I have to go to work. My job is dependent on me and I need my job."

Bryan nodded his head fiercely "*No!*"

Amy then prayed inside for an answer. Bryan motioned and tapped on his throat. "Sing?" Amy said. Bryan nodded yes. So, she hummed and sang, and maybe she could sing her way out to freedom. He watched her, and her face glowed with a light he'd never seen, as the notes bubbled up and out of her from the inside.

The humming and singing seemed to quiet the wildness within him and settle his eyes. He left and then brought some more apples for her to eat. He would release her to use the bathroom and shower as days turned into weeks. He would bring her food, but every time she tried to escape, he would

Chapter 6

catch her and tie her back up. She felt for certain she would be his prisoner for life. He let her use and rewash clothes that she could wear left over from his family.

One day there was a knock at the door. "Bryan, please let me answer it."

Bryan nodded his head affirmatively.

It was the commissioner. "Oh, Hello commissioner," Amy said.

"Hello, I just came to drop the deed to the house off in person, and to see how you were doing in your new home," the commissioner replied. Bryan hid in the shadows unseen. "Is everything okay?" Asked the commissioner—his eyes seeming to pry deeper into the house.

"Oh Yes!" said Amy. "I have been somewhat indisposed—family matters, with my brother and all." Amy lied and felt guilty about it.

"Okay, well, call us if you need anything."

"Sure thing." Amy said. "Why was she lying and covering for this man who held her hostage?" She did not want anyone else being killed, or to enrage him, as he stood nearby in the shadows, listening to everything that was said, ready to strike. As soon as she closed the door, he grabbed her arm back and pressed into her, up against the wall from behind, the mask puffing back and forth against her ear. She said, "Bryan please, I am not trying to betray you. I don't lie. I don't want anyone, even you, getting hurt. I am not that kind of girl. I know all about that. Please you got to hear me!" He knew it, and heard the truth in her voice, and saw it in her eyes, so he released her.

It was her purity that struck him. It was her purity that relaxed him in her song, and it was her purity that allowed her to live. All the others where disgusting to him, them and their sleazy ways. Male and female alike. He still did not know what to do with her, as it was mid-October, and the special day that month that he always killed was quickly approaching. He wrestled with should he kill her then or not? *"What was the THAT she knew about him? She could not possibly know about all the abuse and humiliation. There is no way! For anyone to know about all that would be to be naked in public!"* He became angry with that thought and his eyes started to flash.

Amy, too, was getting nervous about the Halloween date. By now, she was quite sure he would kill her then and Pastor Mark would for sure have found a replacement for her job by now. She prayed about all of it and left it alone. She was being held as a prisoner in her own home…"Or was it his?" The whole thing was crazy. Amy was always curious about this story that cast a shadow over Harding, Indiana and now, here she sat with him face to face. This notorious killer who was strong and scary, yet, almost like a child. He pushed his way into her life and she kind of wished she never met him. She could not understand why he picked her.

"He had the heart to feed her, so he must not be totally evil," she thought or he was waiting for that night that was special to him to kill her. Amy loved fall but did not care for October 31st . She thought it was a dark holiday which meant more than getting candy and Trick or Treat when she was little. She would go with her mother and brother, but she always would dress in something pretty and sparkly, and never anything dark and evil. Mother always called her, her own little Italian Princess. She smiled at the memory.

"Halloween would be in two weeks," she thought, as she kept track of the days and nights in her head, by seeing through a little window in the basement. She calculated she had been here almost a month, and she was sure the police were looking for her, and some people in her church. She had to do something quick to get away. Either that, or the commissioner had said something to the authorities. He seemed to pry his eyes into her house and life that day, when he delivered the deed to the house. She was very good at

Chapter 6

reading people's intentions and she knew without judging people what they were up to. It just came to her, and she was right most of the time.

One night she took out her devotional from her purse and began reading it. Perhaps she could find comfort in it. He came in with her dinner of soup and crackers and motioned for her to eat. Amy thanked him every time for the food and wondered where he got all the food from. Maybe he would go out and steal it. Sometimes he would bring her a slab of meat from wherever. It seemed to taste like rabbit or deer. Amy put her devotional down and begin to eat slowly. She could not figure him out as to what he was going to do with her. All he could do was stare. "Oh no!" The laughter was threatening to come out. Amy quickly diverted her thoughts to something else more serious.

After Amy was done eating, he picked up her devotional and looked at her. He pointed to it and touched his throat, then motioned to her. "You want me to read?" Amy said. "Uh, okay." She did as he wanted. Amy quickly thought of a passage that would be okay to read. Psalm 23:4, "*Yea, though I walk through the shadow of death, I will fear no evil: for though art with me; thy rod and thy staff they comfort me.*" Amy froze. She did not want to read the next verse because it talked about enemies- "nothing to set him off" she thought and went to verse 6: "*Surely goodness and mercy shall follow me all the days of my life: and I will dwell in the house of the Lord forever.*"

If he was really that evil, the devotional surely would have burned his hand like the crosses would do to vampires in movies. She had watched too many of those movies growing up on Saturday night. It did not, and he intently watched her as she read. "Boy, he sure stares a lot!" she thought. She was raised with the idea that staring was rude, but he did not think so. "I guess everyone is raised different," she thought. Over the weeks of her captivity she noticed his eyes were not as crazy, and they seemed to soften somewhat when she would sing. He always wore that mask. She wondered what he looked like underneath. Perhaps, he was disfigured and ashamed, but she somehow knew the deeper things about him from the dreams.

She knew that mask was part of his identity and she did not think it was that scary. His mask was kind of cute. There was a human being—a soul—underneath that mask, and she wanted to know his real appearance. "I like your mask," she said. "It's cute." The comment seemed to jolt him back as he looked at her oddly and tilted his head. *"No one ever told me that, and this mask terrifies everyone,"* he thought. She meant that, but was also trying to soften him, so she could escape. "But would he find her?" No one ever escaped him. She better tread lightly.

That night she was tired and fell asleep. He watched her angel like face; her breathing in and out; and her lips parted once again, to indicate she was in a deep sleep. He could have snapped her neck in at instant. But leaned closer to her and wanted to be close to her face. He was inches from her face when she stirred. *"Not this time will I fall off the chair!"* He thought. The desire welled up in him to touch her. He gently stroked her hair and yearned to touch her face. He did so. *"No, you better not! You have the hands of evil! The hands of a killer,"* came the familiar voices. *"Shame on you! You evil thing you should killed her when you had the chance!"*

He fought these thoughts and touched her anyway. She stirred. He just enjoyed being close to her face and looking at it. For once, it was a face not covered in blood and horror, and he wanted to touch her full lips and gently traced them with his finger. She stirred again and he quickly jolted back. He smelled her skin and it smelled like pumpkin spice. She must have had some perfume in her purse. *"What was wrong with him? Was he falling in love?"* The voices tormented him more, *"She will never love you and you're a monster! You're*

Chapter 6

not worth it you evil demonic thing! Shame on you!" The voices continued cursing and shaming him. He was ashamed at himself. *"Is this what normal people did and was this love?"* A part of him yearned for a normal life and another part of him tormented him for the crimes he committed. It was very early morning and before it got light, he went out to a rose garden a few blocks down. Today he would communicate how he really felt. He picked three roses. These were late blooming roses. Fall had been unusually warm, so the roses were still in bloom. He put them in an old vase he found. It was his mother's vase.

He came in the basement with some cereal and milk he had stolen a few days ago from another house. Once again the family was not home. *"What is with that?"* He thought. He brought the cereal in with the vase of three roses. Amy woke up and gasped. "Uhhm, thank you! Are these for me?" Bryan nodded yes. "Thank you so much! They are my favorite flowers!" The fall roses smelled so sweet. "Bryan, can I go to my house? I-I need some new clothes and I have plenty of food there." Bryan's blue eyes hardened with anger and he violently shook his head, "No!" "I am not going to leave you," she promised! Bryan heard many broken, betraying promises before, from his family and people, and he was not about to lose her. He realized he needed to protect her in some way.

"Is this what someone in love does?" Bryan thought. *"She was so pure and beautiful, and I want to make her mine,"* he pondered. She took advantage of the chance of the moment of vulnerability. "Bryan, can we both go to my house tonight, late, to get my things, where no one can see us. I promise I will not do anything stupid—you can trust me. You can even take your knife if you don't trust me. I want you to know you can trust me." He stiffened, eyes threatening. She looked deep into his eyes past the anger. He stared deep into her soul and knew she was telling the truth. Her eyes were full of light like heaven, and he saw eternity there. They glowed like

brown crystal-clear marbles.

At 3:00 a.m. they set out. Bryan leading the way there within the bushes, firmly clutching her hand. He knew the way where they could not be seen. He did not trust people and all their suspicions. She was different though, and perhaps there may be some good people in this world after all. "Bryan, please not so tight! My hand?" she whispered. "You don't know your own strength." He had not realized he was crushing her hand. His heart was racing wildly at the thought of losing her. His hand was huge compared to hers and just swallowed hers up. They arrived at her house and went in the back door. She made sure she turned off the alarm to not awaken the neighbors. She kept the lights off, just in case anyone would be awake, watching her house.

She gathered about a week's supply of clothes and a good supply of food for the both of them, and she had a stash of money and grabbed it. He followed her through every room, intently watching her closely. She shoved everything into a duffel bag and locked her house back up, and they set out back to his house. It was for sure getting cold, as she breathed in the frosty air. Thankfully, she turned the utilities on in his home. The new furnace was doing its job of keeping the house warm, and the utilities to both places were paid ahead of time by automatic withdraw from her bank account, so nothing would ever get shut off. They saw headlights coming slowly down the street and ducked safely deep in the bushes to avoid being seen. It was a cop car. They both stayed still. "Night patrol just doing their job," Amy thought. They remained still till the car was well out of sight. His gaze remained fixed on her to see what she would do. She did nothing but wanted him to trust her. He was a broken man and she felt pity for him. She believed everything was forgivable, yes, even murder. "We all need a chance to start over," she thought.

Amy knew her life would never be the same after this

Chapter 6

encounter. How could she return to the happy life, friends and work she knew? Her reputation would be scarred and if she did return what would become of Bryan and her reintroduction back into society? She was adjusted into society and he was not; and she thought of the different tribes on islands who never acclimated into a more civilized society. Her Pastor shared this story about the missionaries who have encountered such tribes, and she thought of Bryan right here in the American landscape.

Bryan was her wild man. "What? Her wild man?" She should not even be thinking about stuff like this! Amy shook her head. "Was she falling in love?" She knew how he felt, but him with all his craziness, "How would life be for the both of them?"

Chapter 7

Some people were not too easy to forgive when their loved one's lives were snuffed out. Amy shuttered at the thought. She thought of the three men that approached her that night at the party. They seemed to mean business and were part of the community and did not attend her church. Amy would always see them on the street at events. They were a permanent fixture in her town. She wondered if they were the watchdogs. They were always together and out and about on the streets. She could not help but think about them as Bryan and she walked back and went inside the house. Thankfully the streets were empty and houses dark. Still they remained well hidden along the bushes.

Amy's thoughts were interrupted as he suddenly grabbed her in a strong bear hug and took his knife out, his eyes flashing wildly. "Oh no! Going out of the house must have set him off! This is surely the end," she feared. He forced her into the basement and back onto the bed. He held her so tight she thought she would suffocate. The next thing she knew, he was on top of her, his full weight crushing her, knife in hand, and his masked face close to hers, breathing fast and heavy and the mask's lips puffing in and out. "Jesus help!" she cried. He stared at her stunned for a moment and grabbed her face - then proceeded to almost kiss her. Then his face went down next to hers as if he was hugging her, his full body weight on top of her, arms on each side. His knife dropped to the ground, and his arms went around her body and he held her so tight. He rested on top of her for the longest time. His breathing became slow and steady.

    When Amy thought all was calm, she said "Bryan can you please get off me? Your body weight is crushing me." He was about six feet four inches tall or more to her five feet-five inch frame. He did not move. Was he dead? "Bryan," she called out. He wanted her to think he was asleep, but he was not. He was enjoying being with her. He felt so good being close to her. The voices taunted him and shamed him for his humanness and wanting to feel the touch of being close to another person in an embrace. The only physical contact he knew were blows or needles from people, and the only time he touched people was to kill. He rested on top of her for the longest time and resisted the new thoughts that came into his mind about her. Thoughts he was not used to, and things his human body did. She shifted her body to breathe easier. She too was struggling with thoughts that she dare not ponder on, and she knew one thing would lead to another.

    He finally moved himself off her and sat up staring at her. "Bryan, I am not ready to give myself to anyone. I am saving myself for marriage." The thought infuriated him as he grabbed his knife and struck the nightstand repeatedly, sending wood shards everywhere. "Bryan, PLEASE try to understand I am not like the others." Bryan stormed out and slammed the door. Amy checked the date on her watch and indeed, it was October 31st. "No wonder he was acting crazy! But wait October 31st had come and was almost gone and he did not kill me," she thought out loud. He had initially planned to kill her but did not. Perhaps she was safe after all? Perhaps now he would be calmer in his head.

    It was now November 1st and the first signs of the holidays would be approaching. The town would soon be decorated with Christmas cheer. She wondered about the

Chapter 7

Christmas pageant and wondered if it would go on without her. She wanted her life back, but she also realized inside her heart that there was now another tied to her heart. Did she care for him? She did not even know what he looked like under that mask. Not that, that was important. The next step was to find out what he was under the mask.

He returned hours later with a notebook. He opened it up and he gave it to her. It had a picture of a big red heart he had drawn and the word "love" in the middle of it and pointed to her. Amy said, "I know," and placed her hand on her chest, pointed to him and said, "I have feelings for you too." His blue eyes softened. He just could not stop staring at her. He sat down next to her and moved his masked face closer to her. Their lips almost touched and soon they were in a kiss. This was what he had been waiting for. This was what he wanted. That's why he kept coming close to her face at night. But he did not really know why until now. It was a closed lipped kiss. For the longest time, his masked lips remained on hers. He left and came back with a box and gestured for her to open it. It was his mother's wedding ring.

"Bryan, I-I cannot possibly accept that. That belongs to you. I am sorry." Bryan's eyes narrowed with hurt and anger. "Bryan, I, uh, don't even know what your real face looks like. Can we do this right? I must see your real face. I promise I will accept you for you and will not make fun of you no matter what. Please show me your face. You can trust me. There is nothing to be afraid of. You don't even know my name. I am Amy."

Bryan sighed deeply and paused for a moment as if pondering whether to remove the mask. He sat still like a statue. Then he slowly removed the mask as if in pain. First out came the well-set lips, they were red and perfect. Next came the chiseled cheeks and a scar that ran by the corner of his eye. Next came his hair that was dark brown, straight and tousled. His face was so white. He hung his head in shame.

"Oh Bryan, you are so beautiful!" She had him look in her eyes and held his face. "Bryan you never, ever, ever, have to be ashamed around me. I love you!"

He grabbed her and held her tight and kissed her passionately. Tears welling up inside him, his eyes grew misty. For the first time in his life ever, he was told he was loved. He turned his head to wipe the tears that ran down his face. Amy knew he was crying. Great sobs shook his body and Amy said, "It's okay, Bryan, you don't have to be ashamed." She took his big frame into her arms and kissed his head, wishing she could just take away all the pain he ever had and thought "dear Lord, what did they do to him?" She noticed another scar on the other side of his head and remembered the dream she had about the lobotomy. She just held him tight for hours as he cried. Her shirt became soaked with his tears. This was all he ever wanted to hear, as wave after wave of sobs racked his body. The last time he cried was when his father beat him, but this was different. These tears were tears of healing.

"Bryan, I have to go back to my house to get more food and take these other clothes back to be washed. Do you trust me?" said Amy.

Bryan looked at her apprehensively and motioned please be quick.

"Okay, I will," she replied. It was nighttime, and she quickly walked back to her house and exchanged clothes and grabbed more food. She would wash the dirty ones later. She exited her home and locked her door.

For the first time in his life, Bryan felt like he mattered to someone. Joy welled up in his heart for the first time ever, and he blissfully made sandwiches and chips for the both of them from the food she brought over. Her love and joy spilled over to him and seemed to change him bit by bit. The voices in his head, were all but quiet now, as time had gone on when he was with her. He brought a table upstairs and they would eat like normal people when she arrived home. His thoughts

Chapter 7

were erupted by a loud thud outside. He thought maybe it was her. "Amy, my sweet breath of fresh air," he thought. He went outside in the back yard. It was cold, and he stepped out and inspected the yard. "So, you SOB, you thought you escaped prison?"

He turned and there stood three men with crowbars and bats reeking of strong alcohol. "We are going to teach you a lesson you will never forget! You're in Amy's house and you need to leave now! You demon!" One of them slurred! "We waited for this moment to give you a beat down that you deserve!" The blows came hard and vicious, as the men beat him within an inch of his life. He covered his face and head as he had always done in these situations.

Amy came in and said "Bryan? Bryan? She heard the commotion outside. "NOOOOO!" She cried, "STOP!" He has not done anything to you!" she protested.

"Oh, so now you are fresh with him? His little girlfriend? Get away from him! He is a cold-blooded killer. He is the devil, himself! Get her Tom!" Said one of the other two. Tom grabbed her and hauled her off.

"STOP PLEASE!" Amy cried, and tried to escape his grasp but could not. She cried and pleaded, but it was no use.

Tom said, "I should have got with you when I had the chance!!" He then forced her into his car and took her down to the police station where they drilled her with questions. A psychologist came and questioned her, and after many hours, released her. It was late into the night when they said she could go. The three vigilante watchmen where protected by police, they were related to them as brothers and cousins. So, it was her word against theirs.

Amy rushed back to Bryan's old house, but there was no sign of him. "What did they do with him," she wondered? There was a blood stain in the grass where Bryan had laid. Amy fought back tears. She only wanted to show another human being love, and he so deserved it regardless of his past, and that was what God wanted. "God please protect him," she prayed.

The next day she called her pastor and told him everything. He consoled her for hours. She wept, and he said, "this is a very heavy story." Then she asked about her job. He said "I think you need a few days away yet to process all that has happened to you. Yes, we want you back, but you need some time to heal."

Amy said, "I can promise you I have maintained my integrity and only showed him God's love. He did not violate me."

Pastor Mark said, "I understand, but I am giving you a few more days. It would be your word against theirs…lets pray for Bryan."

"Okay," she agreed.

The pastor was right, it would be good for her to be alone, and so she rested the few days she had to herself. Amy kept herself busy in her first house and did not dare go back to Bryan's place. It was too painful to relive all they shared together, but eventually she would. If he was still alive out there, he was more than welcome to it, for it was cold now and he would definitely need shelter from the harsh winter that would soon arrive. The house was warm and still had food for him if he needed it. She had brought it back that night for them, so he could have it if need be. She prayed for him every night, that he would be okay out there.

That Sunday she got ready for church and slowly walked there, her heart sad. People would turn and stare and whisper about her to each other. She only smiled, but was ashamed at herself for falling in love with the person everyone hated. When she arrived, some church people greeted her with, "Are you okay?" Some were concerned, but others were acting suspicious and hateful, and avoided her like she had a disease. Sheila and Pam came up to her and they locked in an embrace. Faithful always, Sheila and Pam, her two main

Chapter 7

dancers, were there for her until the end. "Thank you," Amy said and smiled. Many cards arrived at her first home of encouraging words and well wishes.

Her pastor gave the message about restoration and hope. The message lifted her spirits and it seemed like she had not been there in years. After service her pastor said, "Are you ready to come back to work tomorrow?"

"Of course!" Amy said.

"I will see you then!" It took several weeks for her to get settled into a routine, but she slowly eased her way back in and her pastor was patient with her. He knew of the trauma situations like this can bring. Before long she was back in the saddle, but Amy's life felt different. She was no longer happy, but sad. Mary noticed this and did not speak too much to her at work. Mary believed Amy should focus on her job and forget about Bryan.

She could not bring herself to forget about Bryan, no matter how hard she tried. Weeks went by, Amy finally decided one Saturday she would go back to his house. She just had to know if there was any sign of life inside the house, she would know if anything was eaten or moved. She turned the key and peered in. "Bryan," she called? No one was there. Her heart sank, and things were still left out from that night. She cleaned up the food and took out the garbage. He had prepared a table for them to actually sit down to a meal the night they attacked him and that's all she had now was a memory. She doubted she would ever love again.

Every Wednesday and Thursday night coming home from dance and play practices she had expected him to pop out of the bushes when she would hear a rustle. "Bryan? Is that you? Please come out." It was nothing. Amy walked on home. Every time she heard a noise it was nothing. Sometimes she wished she had never met him, and life was better before him, but now her heart was wounded, and she doubted it would ever heal. This was much worse than losing

Redemption Has No Limits

her grandmother, and why did the people in her life she cared about and loved always have to die or leave? Christmas came and went, and the pageant took place, but Amy's heart was heavy with sadness as she went through the production.

One Sunday morning, two weeks after Christmas, Amy decided she wanted to go to the bakery instead of church. She just needed some alone-time. She set out to the area bakery. She was soon lost in her own thoughts over some coffee and a donut. These two men in suits, she did not know, walked into the bakery and sat down. Amy tuned her ears to their conversation. "So, they released him? When?" "Sometime in August," the other said. "Who were they talking about?" she wondered. "Yes, his subsequent release. Once a judge releases him on a technicality that was it. Did you also know he kidnapped some girl here in this area and held her for almost two months and now she is the talk of the town?" "She is actually still alive? He did not kill her. That's shocking because he always kills."

Amy hid her face. "Sources say some vigilante group with a family connection to the police hunted him down and beat him severely, and this is the reason why we came to investigate. Also, the two men who were hauling him to the morgue, after they beat him to death, died of an alcohol accident with the blood alcohol content of 1.20."

"Wow," said the other, "that is almost lethal!" "When the police went to investigate the crash there was no sign of the men that was attacked on the way to the morgue. His body, however, was not found. The police examined the area, but could not find it."

Amy's heart leapt for joy! "He was somehow still alive! Or is he? If he escaped, surely he must be somewhere." Amy cried out inside in desperation. A severe snowstorm was headed in their direction and Amy and her town would be snowed in. The news station was predicting 24 inches and her town would be immobilized. The first bands of snow began

Chapter 7

falling early that morning before they were at service…not blizzard-like, but steady.

Amy hunkered down at her first home and made some hot chocolate and watched the news. There would be no going to work Monday if there was that much snow coming in. Amy watched out the window as snow began to fall like a torrent. Through the blinding snow Amy thought she saw a shadow. She rubbed her eyes, but it was nothing but a blob of white snow coming down outside her window, but she could not tell because it was snowing so hard. "No, it's been too long, and he probably would not come back in this storm. Or he was perhaps dead somewhere." She worried about him being out there in subzero temperatures and prayed he was okay. No one in their right mind would go out in this.

Amy shut off the television and called it an early night. It was 9:00 p.m. It would snow all night. She shivered as she heard the howling wind outside. She had some sewing to do tomorrow for the Easter production coming up. "Might as well take advantage of this time off." She got up the next morning to a knock on the door. It was Scotty, one of the neighbor's kids, who always liked to shovel snow and earn his keep. So, he took advantage of the blizzard. "Ma'am, can I shovel your drive?"

"Sure, and I will give you $20.00," Amy said.

Scotty smiled brightly, "Okay awesome!" Scotty was a carrot top kid with a wide smile, who looked almost elf-like in appearance, and he blended perfectly with the snow. "He would make a perfect Christmas elf," she thought. Amy was glad he stopped by because she had a lot to get done with cleaning, laundry, and sewing for the Easter production which was fast approaching.

"Oh," Scotty said. "Pardon me ma'am, but did you notice the foot trails in the snow by your window and around your house over there?"

"No," Amy said but, in her mind, "Could it be?" She missed Bryan terribly. "Maybe it was the meter reader guy," she said to Scotty.

"They come out in all kinds of weather." Scotty replied, "Probably so."

Amy dare not tell Scotty anything he would not understand. Scotty went to work, and when he was done, she gave him the money, and he happily went off to his next job.

Amy went to sewing and doing the various household chores and prepared for the workweek. She sorted all the clothes she would wear each day for the week. It was her nature to be organized. The day was drawing to a close and more snow would be coming in that night, but not enough to get another day off. She was glad she got the last of the costumes done for the Easter production. Amy prepared to go to sleep and she thought she heard something like a bump outside her bedroom window. She looked out and it was nothing but the tree branch bumping against her window. Her heart sank. "Well, I guess I have to move on with life," she thought begrudgingly. "Why doesn't he come back? If he is alive he should. Oh well, I can't force him. He is a man of mystery, yet I know him," she pondered in her heart.

Amy dreamed that night all over again, of the kidnapping, and how she came to know him, and all the times he held her close even though he did not know what to do…if he should kill her or not. As fearful as those times were, she still missed him. She only wanted to remember the good about him. The heart he drew; the three roses, the ring, the first kiss, the way he would not let her go after coming back from her house that night late, the masked face always getting in her face, his relentless stare, his blue eyes, and…that mask. She dreamed about those events over and over that night. She awoke and sobbed, "Lord, is this all I have to remember him by? Please let him come back." She remembered a devotional about the lovesick bride in Song of Solomon. "I feel as she does," she thought.

Chapter 7

She trudged through her day wondering about the dream. "Was it something to come or was it just me wanting and wishing?" Amy could not figure it out, but she continued on in her life, her job, and keeping to her dance and play evening practices. It would be getting warmer soon. It was now March and winter would be over soon.

"Maybe the warmer weather will cheer me up," she said to herself. Easter would be in April and Pastor Mark would give her a few days off for reflection. Pastor Mark always closed the church that week after Easter to visit his family in Florida. He would be back that Friday after. Amy always took her other vacation in the summer to lounge by the beach about an hour away. She would grab breakfast and head out for a day of fun in the sun. It was a secluded area that not many went to or knew about. Amy went there alone to reflect, and it was her happy place. She imagined that place and parts of her life going places not alone anymore, but with him. "Was she only wanting and wishing again, or was it just her imagination?" She could not escape these thoughts. They whispered to her. She fought to dismiss them in case they were just her imagination.

Amy walked home from work and let herself inside her house. She thought of Bryan's house and realized she had not been there since sometime in December, and that was only to clean up the table he had set for their dinner right before the beating. She realized she had to pay a visit sometime to check on the house to see if anything else had been delivered from the county or if anything had been vandalized, since the news got out about her kidnapping and disappearance. The house already had a reputation, so she wanted to make sure nothing was damaged or missing. "Those jerks had it coming," she said to herself. "They had no right to beat him like that! People can change with a little love shown to them." Amy felt angry. She wondered about Tom. No one had heard much about him, nor had she seen him since that night. Amy's thoughts were interrupted by a knock on the door.

Redemption Has No Limits

"Hello ma'am. Good evening." The two men in suits were at her door. The men she saw at the bakery.

"Hello. Can I help you?" She said.

"I am Doug, and this is Jeff. We are here in town and we heard Andrew Bryan Conners, had kidnapped you."

"Okay, how can I help? Come on in." Amy was curious.

"Do you know Dr. Smith?"

"No, never heard of him." Yet, Amy knew who he was by overhearing their conversation at the bakery. She knew to play dumb, releasing as little information as possible. She knew they were up to no good.

"That was Bryan's shrink that kept him doped up, and did many unethical experiments on him. The judge released Bryan on a technicality, and we wanted to chat with you," they said.

"What did he do to Bryan?" Amy questioned.

Chapter 8

"He gave him electric shock treatments at a much higher dose than is legal, a lobotomy, over drugged him with tranquilizers and placed mind-altering drugs in his food. The wardens also confessed to beating Bryan repeatedly at the doctor's commands. They were charged with abuse and assault of a mental patient," one of the men said.

Amy said, "Where is the doctor now?"

"He committed suicide once he realized his license was revoked and reputation ruined," the men answered.

"Oh my!" said Amy.

"Okay, the real reason we came here is to talk about you. You survived the ordeal. We want to hear your survival story. What was that like? Do you know where he is?" The men queried.

"No, I don't. I have not seen him since that time," Amy replied.

"What time," they questioned?

"The time he kidnapped me and released me."

"What? He released you?"

"Yes," she said. Amy did not dare to tell too much, or that she loved him. The men were fishing for information and she was not going to give them too much to chew on. Finally, getting frustrated inside, Amy said, "Please hear me out. If you are expecting a long drawn out story, Bryan did not talk, so there is not much to tell because he is mute. He also did not rape me, so there is nothing there. What do you want me to say? My faith allowed me to survive, not Bryan."

They were satisfied with her answer and bid her "Goodbye."

"People did not want to talk about stuff like faith these days," Amy thought. She shut the door and breathed a sigh of relief. That's the last she would see of them as they traveled back to the area they came from. Their car exploded from a gas leak in the engine after their stop at a restaurant.

"Amy, I want you to work on a special flier for spring. I am planning to host a creative arts event. I want people to use and display their talents. We have had a harsh winter and the event might lift people's spirits up. Easter will be one week after that, so think of something creative and special for the flier.

It's April 1st, at 6:30 p.m. on Friday," Pastor Mark said.

"Sure thing, you got it," Amy said.

Amy set to work on creatively organizing the event, where people could show off their talents for the first hour, and they would a worship and prayer time afterwards. The flier would invite people to come and display their talents or just come to the event and enjoy the talents of others. Finally done with the flier, Amy was pleased with the colors and letter style she picked. Pastor Mark said, "That looks good. Okay, let's run it off and send out the fliers."

"Sure thing," said Amy. Pastor Mark always had Amy make the fliers, and Mary did the more administrative duties of the office. Mary was the nuts and bolts of the administration of organizing pastor's schedule.

Amy was not as close to Mary as she used to be, but they worked together peacefully. Amy kept the conversation with her light and happy. Amy was okay with that and it was well. She knew talking about Bryan was a big no-no in the office, and she was wise about that. Mary did not care to hear

Chapter 8

anything about him. She was finished with that conversation and would have had Amy forget him too.

Walking home from work, Amy thought of who could be in the show. There were many talents in the church to do skits, dance and sing. She asked around church Sunday, about six people signed up, and she would sign up too. Some signed up for skits, others to sing a song, and a few to show their art. Amy signed herself up to dance, each one would get about ten minutes to perform or show off their crafts. It was going to be a good time, everyone needed some kind of outlet, especially creative people, she thought. Everyone was on their own to come up with something and they would get a chance to express who they were.

"Amy wait up!" Amy turned, and it was Tom.

"What do you want!?" Amy said angrily.

Tom said, "I just wanted to see how you were since the ordeal."

"You had no right to do that to him like that!" Amy said.

"Are you kidding? That man has no soul, and did he get with you?" Tom said mockingly.

Amy slapped him hard. "How dare you! You know what I am all about!" Amy expressed vehemently.

"Well, you know he's still out there, don't you Amy?" Tom sneered.

"I know nothing since the night you all brutally beat him senseless!" yelled Amy. "How are you much better? Two wrongs don't make a right!" Amy screamed.

Tom said, "Obviously we did not kill him, and when he does come back, I have a bullet for his brain! Amy you know I wanted you to be mine since we were in high school, and mark my words, his hide is mine if I ever see him again!" Tom's eyes flashed a vow of rage, and his black hair glistened against his pale skin. If anyone seemed evil, he was.

Amy stormed away as he glared at her. Amy was hot with anger and shook up. She rushed home and needed to find a peaceful place, and quiet. She turned on her inspirational music and finally fell asleep. She awoke with a pounding headache and took some aspirin and made some dinner.

It was the week of the creative arts event. Amy was getting excited. She hoped that perhaps, she could try to put the past behind her, and preparing for the event would take her mind off Bryan. Amy was almost finished with her work week, and that afternoon, first things first, she decided she was going to finally stop back at Bryan's house just to check on things and to perhaps heal.

So, the Thursday before the arts event, she was planning to stop at Bryan's house. She walked over in the warm, spring sunshine, the trees started to show new growth and the lilies were coming up. They seemed to bloom early this year. Her favorite flowers were roses and lilies.

Amy turned the key to the door of Bryan's home and walked in. She checked all the rooms. She breathed a sigh of relief when she saw nothing had changed, and nothing was damaged from vandalism. She thought of Tom and what he may do, but the house was in her name, so she did not think he would disturb it. People would know it was him because he was breathing threats, and that was how she knew him, as one that was very vocal when he was mad about things. He had always been that way, loud and boisterous, with a hot temper. She recalled him punching someone's face, in a fight and shattering their nose and jaw, so he was nothing to play with. She knew what Tom was capable of and feared for Bryan. Even though she knew Bryan was very strong and quite capable of killing him with one blow. "Lord, please protect Bryan because he does not deserve this, he is trying to change and not be the same way he once was," she whispered.

Amy went in the basement and checked out everything. Everything was still intact, and she imagined, once again, the events of the kidnapping and she saw his mother's ring hidden in the corner of the room. The bed, chair, and nightstand still

Chapter 8

intact. The nightstand still displaying the gouges Bryan made that night. She slowly made her way upstairs and went to the kitchen. Wide eyed, she gasped. There were three lilies with a piece of paper folded next to them sitting on the table in his Mother's vase. She became so excited! "He was here!" She checked the food in the pantry and found it was empty. He had been eating it. "Oh my gosh! Oh God, please come back!" She cried in tears of joy! She was so glad he had a place to stay warm for the winter. She rushed home and stuffed a duffel bag full of food, and returned to his home to lay it on the table for him, so he would not have to steal. She opened the piece of paper and it was another heart drawn, with "Love" written on it. She took the lilies, picture, and vase, so he knew she accepted the gift.

Tom had been watching Amy's every move from a distance and he would make sure Bryan would not return. He left Amy's second house alone because she knew if there was any damage, she knew it would be him at fault. So, Tom waited for Bryan to come back instead, he would finish what he started, Tom thought out loud. He wanted Bryan's blood, and the thought of Amy and Bryan together, made his blood boil with rage, and he vowed to get rid of him once and for all.

Amy soared through the workday that Friday, singing and humming. "What is up with you?" Mary said. "I have not seen you like this in months."

"Oh, it's just the event tonight," Amy replied.

Mary said, "You must be getting back to your old self. I mean, I am sure it was quite traumatic to go through all that."

Amy said, "Well, we all have to move on from troubling things that happen in our lives."

"That's the spirit," Mary said.

Amy was so excited as she bounded home, she did not notice a slight movement in the bushes, or Tom in the far distance of the street. She just sang, and with a smile on her face, soared home. Amy could not eat her dinner of tacos she had fixed the night before, she was so excited! "How could she be able to see him again? Perhaps he was ashamed to face her, or disfigured from the beating," Amy wondered. She did not understand why he had not come back to see her. Maybe he knew Tom was looking for him. He was pretty street smart and always seemed to elude people that were after him and had a way of playing hide-and-seek, almost like a ninja stealth warrior. She had witnessed it firsthand the night they went to her house together to get food and clothes.

Amy jumped in the shower and got ready for the event. She put on a greenish - blue flowing chiffon dress garment, and her white dance pants. She strapped a shiny gold belt to her waist and slipped into some shiny gold shoes. She looked like an angel in the flowing garment that went so well with her coloring. "All set for spring and new things," Amy said to herself.

She slipped a jacket on and walked to the church in her outfit, which was more convenient than changing at the church. The first person showcased their art and told the audience about it. The next two groups were ten-minute skits, the fourth person was a solo that sang a few songs. The fifth person played a guitar. The sixth person shared her poetry and finally, it was her turn. She danced to a slow worship song that drew the people in as she moved. She imagined she was dancing with another for a split second. She snapped out of it and focused on the reason for her dance. "Was I imagining it?" she thought.

He watched her from outside the church quietly. She was so beautiful. Heavenly light came from her face as she danced. He could not stop watching her from the bushes. His heart beat fast and his breathing deepened through his mask. He had not seen her since the blizzard. He cursed himself for even being involved with her. "Why did this happen? Those men, were they any of her boyfriends, or was there another?"

Chapter 8

He limped deep into the woods after the beating and spent the night there. He made a makeshift shelter and broke into a camping store to get some blankets and medical supplies. He nursed his wounds as he was used to doing when he got shot and stabbed and he knew how to remove bullets, stitch up wounds, and keep them clean and medicated. So, they would not get infected. These were survival skill his grandfather taught him.

He killed deer and rabbits for food and kept warm by the fires he made at night. When it got so cold, he couldn't bear it, he went back to his house. The night of the blizzard, he made his way back to his house unseen. He snuck up to her house and watched her before going to his. As for his Amy, he was too ashamed to face her and his humiliation kept him away, and he already knew Tom was after him, but because of Amy he resisted killing Tom. He so wanted to kill him, but he knew if he did, he would never see Amy again. His heart would not let him forget her. He had to see her again. No matter what the risk was.

Chapter 9

The night wore on, as he waited in the bushes by the church. They began to sing, and the melodious music soothed him. He felt a drawing to be inside. But he was so afraid to be seen, the place was full of people. The voices in his head were screaming at him to not go in there. They would haul him back to prison and he would never see Amy again. "You are not worthy! Who do you think you are, you dirty rotten sinner! You're going to hell! You're the devil!" The voices thundered, as he grabbed both sides of his head with his large hands.

Most of the people that showcased their talents had left, and there were just about 20 people still there. He became so enamored with the music happening from inside the place and lost in it, he did not realize he already had stepped foot inside the church. The music stopped, everyone froze and gasped! Amy began sobbing and ran up to him. He took her in his arms, for the longest time they embraced. Her feelings were out in the open and now everyone knew the truth. Even Mary, who sat there stunned. The two of them holding on to each other was all they needed. The felt that everyone and everything else could just disappear, and they would just be together in this bubble of love. Amy led him up to the front of the church, the alter, and Bryan just fell on his masked face and wept.

Redemption Has No Limits

Something was cleansing him from the inside. He felt something was pouring over him, like liquid oil. Then he came to the realization that it was love…yes love. He cried and cried. All the pain of his life came out in each tear. All the abuse and humiliation, which he experienced all his life, was being obliterated. All the ugliness came out tear after tear, as he cried in heart wrenching sobs. He looked up at the cross and he pulled the knife out and laid it down on the altar before the cross. He understood about the blood now. The songs that they sang made perfect sense. Jesus died and shed his own blood even for him…yes, him! *"If this is what Amy has, I want it too!"* He thought. That light he saw in her, and the lack of fear she had at him trying to kill her. He did not know how to pray, but only could say inside himself, "Save and forgive me!" The inside of Bryan's mask was drenched with tears, but he still kept it on.

Some people in the church wept and cried, but others were still suspicious and indignant. They did not think Amy should be involved with the killer and she could do much better. Pastor Mark stood by Bryan in awe. He had seen things happen like this, but never with a person like this. He too shed tears at the miracle that just happened.

Just then, there was a loud crash in the back of the church, and in stumbled a drunken Tom through the doors, holding a handgun. "I told you I would come again and finish what I started, didn't I Bryan? Remember that night we beat you so badly you could not see straight?"

"Not in here!" Pastor Mark said. Bryan stood up ready for whatever was coming to him.

"I told you to stay away and out of Amy's house, you evil devil!" Tom cursed a nasty stream to Bryan.

Pastor Mark said firmly, "Watch your tongue!"

Tom grabbed and yanked Amy to himself. "NO! Please Tom, NO!" Amy screamed.

"You're my girl, and I will have you!" Insisted Tom!

Chapter 9

"Let me go! I was never your girl, and nor I will never be!!" Bryan grabbed his knife ready to kill Tom. "NO Bryan! Please NO!! That's what he wants! You're not what he says!" Amy cried.

Tom raised his gun a squeezed the trigger the bullet hit Bryan in the thigh and he slumped down on the floor. Blood dripped onto the carpet creating a red stain. "STOP IT TOM!" Screamed Amy.

Just then a police officer heard the commotion from his car and burst inside, gun poised, and not related to Tom, said, "DROP YOUR WEAPON NOW!" Screamed the police officer. "LET HER GO!"

 "Not till I finish him off! That SOB needs to die!!" Tom said and then pointed the gun to Amy's head. "If I can't have her no one can!"

"I SAID DROP YOUR WEAPON NOW!" Commanded the police officer. Just then Amy stomped on Tom's foot with her heel as hard as she could and broke free.

"Ugh!" cried Tom! He pointed the weapon at Amy, the police officer fired at Tom. The first bullet from the police's gun plunged into Tom's chest, followed by a hail continuous of gunfire until he slumped down with blood splattering out of his chest onto the carpet.

Amy rushed over to Bryan's side and fell on his chest and cried out, "Are you alright? Oh my God, please tell me you are!" Bryan's eyes were half closed.

Pastor Mark said, "We must get him to the hospital right away—the wound is deep!"

"I will go with him," Amy said. The ambulance came to take Bryan to the hospital. On the way there, Amy stayed with him. She was crying and holding his hand. The paramedic started to take Bryan's mask off, and his eyes flew open in rage. Amy knew that look well. "Please don't" Amy said. "Leave it on!"

"Okay, suit yourself, but we are only following procedures."

"In this case, you don't need to. He will be okay with it on," said Amy. At the hospital, they treated the gunshot wound, numbed it, took out the bullet, and stitched it up. They had to cut his jumpsuit up to the thigh. Bryan eyes flashed anger at the sight of his milk-white scarred thigh being exposed to others. Amy said, "Bryan please don't worry, I will get you another suit. Please, this must be treated and that is their job. There is nothing bad about it." He did not like being exposed to anyone. Even something like a thigh injury. He looked deep in her eyes and touched his chest and pointed to her. "I love you too," Amy said. Bryan relaxed and let them treat his injury.

"He will have to stay overnight for observation. One other thing. He does not have any insurance, so we need a payment upfront," said the critical care nurse. Amy said, "I will pay for it." So, she did. Amy hated bureaucracies and all they stood for. To her they were money-hungry organizations ready to milk people of their money. She gladly paid the bill, so her Bryan could be well. He was worth it.

"You have to leave now. Visiting hours are over," said the nurse.

"No, I won't be leaving. You must accommodate me," begged Amy.

"Orders are orders, and you are not family," the nurse replied.

"I will not leave. Let me speak to your supervisor," said Amy. The night supervisor came in. Amy said, "Do you realize I was almost shot and killed tonight, and he tried to protect me? Yes him! Please let me stay. I must be here for him," she said.

"Okay, we will bring a cot for you," said the night supervising nurse when she saw the desperation on Amy face.

Chapter 9

Amy did not realize Bryan was smiling at her through his mask- his eyes tearing up, he thought to himself, "she truly cares about me." She laid her head on his chest and said, "I will not leave you this time, ever." She heard his heart beat steady and soft.

Amy stayed with him all night, and the hospital released him quickly the following morning, because they did not know what he would do. They all knew who he was and viewed him as a threat. He and Amy took a cab back to Bryan's house. Amy helped him up the steps. It was awkward - his size to hers. She helped him down into the basement and then helped him on the bed. His leg was bandaged up, and the bandages would be on till he was healed.

"Bryan, I must leave to get you new coveralls. I will be back."

Bryan glared at her and shook his head "NO!" He viciously pointed to his heart and to her.

"Okay, I will stay. I won't leave you, not right now, but you must know my life has a duty. Do you know what that means Bryan?"

Bryan shook his head, "*no.*"

"It means people do things in their life to take care of things, in a nutshell. Like work a job, go grocery shopping, and take care of the loved ones, like you. I love you Bryan and I am taking care of you. Please trust me to come back. I will. The ones that hurt you so bad are gone and they will never hurt you again. All of them are dead or in jail themselves. They cannot come back from the dead. I know you have escaped death more than once. You are not cursed. I believe you are actually blessed beyond measure."

Amy continued, "I am so very sorry, people have said you are worthless, bad and even cursed to you all of your life. But this is what I know, God kept you alive for what you did before the cross, last night. You have to believe me. This will explain it." She pulled out her devotional. "Please read this. I promise to be quick! Please don't go outside. I will safely lock up. What color coveralls do you want?" He pointed to the ones he had on. "Okay, black," Amy said, and stepped out. Amy hurried to the store and bought him several pairs of coveralls of the same color, underclothes, food, towels, a coat and toiletries with which he could clean himself up with. He could use a much-needed shower, and these things would help.

She passed the church and there was a crowd gathering. News stations came from all over to get the update of what happened last night. They saw Amy and rushed over to her, asking all kinds of questions. She was brief with her answers and kept her promise to Bryan. The story made the national news, and one newspaper's title was "Who's the real monster?"

Amy did not care about being on TV. She just had to get back to Bryan. She came in and quickly went to him. Bryan's eyes brightened when he saw her. "Hi Bryan, I got you all kinds of goodies, food, toiletries, coveralls, and a coat. The coats were on sale, so, I got you one. Would you like a shower, so I can dress your wounds? They said it had to be kept clean. I will go upstairs until you finish, so you can have your privacy. I won't be far." Bryan hung his head.

"Oh no, I did not mean it that way. I am just concerned about your wound. Here is some underwear." Bryan hung his head again. "Oh, Bryan, please don't be ashamed, we all wear them. It's okay. I will be upstairs." Bryan nodded his head. Amy quickly went upstairs and left him, so he could shower.

Amy wondered why he was so sensitive about his body. Perhaps, she was getting to his tender side. Amy could not wrap her head around it. She began to wonder how abused he really was, his body was very scarred and he must be embarrassed by any form of exposure. That had to have been it, because of the beatings he received.

Amy did not care about any of that. She was just glad to be with him again, and she knew they would work through

Chapter 9

this all together, no matter what. She would be there for him, never to be separated again. She realized every time he tried to get up and have something happy happen in his life, people would knock him down. She never wanted to do anything to cause him pain again...like leave. She noticed the welt-like scars on his thigh, probably from an old injury or being beat as a child. "Maybe most of his body is like that," she thought. She missed church due to taking care of him; and she stayed at his house for most of the weekend. They slept in separate rooms upstairs, but she wanted to be near, because he needed to know she would not leave again.

Chapter 10

"Bryan, I have to work today, but I promise I will be back, in only six and half hours. She knew Bryan needed a time frame to hold onto while she was gone. Bryan pulled her into his arms and Amy knew this was not going to be easy for him to let her go, but she explained and reminded him again how people have duties to do. "Bryan, if I don't go, I don't get a pay check, and other people are dependent on me to serve the community," said Amy. Bryan released her reluctantly with sadness in his eyes. "Bryan, you never have to worry about me leaving you for good. I am here to stay, I love you," Amy said.

He embraced her and let her go. He sat there and wondered why she had to go away. He picked up her devotional and read a story about a Man that was rejected and full of sorrows. He kept reading, and realized his own life was similar to this Man's. This Man was beaten to a bloody pulp and not recognizable and humiliated in every single way. How they called him a demon. That part struck him hard. He began to tear up realizing he was not alone in his situation. Someone else went through it too! He stumbled across Isaiah 53:4 "*He is despised and rejected of men; a man of sorrows and acquainted with grief: and we hid as it were our faces from him; he was despised, and we esteemed him not. Surely he hath borne our griefs and carried our sorrows: yet we did esteem him stricken, smitten of God, and afflicted. But he was wounded for our transgressions, he was bruised for our iniquities: the chastisement of our peace was upon him; and with his stripes we are healed. All we like sheep have gone astray; we have turned everyone to his own way; and the LORD hath laid on him the iniquity of us all. He was oppressed, and he was afflicted, yet he opened not his mouth: he is brought as a lamb to the slaughter, and as a sheep before her shearers is dumb, so he opened not his mouth. He was taken from prison and from judgment: and who shall declare his generation? For he was cut off out of the land of the living: for the transgression of my people was he stricken."*

People had cursed and hated him all his life and now he saw his name penned in this passage. This Man went through it all too!! He wept in great heaving sobs and he understood more of why Amy was so special.

She did not respond the same way others did, in sheer terror, when he went to kill them. She seemed shook up, yet at peace, the whole time she was with him during the kidnapping. He saw eternity and heaven in her eyes. He read for hours and needed to know more. He kept crying even when Amy walked in the door. "What is it?" she said. Bryan motioned for her to read to him and he indicated he needed to know more by his gestures. He opened her devotional and pointed to the Man's name. "That's Jesus," and she told him all about Him.

Bryan took her into his arms, sobbing, and laid on top of her for what seemed like hours and cried. He held her so tight and kissed her through his mask. "Bryan, remember you are crushing me," Amy said. He acted as if asleep. She just felt so good to be close to. He did not want to stop being close to her. The voices shamed him for his humanness, but he just ignored them. The voices came and would torment him. However, they would come much less since the night

Chapter 10

he boldly came into their meeting before getting shot. They were still there, but not inside his head anymore. They seemed to be around him, faint, but still there. Amy was so beautiful that night and he watched her float across the floor like an angel in her blue-green dress through the bushes and stained-glass windows. The image of her would be always sharp in his mind of that night. He eventually got off of her and sat up. Amy exclaimed, "I better check the wound," then pulled his pant leg up. Somehow it was healing very quickly. "Wow! You heal quick!" She said.

It was getting dark and Amy said, "I will go upstairs, set the table, and make us dinner." She made a Mexican casserole and Bryan seemed to enjoy it. He ate almost the whole pan of it to her single portion. "Dinner at this table is long overdue," she said. He nodded in agreement, eyes glistening with joy. She noticed when Bryan ate, he either rolled up his mask to the mouth or ate through the mouth hole. She never pressured him to take it off, because she knew how sensitive he was about it. She loved him for him, mask and all. He would take it off when he was ready. She finished the dinner, washed the dishes, and put the leftovers in the refrigerator. "You can have this tomorrow for lunch. I am going to have to make my way back to my house." Bryan's heart sank. "Wait a minute, do you want to come with me to my house? Your leg seems much better?" Amy asked.

Amy knew the risks associated with him leaving his house, but she was willing to give it another try. He reluctantly decided to come. He led her to the bushes. "Bryan, I don't think we have to hide anymore. Everyone knows about us."

He insisted and pointed to his mask."

Okay," she said. Bryan just did not want to be seen as he led her back to her house. It was much earlier this time at night, and people now had their lights on. Amy and Bryan did not need jackets, because of the warm, spring, evening air. They got to her house and came in the door. "Bryan, do you want to watch a movie? I will pop popcorn." He nodded "yes." So, they watched a movie and enjoyed each other's company. "Let me drive you home," Amy commented. "It is getting late and I have to work tomorrow. You know... duties. I will give you one of my extra sweaters, so you won't have to feel so alone. I will be over as soon as I am off work." She sprayed it with her favorite fall fragrance.

"Here is my sweater and you can keep it for good." He breathed in her scent and deeply clutched the sweater to his face. He held the sweater close to his chest as they went out to the car. Amy thought it was so cute, how he was with the sweater, and to be wanted that intensely. "Gosh, he just does not want to let me go!" Her heart swelled with joy.

"Ohhh, look at the Freak and his girlfriend," came the voices from the bushes mocking him. It was a group of teens on the street. Bryan stood poised, ready to strike, his eyes flashing and blood boiling. He hated teenagers.

"Stop it and knock it off! Go home, its past your bedtime! I'm going to tell your parents and I know where you live!" They ran off. "Come on Bryan, I need to take care of this right now!" She took his hand to divert him from going after them. He followed her. Amy was very angry and marched right back into the house and called their parents.

"What," inquired a mom.

"Yes, they are harassing my company and I don't appreciate it!" Amy did not tell the parents who her company was. She had friends over from time to time.

The parent she called said, "We will deal with them when they get to my home. My son was supposed to be doing homework at his friend's house, but obviously not."

"Thanks," said Amy and hung up.

Bryan admired the way she stuck up for him. He knew he would always protect her, but he also knew if he acted the old way, he would lose her, and society does not like what he did. So, he also had to play his cards right. Amy said, "Bryan, some people have a hard time letting go of things others do. Even myself - some people still hold me in contempt for things I have done, and there is not one of us that is perfect." Bryan hung his head. "I don't hold you in contempt, and all things we do are forgivable, so don't be ashamed." Bryan teared up, hugged her, and smiled. Amy drove him home and walked him into the house. He was still clutching the sweater, staring at her. "Yes, you can keep it and I will be over tomorrow after work," she said. Bryan went into his house to the basement and got ready for bed. He never let go of the sweater and fell into a sound sleep, clutching her sweater wafting in Amy's scent.

That night he dreamed of distant memories from his past: of the humiliating beatings, over and over from his drunken dad, and all the mockeries of him and many things that happened in prison and Dr. Smith's shocks and lobotomies. He relived the nightmare over and over again, as he saw many fingers pointing at him. Then he saw Amy in the arms of another man. He awoke in a sweat, heart racing. He jumped out of bed and went to her house in the middle of the night. Bryan did not care who saw him out on the street. He was trying to run from his past.

Amy awoke to the sound of the doorbell. It was 2 a.m. She wondered, "Who would be ringing my doorbell at this hour?" She opened it and Bryan came in waving his arms crazily. "What is it? What is it? Please write it down!" Amy got a notebook and pen. He wrote, "*Nightmare and very bad things.*" It came back to her mind what she saw in her dreams about him. He continued to write, "*Amy in another man's arms.*"

Oh, Bryan, I am so sorry all those things happened to you. I-I know about them. When you kidnapped me, I dreamed of all that happened to you in your life." Bryan got wide eyed as if he was exposed. "I know it sounds crazy, just some gift I have. Some call me prophetic, others say it discernment. I don't know, I just see things inside of people's hearts and into their hurts." Bryan hung his head. "Oh, Bryan I love you, and no matter what happened to you, I love you for you! The past does not matter, and it will never matter!" Bryan pointed to the sentence he wrote about the other guy. "No, not a chance! You are my only man - no one else. Other guys have wanted to date me, but you are the only one. You have my word on it.

Sometimes we have to forgive those who hurt us and release them too. That's for our own peace - not others. "Bryan wondered what he would ever have to offer her when so many other guys had stable jobs, careers, families, and sound minds. He pondered her words about forgiveness. Amy could have easily wound up with any one of the guys in town, but she wanted to be with him, and he did not give her much of a choice. He made her choose him and they fell in love. He realized he pushed himself on her, or was it fate? Nevertheless, she was his and always would be. She drove him home and reassured him she would be over after work.

Amy went to work in the morning, very tired from the long night. She trudged to work. When she had arrived, Pastor Mark and a group of church leaders, along with Mary, were sitting in the conference room. "Amy sit down," said Pastor Mark. Amy sat down and was puzzled. Pastor Mark began, "As you know, the series of events last Friday have caught the attention of the news stations and newspapers across the nation." Some people at the table had a critical stare.

Amy said, "Yes, I do."

"Well, because of the events that happened, and your involvement with Bryan, we are going to have to let you go."

"Why?" Whimpered Amy. "I have been faithful to the job and never resisted anything you asked me to do!"

Pastor Mark said, "You seem to be in fog lately, and cannot seem to focus on the tasks at hand and Mary had to

Chapter 10

re-do a few things I had asked you to do. With the community knowing about you and Bryan, it is too much of a risk, and is bringing to much unwanted attention to our church and community."

"I can promise you nothing is going on, and he tried to save my life!" cried Amy.

"I am sorry, and what if he snaps again and does the same things?" Pastor Mark asked.

Amy said, "He is not going to. Don't you remember that Friday night he came to the alter? What about that? It was YOU who told us in your many sermons, all can be forgiven, and no wrong is too great! What about now?"

"I am sorry," Pastor Mark said, and hung his head. "Please turn in your key and clear out your desk." Amy threw her key on the table, stormed off in tears, quickly emptied her desk and left.

"Okay, so that's why Mary had been acting so cold to me lately?" Amy thought. Ever since that Friday night at the talent show, she had not spoken to her in the office. "No Good morning - nothing."

Thankfully, she had her Grandma's fortune trucked away for a rainy day and now this was a rainy day, and money would not run out anytime soon. It gained interest and she could live off the interest till she found another job to occupy her time. Amy did not need to work, but she chose to. Laziness was not in her nature. Hmmm, she thought momentarily, she could open a boutique, so she and Bryan would never have to be separated again. She knew how to sew and make things. "Why not?" she thought.

Amy went to his house afterwards and he looked at the clock puzzled as to why she came back so early. She explained and slumped down on the couch. "They let me go, they fired me, because of what happened that Friday." His eyes flashed threatening anger. "No! It was not you! If Tom had not did what he did, they would not have wound up in the news."

Redemption Has No Limits

Bryan's fists grew whiter than the rest of him from clenching them. He grabbed another knife out of the kitchen drawer. "Bryan, PLEASE NO! What we have here together is so much more important than that stupid job. I have resources you don't know about, and I will be okay! I have a plan," Amy said.

Amy realized she slipped when she told him a little about her fortune. "You are more important than any position or job in life. You know how I told you we have to forgive?" Bryan nodded and lowered his knife. "That means me too. People will not always act like they should, and we all fall - even those we look up to but, I am with you and will still remain," Amy said. Bryan put the knife back down and hugged her close. She could feel and hear his heartbeat against her ear through his strong chest.

Amy attended another church that Easter Sunday, because she was in a conflicted state about the loss of her job. She was ashamed and did not want to face the people at her church. Amy drove to the other side of her town to a larger church, and hopefully she would not be recognized. She sat in the back and quickly dodged out before the end of service, before anyone could see her. Bryan did not want to go to church, just yet, because of what happened with Amy. She quickly drove home and went to her house. When she got there, Bryan was waiting for her in the back of her house. She fixed a nice dinner and they enjoyed their time together.

Monday and the usual workweek loomed up ahead, but Amy was not used to being home, so she checked out the help wanted ads and went out and applied for a new job somewhere else. The answer was always the same. "We heard about your ordeal at the church and with Bryan. No thanks, we already filled the position." Amy said to herself, "Geez, am I that unemployable because of who is in my life? Maybe that boutique idea is not so bad after all. I will look around for more places of employment this week," she pondered.

Chapter 11

After weeks of job hunting and looking at shops for potential small business, it was now early May and soon to be summer. The flowers were in full bloom and Bryan always brought her new flowers of her favorite kind. She kept his mother's vase on the table to show him she truly appreciated the gifts.

Amy heard a knock at the door one afternoon. It was Sheila and Pam. Both ladies were blonde, angular shaped, and plain looking, but so much fun to be around. She was so happy to see them. "Hey ladies how are you doing? How has life been? It's been so long since we last seen each other!" said Amy.

The three ladies hugged in a warm embrace. Sheila said nervously, "where have you been? It's been weeks since we last saw you!" Amy told Sheila and Pam of how she was let go from her job, and that she was busy looking for another one and maybe to open a boutique.

"You know, not much was said about letting you go," Sheila said.

"As for that boutique that is a fabulous idea! We can help you! It still was not right for Pastor Mark to let you go though," Pam exclaimed.

Redemption Has No Limits

Amy said, "You know, come to think of it, I think it was more pressure from the community, clergy, public, and all the exposure on the news. I had to forgive them. I have been attending another church. The whole situation would be awkward - going there after being fired and all."

"We understand," the ladies said.

Bryan had been in the shadows listening to their conversation in the other room and stepped out into the kitchen. The two ladies gasped and started to leave quickly. Amy said, "Wait, wait, please don't go! He is not going to hurt you. He does not talk, he just wants to say hello."

The two ladies waved hello. Bryan tilted his head and nodded. Amy explained, "It's not what it seems. They are making him to be a monster, but you know what we can all be monsters inside at times." The two ladies nodded, and Amy said. "He has not done anything to me that is hurtful. He just wants to be forgiven and given another chance at life, society is not giving him much of a chance to show them he is not the same person. He gets picked on by teens and I am ostracized in this town now because of my involvement with him."

The two friends were saddened by this news. "Wow! That is so wrong. We don't have dance practice. The arts department has dissolved. They didn't bother hire anyone to take your place!" Sheila said, "You are missed by many. We all want more dance and play events. Where is no outlet for the arts there anymore."

Amy hung her head. "I don't know what to say," she said. "It's been about two months going on three since I was let go."

"Well, hopefully something can be done," Pam said.

"Let's hope so. When the arts thrive, the community thrives. The arts create opportunities for up and coming artists, dancers, and plays. There are so much the arts have to offer besides job opportunities, and it is chance to express oneself," Amy said. Bryan sat there listening intently to the

Chapter ii

ladies talk and tilting his head at times. He did not understand the arts, because no one ever taught him anything in the arts. But he knew from watching her sing and dance, it was beautiful to behold.

Sheila and Pam paced back and forth and were in deep thought. Sheila sopped, looked up and said, "What can we do to fix this?"

Pam replied, "Yes, we must do something to help Amy. I mean, she has been there for us through many things and now it's time to be that friend to her." The ladies thought for a moment.

"I got it!" Sheila said. "Let's start a community petition!"

"You know," said Pam, "that's a great idea. I will be a lot of work, but Amy is worth it!"

Sheila said, "Lets meet at my house tonight to make the plans."

"Sure thing! I'll be over at 7:00," Pam said.

"Deal," said Sheila.

The two ladies met and began to work that night on a plan to restore Amy to her position as the creative arts director. Sheila typed up the petition, the cause, and how it should be worded.

"What shall we name the petition?" asked Pam.

"We will name it, 'Reinstate Amy.'" The two ladies worked into the night and did not stop until the petition was complete.

The petition presented the reason why Amy's position was needed for the community and how much the arts have impacted the community. "We must go door to door for this cause," said Sheila.

"Let's do it!" Sheila and Pam took special care not to let their church know of their activities in helping Amy. They did not go to church members homes and knew they all lived very close to church.

The next day they set out and cased many other area neighborhoods. "Oh, my gosh, that would be wonderful!

Redemption Has No Limits

Where do I sign?" Said person after person, as the two women went door to door.

"How can I help get the word out?" said one family. One signature after another was taken and many offered to help distribute flyers and information. Pam and Sheila printed off many fliers with Amy's picture and cause and distributed them all over the town.

It took about a month to get about 50,000 signatures, and pretty soon the news stations caught wind of what was happening in this community. Once again, Pastor Mark was interviewed as to what happened with Amy and her position. The Pastor was shocked that this was going on and seemed touched as well. He remembered, and was convicted in his heart, and humbly admitted he made a mistake and did not realize what an impact her absence made in the community. The impact of the signatures was very powerful. Sheila and Pam planned a surprise rally for Amy at her house. Amy did not know anything about it, as the two women worked hard to plan the event. The Rally was set for June 1st.

Amy had just woken up and decided she was going to go to the park and take a walk. She showered and got ready for her day. It was Saturday. She scrambled some eggs and made some toast and coffee and sat there wondering what to do during the day. The weather was getting nicer, and she put on some aqua shorts and a sea green, modest, thick-strapped tank top. She prepared to go take a walk, because she needed some alone time to think.

However, Bryan came over very early that morning to visit. He had gotten used to being at his house and he knew he would always have a friend in Amy. But he still kept her sweater to remind him of her scent. That way he knew he would never be alone. They always spent time together and he still enjoyed the occasional stalk. He would sneak up on her and surprise her, but it was no longer to kill, yet stalking was still a part of him. Amy found it mysterious, delightful,

Chapter 11

and intriguing.

Amy did not want to tell him to go away. She enjoyed his company and he could come anytime if he wanted to. He had been rejected enough in life and she was not going to add to it. "Would you like some breakfast?" asked Amy.

Bryan nodded his head, "Yes." He stared at her from across the table and he loved the colors she was wearing. Amy was very careful to dress in a modest way. That was her style and because she did not want to set him off, as she knew he would be disgusted by it. Her olive toned arms and legs glowed with a bronze sheen of a beginning tan. *"She did not need to go out in the sun as she already had a natural color,"* he thought. *"I wonder what nationality she is, because she looks different from me, and my pale white skin. There is that inner glow she has, I cannot not dismiss and those crystal-clear, dark brown eyes, and flawless complexion. She looks very ethnic..."*

"Bryan, I am planning to take a walk to the park today. Would you like to come with me?" Amy asked. Bryan cocked his head. He was still unsure if he should go out in public. His mask and presence were still very much a threat to most in the community. "I need to think about some things," Amy said. Bryan's eyes narrowed, and he stood up and grabbed her, held her tight, and pressed against her.

"No please! I have to think about the next step to getting a job. Sometimes, I like to walk and think. It's not about you at all. I just need to figure out what to do with the rest of my life, and I can reassure you my life is with you. Please don't think any different," Amy said. Bryan then released her, tilted his head and she said, "Oh Bryan! What am I going to do with you? You are so sweet and possessive!" Amy laughed. Bryan just looked at her and tilted his head. "Oh, by the way, I love your head tilt!" Amy laughter seemed to mock him.

Bryan looked sad. "No Bryan, I am not laughing at you. I'm laughing because it's cute! It's just the way I laugh. I laugh at a lot of things, and find joy in them," Amy said. Bryan

Redemption Has No Limits

seemed to understand and hugged her again. Anytime Bryan ever heard laughter in his life, it was people laughing at him, teasing, and mocking him. Amy's laughter was different. She had a giddy, delightful, joyous laughter he could not explain or understand, but it touched him, tickled, and tantalized him inside. He trusted she was telling the truth about it. He would never forget that laughter-the way she would throw her head back and laugh at things. It was unusual to him, as he never grew up with laughter of any kind. There was never smiles or laughter in his home, but now he was in the presence of someone always happy and a person who loved him.

"Bryan, I will stop back at your house after I come from the park," Amy said. Just as they were to part ways, Bryan got up to slip out the back door to make his way along the bushes to his house (so he would not be seen), the doorbell rang. Amy answered it, and to her surprise, she was greeted by the whole community, and her two friends Sheila and Pam, the commissioner, and the Mayor.

"Surprise!" they shouted. Amy was totally shocked and said, "What is this about?" The groups had displayed banners that said, "Redemption has no limits and, love wins." Sheila and Pam bounded up to her and said, "Amy, we started a petition a about a month ago to reinstate you back to your old job and it looks like, judging from the crowd, it had quite an effect!"

There were thousands of people who had signed the petition, and were there to support, and the news stations as well. Amy said, "Oh my God, you did not!"

Sheila said, "Yes we can, and we did!"

Amy shook her head and said, "Sheila, you and Pam… what am I going to do with you both?" The trio hugged tightly.

"Amy?" Called a voice from inside the crowd. Amy turned, and Pastor Mark came out from the crowd and said, "I am

Chapter 11

very sorry I did you wrong, and I bowed under pressure by the longstanding members of my board. I was more concerned about what people thought, instead of how valuable you are to our church and this community." Pastor Mark then spoke up and called out to the community, "Listen everyone, to all of you, I repent before you. I realize I need to take full responsibility for doing what I did and as of Monday, Amy will be reinstated to her job, and I will double her salary! She is a valuable part of our church and this community and I am so sorry. I just did not want that night's events to be all over the news and if God changes people, even people like Bryan, He can—and wherever Bryan is, I'm sorry I failed you too."

Just then, Bryan stepped out from the shadows and stood behind Amy—mask on, and the black coveralls. The whole crowd gasped in fear and terror and started to run away. "WAIT! Amy cried. "This man did not do anything wrong to me. I want you all to know he has not harmed me during the time of my kidnapping. He only wanted to be loved, and another chance to start over in life. Please give him a chance! He cannot talk, but he only wants to say he is sorry. You know we ALL fall short, and if God can forgive each of us, He surely can forgive him. PLEASE, folks. Yes, he has done a lot of things wrong—as we all have, but we must forgive."

Bryan stared out at the crowd, then held up the notebook with a message he wrote to them in large letters, so everyone could see it. It read, "I'm sorry." Bryan then went back inside, as he was not used to crowds or being with other people. He only wanted to be with her. The crowd seemed moved and applauded. The crowd celebrated Amy's return to her position by furnishing a cake and ice cream. The police stood back a little ways just in case there would be trouble. They were still leery of him, being their three vigilante henchmen relatives where all now dead. So, they stood watch with batons from a distance in case of trouble. The crowd eventually thinned, and Amy said, "Thank you so much," to her two friends and

Redemption Has No Limits

everyone went their separate ways. And then it was just her and Bryan.

"Well Bryan, now would you still like to take that walk with me?" Bryan seemed to smile as to indicate a yes. "Let us go!" Amy said.

It would be Bryan's first time out in public, free from shame. They walked among the flowers that were in bloom. Roses, lilacs and various sweet-smelling flowers, filled the air with their fragrance. Bryan's eyes seemed to sparkle with life as he walked with his Amy down the path. He could breathe the fresh, warm air of the sunny day and not be ashamed. Amy said, "I am so glad I got my position back and I look forward to planning some new events for the community. Bryan, would you like to be a part?" Bryan just stopped, and held her close, and kissed her through his mask.

He seemed happy, but sad, knowing that they would not spend time together and Amy sensed this and said, "Bryan, I will have Fridays off as an option, and evenings and, by the way, my summer vacation is coming up and we will be together then. You have to remember the duties I talked to you about. We may be apart, but I always carry you in my heart."

Bryan pointed to his own heart, then back at her. He grabbed and kissed her again.

Amy joyously went to work that Monday morning after the weekend, and Mary greeted her with open arms.

"How are you doing?" Mary asked.

"I am fine, and I am a survivor," Amy responded.

Mary said, "Look, I'm sorry for what I did, and I was more concerned for my own safety instead of your well-being and income. Will you forgive me?"

Amy said, "Of course, let the past be the past." The relationship was restored.

"Uhhuum, how is he after all?" Mary was curious as to what it was like being with him.

"Well, he does not talk, but he sure knows how to show

Chapter 11

love, and that night he came to church and got shot really changed him. I hope the community will eventually accept him, because he really means it."

Mary said, "That's great." She was still nervous to see how everything would play out, and how time would tell. "Let me buy you lunch to make it up to you! Your pick, we can talk more about it over lunch," said Mary.

"Thanks so much!" Amy answered back. The two ladies headed out to lunch.

Amy started to explain, "You know Mary, I really felt protected the whole time I was being held there kidnapped. Bryan has his own place to stay, and I gave his house back to him, because it is only the right thing to do."

Mary said, "You know I have to ask, because curiosity is burning a hole through me. Did he?"

"Did he what?" Amy asked.

"Well, you know… touch you inappropriately?" replied Mary.

"No, not at all-although there were a few times I did not know what he was going to do with me…like, kill me or not and I read somewhere, raping people is not like him. He did nothing like that."

"He was not stable at the time, but it was revealed to me far more sad things that happened to him, than what met the eyes… if you know what I mean," said Amy.

Mary said, "Yes, but he did kill a bunch of people. He…" Amy interjected, "But he wants a new chance at life. Should not he be given one as we have??"

Mary said, "Your right, but some wrongs are greater than others."

Amy said, "Yes, but we are all human and need a chance to start over."

Mary said, "How did you know about him?"

Amy said, "I know this sounds crazy, but I had dreams and somehow knew that I was shown what was really going on inside him and remember, you did tell me that dreams are sometimes God's ways to get our attention a long time ago."

"You know, I do remember saying that," said Mary.

"Well, come to find out, it was true," replied Amy.

He waited for her to come to his house after work daily, and patiently waited all day just to feel her embrace and smell her scent of perfume. As usual, she would be over at the same time every day and they would either spend time together at his house, or time together at her house, but he would only try to go out at night as he was used to and to be seen during the day was very rare for him.

It was the middle of June, and that Friday, Amy decided to take off for her weeks' vacation. "This is a well-deserved break, and I get paid too, for the week," she thought to herself, as she headed home that Thursday evening. "I think I am going to go to spend the day at the beach tomorrow. I need some alone time to think-and relaxation. The last eight months have been a trial, and unusual events."

About 7:00 a.m., Amy made plans to go to her quiet place by the beach. She put on her aqua, blue-green, one-piece swimsuit, and matching flowy wrap and slipped on her golden-jeweled sandals. She looked every inch of a bronze-skinned Italian princess, as she quietly slipped out of her house.

"It was going to be a hot sunny one today," she thought. "Certainly, Bryan would be asleep and resting at his house in the air conditioner. He would burn himself, being so pale, in the hot sun and he was not one to go out unless it was dark," she thought. She bought a used mustang convertible to drive, in the warmer months, it was her favorite sea-green color. She loved having the wind whip through her hair, and when she drove this car, she imagined she was on the beaches of a tropical island, or the Mediterranean beaches of southern Europe's warm climate. Amy packed a picnic basket for herself and headed out.

Chapter 12

Amy picked up a morning coffee and got gas on the way there. She drove singing her favorite songs, and it was just a joy to be free from all the obligations of her job, but she did not mind it. "It sometimes is good to get away!" She thought. She wondered what Bryan would think, had he found she left town for the day. "Would he be mad? After all, they were not married." Amy hoped he would not be upset, and maybe he thought she would run some errands and then be there late. They spent time together every day, and perhaps, he would get tired of her. "Sometimes a day or two away makes the heart grow fonder," she thought.

She drove on until the roads became a country road, with less and less houses and then became woodier, with lakes and beaches all around. Some were owned by private owners and others were just rental properties that would never be occupied for very long. This was a time she could go to the beach unnoticed, and in her area, there were no laws about trespassing. There was an extra place that was not owned by anyone, and she would go there and spend the day. She parked the car a distance away from the beach and started down the path that led to the place she wanted to just "be." It was a woody area with a dirt path that had bushes, trees, and vegetation on either side. The ground was warm and sandy, and Amy took her shoes off to enjoy the sand under her feet. She strolled down the path and enjoyed every step. She started to feel like it was a vacation just by her surroundings.

She heard something behind her that sounded like footsteps. "No way!" she thought. "He most certainly would not follow me here, and he does not even know about this place." She would find out how wrong she was in the hours ahead. She turned and looked behind her and it was nothing. She went on. It would be a half hour walk to her private place.

Amy kept walking, she thought she continued to hear steps behind her, but each time it she looked back, it was nothing. The beautiful beach loomed ahead, beckoning and welcoming her to come. "It would be so refreshing to swim in those waters," she thought to herself. She spread out her blanket and sat down with her devotional, and let the warm sun brown her olive skin. "Aahhh! This is heaven!" she thought to herself.

The crystal waters beckoned her to come, and she swam the morning and afternoon away, in and out of the water. She relaxed, meditated, ate her lunch, and rested. "How blessed I am to be able to have my vacation of bliss." She still could not help but think about Bryan back in town. She shrugged the thoughts off and went back in the water.

She came out of the water and headed to her beach blanket. She looked down at her arms and admired how easily the sun bronzed her complexion and her tan was already darker than most of her friends, and needed almost no time in the sun. As she was lost in her thoughts of fun in the sun, she heard a noise. She snapped her head up and it was indeed Bryan! He was furious, with his eyes blazing, as he assumed the position of a mad man. She quickly wrapped herself in her wrap and cried out, "Oh my gosh, Bryan, how did you? You don't want to see me in my swim suit!" She quickly got the wrap on.

Chapter 12

He quickly grabbed her up and put her against a tree and pressed against her hard, eyes wild with anger and hurt. His masked face puffing in and out, in her face. "Bryan, I-I am sorry I did not tell you I was leaving for the day, and I just needed some alone time." He did not relent. He held his anger and her up against the tree for what seemed like eternity. Amy said, "Please Bryan! Try to understand…I-I thought you might get tired of me and I thought you needed a break."

Bryan viciously shook his head "*No!*"

"Bryan please put me down. You are hurting me, and I can explain this getaway." Bryan slowly and reluctantly put her down and Amy said, "can we sit on the blanket?" Bryan was hurt, and Amy could tell by the anger and sadness in his eyes. "Bryan, I am so very sorry about hurting you. I did not think that a little getaway would affect you like this. I know you have been so hurt in your life and I never wanted or intended to hurt you. I just needed some time to…" Her words were interrupted by Bryan slamming his fist on the ground. He grabbed her and got on top of her, stared at her face to face, then put his head down besides hers and held her until he calmed down and his breathing slowed. So, they laid there in silence for the longest time. Amy realized she needed to give him time to cool off before talking about anything.

He was still in his coveralls and mask. "*How could she do that me. She said she would never hurt me!*" he thought.

He was so angry with her and he thought she went to meet another guy away from town and would forget about him. He was glad she did not, but he could not understand why she left town when they were always together. He had never been anywhere before, and the only time they went away with him growing up was to visit sick grandparents. It did not matter because he was beat there too. This thing of her leaving for the day infuriated him and he was tempted with the old temptations of hurting her. But he knew he never wanted to harm her because his love for her was greater than the hate that taunted him with old memories.

Redemption Has No Limits

"Amy indeed looks so beautiful and her skin was so rich and dark, those colors in her swim suit and covering made her shine like a person from the tropics," he thought. Did he want to see her in her swimsuit? Bryan struggled back and forth in his thoughts with that and realized he did. His anger was much stronger than to think of things people usually thought of about those things, because he could not bear being apart from her, and could not believe she just left. He felt she betrayed him by going away, or she did not want to be around him anymore. Her skin was now darkened by the sun compared to his whiteness. He loved her coloring even more. He too, wondered briefly, what it would be like to be out in the sun. She felt so good to him when they were on the blanket together. She somehow had a way of calming him when he did that, but he did not understand how. Because no one ever had that effect on him before nor, had he been close to anyone before. He had watched her in the blistering sun for hours, before he decided to make his move to let her know he was not pleased.

Amy waited until all was calm and said, "Bryan…do you know what a vacation is?"

He tilted his head and shook it "no."

"Well," said Amy, "it's a place you go to forget about the daily things of life." Bryan just stared at her. "It's a place you go with others, or alone, to rest and relax. Did you ever do that growing up?" asked Amy.

Bryan shook his head no.

"People do that when they need to get away from the same things they do every day and the human body needs rest."

Bryan grabbed a notebook that stuck out of her purse and wrote, *"You hurt me, and I thought I lost you."*

"Oh no!" Amy said. "I would never do that Bryan. I love you and I know without a doubt you love me too and to follow me all the way here…Oh, what will I ever do with you

Chapter 12

Bryan? And to do that, you must be in love!" she laughed. Bryan just cocked his head at her, stared and listened.

"Would you like something to eat?" Amy asked. "I have some chips and some fruit in my basket," Amy said.

Bryan nodded his head "*Yes.*" Amy opened her basket and gave him some food. To her surprise, he slowly removed his mask and began to eat. Once again, Amy saw his blue eyes, that pale, chiseled face and that dark brown, straight, but tousled, hair and that well-set ruddy mouth. How sweet that mouth was. Amy smiled and thought, "Maybe he got too hot in that mask. He is so cute and so crazy-possessively wild!"

Bryan leaned over and kissed her. He could no longer resist kissing her or stay angry for long with her. She giggled and said, "You know Bryan, I am glad you're here, and we can come again if you would like and next time, I promise I won't leave you back home."

Bryan nodded his head excitedly, "*Yes.*"

"By the way…How in the world did you get here? It's an hour away." Bryan smiled with a gleam in his eye and said nothing. "That's one of the mysteries about him I don't understand," Amy thought and packed up. "Let's go get some ice cream," Amy said. Bryan put on his mask and they went back down the path to the car. They stopped on the way back to town at the drive through.

The clerk chimed in, "Is it Halloween yet?"

Amy fired back, "You need to mind your own business and you don't know his story." The clerk was embarrassed and said she was sorry. Bryan's fist turned white in anger. Amy seen it out of the corner of her eye. "We will go somewhere else then." Off they quickly went to another ice cream place. Amy knew the challenge of being with someone like this, and she was ready to stick up for him. She loved him for him, and nothing would ever change that.

Redemption Has No Limits

The week of her vacation flew. Amy and Bryan spent every day together, as she promised it would be. There was something that was bothering her though. She was wondering the next time Bryan would bring it up about his mother's wedding ring. It was still tucked away in the corner of the basement. "I mean he did want to marry me," she said to herself. She was conflicted inside what would life be like if they did get married? "Would people accept him? If they had children, what would they be like? Would life ever be normal, or would he always wear the mask?" She firmly decided, she did not care if he wore it or not and she liked his mask and thought it was cute. Her mind was made up to love Bryan for who he was, and he would remove the mask when he was ready. As for church, she never pressured him to go, but he read her devotional, and would watch Christian television. That was Bryan. He just did not like being in crowds.

The 4th of July came. They spent time in her back yard and had a cookout and watched the fireworks brightly light up the sky on a blanket that night. The weeks of summer went quickly by, and soon the anniversary of her kidnapping would be coming up. Bryan never had so much fun in all of his life and realized, *Certainly, this must be what normal living is like!* He loved it. No more run-ins with the police. No more getting shot or stabbed. The thing that excited him now, was just to be with her.

That night he had another dream. But this time for the first time in his life that he could remember, it was a happy dream. This time it was about her. They stood face to face, as he slipped his mother's ring on her finger and then he woke up. A few nights later, she dreamed she was in a faraway place, dancing with Bryan, and she was dressed in white, and then woke up. They were both consumed with thoughts from those dreams and could not stop thinking about them. Unknown to Amy, he was planning to stake his claim, and it would be soon before she may slip away. He had pondered a

Chapter 12

plan and set it in motion, of how to make her his forever, and seal the deal. He had been watching TV to learn how people got engaged, and how he could set his plan of asking Amy to marry him into action.

One Friday night, she went over to his house and fixed him a spaghetti dinner, and they sat down to eat. The table was set with a big bouquet of her favorite flowers. "Oh Bryan, they are so beautiful, thank you!" He dimmed the lights and lit some candles set on the table. "This is so nice!" Amy said. Bryan gestured for her to hold on before they ate and went downstairs. He came back up with something in his hand. He got down on one knee, slowly removed his mask, set it on the table, and opened the box. It was his mother's wedding ring. He questioned her with his eyes, as he looked from the ring to her eyes, then back at the ring again and Amy knew what he wanted.

"Yes!" she cried. "I will marry you!" Bryan stood up, smothered her with kisses, grabbed her so tight and whirled her around, she thought she would suffocate. "Bryan, uuughhh…please…you're crushing me!" Bryan then released her, and she realized he was crying. This was what he wanted the whole time, from that first encounter, was for someone to love him and had not she been thinking the same thoughts?

He gripped her so tight, kissed her again, and would not let her go. "Okay, I am yours. Bryan, you are crushing me again," she chuckled. What a passionate man this was, and she would find out even more on that special day.

Chapter 13

That Monday, Pastor Mark invited Amy into his office and this time his wife Chrissy was with him. Chrissy was seldom in the limelight, and she was a very quiet, meek, and behind the scenes person. She had a with a mousy appearance, with brown hair and glasses. Pastor Mark and Chrissy were a middle-aged couple that never had children and they were content in their lives as they served the Lord and community. Their lives were focused with activities in serving.

"Amy," Pastor Mark said, "come in and sit down. We need to speak with you."

Amy thought, "Oh no, what now?"

Pastor Mark's demeanor this time was gentle and loving and he said, "I'm not sure how to approach this, but I know you and Bryan have been spending a lot of time together, and I cannot help but notice you have been different. I would like to talk to you about your life with him." Amy listened calmly and told Pastor and his wife that Bryan was unique and explained that he did not like being around other people. "That is understandable, being where he came from-the horrible abuse and all from his family," Pastor Mark said.

Amy said, "How did you know?" "My older brother lived next door to their house years ago and would hear all the beatings, whippings, and Bryan's cries of pain. Police were called, but nothing was ever done because in those days what happened in the home stayed there, and no social services were in our area."

"That's so sad!" Amy said.

Pastor Mark said, "I am going to ask you this…has ever he hurt you, physically I mean?"

Amy said, "No, he has different ways of expressing himself, and not during the kidnapping either. He tried, but he was stopped for some reason," Amy said.

"Do you love him?" asked Pastor Mark.

Amy began crying and replied, "I do so much! He asked me to marry him and I said yes!" She then showed Pastor Mark and Chrissy the ring on her finger his mother had. Then then told them how he asked her to marry him without saying a word out loud.

 Pastor Mark said, "Well girl, you better get to planning the wedding and just a word of caution. Make sure Bryan is happy with the type of wedding too and try to be sensitive to his fragile situation. I also believe time will heal him. When the special day comes, I offer my services to marry you!"

"Oh Pastor, thank you so much, and I sure will!" Amy said, and hugged them both. With her pastor's blessing, Amy's heart soared. But would Bryan be okay with it? Amy had to plan carefully, and who to invite those who would look past Bryan's mask, in case he would wear it that day and she thought he would.

Amy's was grateful for her pastor's blessing on their special day. As much as a social butterfly Amy was, she realized she had to consider his needs now. She would have liked a bigger wedding, however, Bryan may not want a lot of people there, and she was okay with it, if that would be easier for him. She just wanted what was best for him, and he would not feel judged or bad for who he was. So, she had to pray and plan carefully. She also realized that whoever she would

Chapter 13

invite would have to accept him, mask and all, so she began working out a plan to talk first to people she had planned to invite.

"Bryan! Bryan!" Amy cried, as she bounded over to his house after work. He came out to the living room. "My Pastor wants to be the one who marries us! We have his blessing!"

Bryan hung his head and was sad.

"What's wrong Bryan? Can you write it down?" She handed him a pen and notebook. "*I have never been in a church or felt comfortable around a lot of people and I am afraid if something might anger me, I would lose you forever.*"

"No worries Bryan, I am going to plan it in such a way that you will be okay with everything. In fact, it doesn't have to even be in a church. How would you feel if it was in my backyard? There certainly is enough space and shade, being no neighbors will be able to see."

Bryan nodded "*Yes*," and seemed relieved.

"In fact, we can plan it together," said Amy. Bryan was happy with that, and they would pick out the colors and details.

They sat down that night and came up with ideas to have a wonderful wedding that both of them would be okay with. Amy checked her calendar and realized fall would be coming up fast. It would be a year since her grandmother passed away and the events of the kidnapping. It would have been so nice to have grandma see the wedding, but she knew life is not forever. Amy wrestled with the idea of inviting her brother. He might be one to say something smart, but he would probably be upset had she not invited him. They have not spoken in months, because it always was so hard to reach him. He was busy chasing money and the larger lifestyle of wealth. Amy would deal that later, but now she had to focus on planning the wedding.

"What month would be good for a wedding? What do you think?" Amy asked Bryan one afternoon. They sat

Redemption Has No Limits

together on the couch and she thumbed through August. He shook his head no. "How about this weekend in September? The weather is still warm." Week after week in September, she pointed on the calendar, but Bryan kept indicating no. "You mean October?" she said.

He pointed to October 31st. "What? On Halloween?" That day happened to fall on a Saturday that year and would be perfect.

Bryan excitedly nodded his head yes.

"Are you going to be okay that day?" asked Amy, nervously recalling the events.

He nodded his head, and grabbed the notebook and wrote, "*I want a fresh start, and I purposely picked that day to start new, and to let the dark things of my past go. I want to declare that I can begin a new life, that is a normal life and it's always been one of my dreams to have what everyone else has, and that is to be loved by another.*"

"Oh, how sweet! Okay, October 31st it is!" Amy said. Bryan did not care about the other details, he just wanted to know for himself, and declare to others, that he has changed. "Bryan, I will also be busy calling about flowers, food, cake, and other loose ends. There at a lot of things that takes place in planning a wedding. Are you going to be okay with that? I may be home late some nights."

Bryan nodded "*yes.*" He trusted her.

Amy joyfully and tactfully began planning the wedding. She had also contacted the people that would be present at the wedding, to consider the sensitivity of the situation. She picked out the fall roses of every hue, and wine-colored lilies, the caterer, chocolate cake and fall colors decorations. She had to balance work, her practices, and wedding planning. There would be about ten people, her closest confidents, there. The less people at the wedding, the better, for Bryan's sake. It was a clear, warm, sunny, fall day and Amy went to Bryan's house

Chapter 13

after work. "Would you like to take a long walk?" Amy asked.

At first Bryan hesitated, and then he nodded yes. "I will fix us some pumpkin spice coffee we can take it with us in our cups." So, she heated some up and off they went. Amy carried a notebook with her in case, Bryan wanted to talk to her. They decided to go into the woods and would find out later it was a mistake. They walked and enjoyed each other's company. They found a bench and sat on it. "I was always curious what made you choose me," Amy inquired.

Amy gave him the notebook and he wrote, "*The day I saw you at your grandmother's funeral, I saw you look right though me, as if you knew I was there in the bushes and I saw something I never seen in another's eyes, that I saw in your eyes that made me pursue you. Your eyes had heaven in them. Your eyes had me transfixed and I had to know more about you. I know now, you have eternity in you. It was what I was searching for my whole life, and I thought killing others would make it happen, and fulfill the deepest needs in my heart for peace. It was then I loved you and did not know how to express it. Your eyes were like the eyes of an angel. I had to possesses that. I had to have you to myself. I had been stalking you, to the places you go, for weeks and could not get you out of my mind. Then you loved me back. No one ever loved me in my life. I had plans to kill you but could not. I became insanely jealous at your happiness, your friends, and other people wanting to be with you - especially other guys. I could not bear it, and because of you, I could no longer kill and hurt people. No woman ever wanted me. They would make fun of me, because I am different. I hated everyone because I was never accepted for me, but continually rejected and made fun of. You are the only one who has ever loved me, and because of that, I will forever be grateful.*" Bryan began to cry as he wrote.

Amy teared up too, and said, "You have nothing to worry about because I will always be yours. When I said yes, I meant every word of it. My heart is yours. I love you for you - mask and all." He embraced her in his strong arms and held her so tight and gave her a long, passionate, closed-lips kiss, through his mask. They sat and enjoyed each other's embrace, and enjoyed their coffees, and watched the fall leaves gently sway in the wind.

"This was the very thing he wanted to hear all his life-for someone to love and accept him for him. Amy thought to herself, "This is the most he has ever shared with me, and he is so jealous for me."

Amy's thoughts where interrupted by a commotion of five ski-masked teens on mopeds. "Oooh, look at the white-faced freak and his girlfriend!" They circled around them, riding back and forth, and began to tease Bryan and taunt him. Amy knew this would not end good, and she looked at Bryan and his eyes were blazing with rage, and his fists whiter than white. He tried to lunge at them, but they were too fast, and kept zipping back and forth on their mopeds. "Freak! Freak!" The youths cried and hurled all kinds of insults and mocking laughter at Bryan.

Amy yelled, "Go home to where you came from! Leave us alone!" One cocky youth got too close, and Bryan quickly yanked the youth off of his moped and shoved him so hard, to where he flew through the air and landed on the ground, with his moped careening down the hill.

"I'm going to tell my dad, and they are going to lock you back up!" The youth yelled, as he slipped over his own two feet, scrambling away. Amy saw white things in the other teens' hands, as they came by Bryan, and threw eggs at him. The eggs landed, splat after splat, onto his black coveralls. They mocked and laughed the whole time, and quickly sped away as Bryan went after them.

"Bryan!!!" cried Amy, but it was too late. "Certainly," she thought, "he would be put back in jail. He had worked so hard to show people that he was not that way anymore,

Chapter 13

but the snotty-nosed boy would certainly squeal on him. Kids today have more of a voice than they did when he was growing up. The authorities would consider his previous record compared to theirs and lock him back up."

Bryan was gone, and Amy made her way back to his house. Bryan was there, with his eyes flashing rage through his mask. Amy noticed the house too, had been egged. She realized the youths had been tracking them the whole time. "Bryan, I-I am so sorry about what happened to you. I thought people would be different once they seen you were not the same way."

He just stood there with his dirty coveralls, ashamed and full of rage, wanting to once again kill someone or something. Bryan stormed out.

"Bryan, please! Where are you going? Oh God, please don't let him kill anyone! God, PLEASE!!"

Amy quickly cleaned the eggs off the house and called Pastor Mark and his wife to tell them everything that happened and they said they were praying for justice to be done, and that Bryan would not go back to prison again. The wedding was weeks away and Amy was now worried. She cried when he never came back all that night, as she waited for him at his house. Amy cried herself to sleep and wondered will people ever leave them alone, so they could live a life of peace and happiness? It was very early in the morning when Amy sought to find him. She drove all over town, and even scanned the woods to see if she would find any trace of him, but there was nothing. "Not again!" she blurted to herself.

Amy desperately prayed and figured out what to do next. She went to work as usual, but was very tired from all the events of yesterday. She stumbled into work, nearly falling over the rug before her desk.

Mary asked, "Amy, are you okay?"

"No," said Amy, and began to break down and cry. Amy then told Mary what happened.

Redemption Has No Limits

"Some kids have no respect for their elders," said Mary. "I hope nothing happened to him, and I will have my ladies prayer group pray for him."

"Thanks," said Amy.

Mary hugged her and said, "everything will work out--just wait and see."

"I hope so," said Amy.

Amy made her way home after work to her house and was greeted by Scotty, the red-headed boy who would always shovel her snow, or always was looking for work, like raking leaves, or mowing the grass in the summer.

"Oh, Hi Scotty," said Amy.

"Hello... I need to talk to you," said Scotty.

"Sure," Amy said.

"Do you...umm, is that white-masked guy your boyfriend?"

"Yes, why do you ask?" Amy said.

Scotty responded, "I need to tell you what happened at school today."

"Okay," Amy said, with her ears perking up.

Scotty said, "I overheard some of the older kids at school, two grades or three years older than I am, talking about what they were going to do to Bryan when they caught him out with you in public and that they were going to egg his house."

"Oh wow! Are you serious?" Amy replied.

"Yes," Scotty said. "I know the boys who did it. It was Dean, Rick, Mark, Ryan, and Tim."

"You know what?" said Amy "I truly believe you, and I just need to find him. He disappeared after that happened. I don't know where he went and..."

Scotty said, "No worries, he was picked up by police while he was walking down the street."

"What... no!" Amy said, relieved they had found him. But, "did he kill anyone or what did they do to him?" she wondered. She remembered, "He was beaten in prison and

Chapter 13

certainly they might do it at the county jail too." "Scotty, I want to thank you so much! This means the world to me, and next time you come to my house for work, I will pay you double for your trouble!" "No worries ma'am, I just look out for my customers." Amy marveled at how responsible Scotty was for his age.

Amy raced to the county jail and went to the front desk. She was greeted by this not-so-friendly female officer who asked, "Can I help you?"

"I am here to see Bryan Conners."

"Well, you cannot."

"Ma'am, it is my right to be able to do so."

"I told you, you cannot."

"Well ma'am, where is your supervisor?" "I am the night supervisor here now," the officer replied.

Just then, Amy saw Bryan being led down the hall, limping in chains, with three police officers around him with batons. "Bryan!" cried Amy. Bryan turned his head.

"I told you, you cannot see him now. You must leave!" Sneered the female officer.

Amy was stunned and saddened, she said, "But it is my right."

"Well Missy, in dealing with an inmate like him, he has no rights and neither do you. Now go!"

"We will see about that!" Amy's eyes flashing anger. She began to stormed out.

Another officer said, "Hold on ma'am! Here are your subpoena papers." "What?!?

Amy asked. "What's this for?"

"Bryan has a court date for October 20th and he has to appear in court that day."

"What? He has done nothing wrong!" "Well Ma'am, your wrong. He put his hands on some kid."

"No, they came and were harassing us when we were minding our own business."

Redemption Has No Limits

"Ma'am, you will have to tell that to the judge."

"You bet I will! What a twisted story and a twist of justice! Did you not see how he has changed that day when you all where at the rally?" protested Amy.

The officer said, "I am sorry, but orders are orders, and due to his past, and what he…"

"People can change!" cried Amy.

"I am sorry, but I am just doing my job."

"I know," said Amy, "but certainly there must be something to be done. This is not right!" Amy stormed out and went home.

"Alone again," thought Amy. The wedding plans were well under way and now set. The wedding would be at the house after all, and Amy had to trust everything would be brought out in the light, and the truth be made known. Amy was at work the next day and excused herself, so she could call down at the police station. For such a small justice system in her town, everything moved quickly and the court system was attached to the police station, so whatever administrative things that took place, were quickly dealt with.

"Hello, can I speak to the day supervisor?" Amy said. "Yes, hold on," came the voice of the operator. "Hello, yes, I am inquiring about an inmate--Bryan Conners, and I need to know if I can see him?"

"Hello, and yes, of course. My name is Tim," said the male Chief of Police.

"I was down there at the jail last night and told I could not see him," said Amy.

"No, that's not true and you can see him whenever. Who was working last night?" asked Tim.

"I think her name was Jane, and she said she was the night supervisor."

"No," Tim said, "she is not a supervisor; and I will be talking to her." "Okay, so I can come tonight?" said Amy.

"Yes of course," said Tim. "Come anytime. I know you as

Chapter 13

an upstanding individual in the community for the arts. Yes, you may come."

"Thank you so much!" cried Amy!

Amy raced over after work, only to encounter the same female police officer.

Jane said, "I already told you, NO!"

"Well, I spoke to Tim and he said yes, I could see Bryan," Amy answered calmly.

"When are you going to…"

"Jane?!" said a male voice behind her. Jane turned and was shocked and unknown to her, Tim had still been at work, because when he would leave, then she could take over. "Come here Jane," Tim said. Jane walked over to Tim. Tim said, "Is this how we treat the public? I know Amy very well, and she has influence in this town. You will not speak to her or any one else like that ever again! I am going to have to write you up, because that was uncalled for."

"But…" Jane protested.

"Jane, you are not a supervisor. You need to know your place, and if you ever want a promotion, you would not get it, because that is not how we deal with the public. A police officer must be professional, at all times. Whenever Amy comes here, she will be allowed to see Bryan, and will not be disrespected." Amy overheard the conversation and knew Jane was getting in trouble.

Amy thought, "Maybe for Bryan's sake, things are turning around, and people will see that he is not that bad of a guy and wants to show people he has changed." However, the image of him limping down the hall disturbed her and what they may have done.

"Come with me," Tim said. Amy followed him down the hall to where Bryan was. He let her into his cell.

"Oh Bryan!" How are you?" said Amy.

He nodded he was okay.

Redemption Has No Limits

Amy noticed he was chained up like an animal. He had a heavy brace around his neck, chains and cuffs around his hands and feet. "Why must he be chained like this?" Amy said to Tim.

"It is due to what he has done, and orders are orders." Amy was sad that they had treated him as such. When she passed other jail cells, the others were not chained like this, but were free. This upset her, that people still judged him according to his past and did not see him as she saw him.

"Bryan, did they beat you?" Amy whispered. He hung his head and nodded yes. "Do you know who they were?" Bryan nodded "No." He made a gesture of how they were disguised. Amy understood there were even those in the police force in her own town that were monsters. They must have heard what happened while he was in prison and thought they would get away with the same thing. Amy would let Tim know about this. She was sure he would be questioning those who beat him. Amy was so happy to see him, but also wondered what would happen to him when his court date would take place. She visited him every day up to the court date. She wondered if other lies would be told on him. He was framed and it was not fair.

The next day would be a Friday. Amy took time off to see Bryan and speak to Tim. She set out that morning to the police station. "Officer Tim, can I speak to you?" Other police and employees where there, they all turned and looked at Amy.

"Sure, what is it?" "Can I speak to you in private?" Amy asked.

"Sure, please close the door," Tim said. They walked into his office and Amy shut the door. "Please have a seat and get some coffee."

Amy said, "No thanks. I came to talk about why Bryan was limping and why he was chained. They beat him a lot while he was in prison, and now, I fear the same thing has happened to him here."

Chapter 13

"Oh no! Are you sure?" Tim asked.

"Yes, police are here to protect, not brutalize others, especially when he has done no wrong," Amy said.

Tim replied, "I don't know about that, but let's go take a look, to be sure. If any of my officers who violate prisoners just for kicks, will be dealt with on my watch! That is not what we are here for, but to serve and protect the community. When they do bad things like that, it will come back on me."

They went to his cell and went inside. "Bryan, can you walk for me?" asked Tim. Bryan stood up and walked across the cell, with the limp, and still in chains. "Now, let's walk down the hall and back." Bryan limped and hobbled back towards the cell. "Can we go to the bathroom? I need to see something on you, like bruises," Tim asked. Bryan's eyes flashed anger, it was as if he already knew what Tim had to do. He hated being exposed and humiliated.

Amy said, "Please Bryan, he needs to see evidence that you were beat." Bryan calmed down, and they went into the bathroom, and Bryan let Tim see the beatings on his legs, back, and backside. There were indeed black and blue bruises all the way down the back of his white legs and backside. "He was indeed beaten, I will get to the bottom of this," Tim said.

Amy replied, "Thanks so much!"

That afternoon, Tim called an immediate mandatory meeting, and they sat in the board room. Everyone filed in and sat down. Tim said, "First of all, I want to address the matter at hand. Folks, this is really important--that you all need to hear this and take heed. A matter was brought to me that a prisoner was reported having signs of police brutality on their body, and I need to speak to each of you, and a memo will be immediately sent to everyone stating that, for no reason will anyone ever beat a prisoner without just cause, regardless of who it is. It is not professional, and it is not ethical and as police officers we are to be professional. Now, there is a time for forceful intervention, but to beat someone for no reason other than the fact of who they are, is totally unacceptable, and if anyone is found out, they will be terminated."

Tim was finishing his day up, walked out of the office and was greeted by Police officer Randy, who had just come back from inspecting a robbery.

"Tim, can I talk to you?" Officer Randy nervously looked around and made sure no one was in the parking lot, or around.

"Sure," Tim said.

"If you promise not to let people know I ratted on them, I know the four men who beat Bryan. It was during third shift. They had planned it out and cut all the lights off, so Bryan would not see their faces and they went in his cell and proceeded to beat him. I happened to be working that night and I knew what they were up to. I heard Bryan's grunts of pain and he had done nothing wrong. They just wanted revenge for the three watchmen vigilantes who died, not at his hands, but of circumstances. So, they took their wrath out on Bryan, even though he had nothing to do with their deaths."

"Okay, I need to know who they are, and I promise you won't be revealed to anyone," said Tim.

"It was Officer Loft, Officer Williams, Officer Ray and Officer Keys."

"Oh, okay…they are all related to the three watchmen who died: Ted, Tom, and Doug.

"Okay, I see where this is going and what I need to do." Bryan indeed had nothing to do with their deaths and it was their own undoing. He knew how strong drink can affect a person's judgments, and he knew all three men had been heavy drinkers.

The next day Tim called a meeting with the four officers and terminated them. He explained, "We don't do things that way, and a person is innocent until proven guilty--no matter

Chapter 13

who they are. Turn in your badges--you're all fired." The four men turned in their badges and stormed out the door, vowing revenge, and to seek out the person who told. They would never find out, because Tim would never let them know.

They also walked out breathing threats against Bryan. But their threats were never carried out, because they all died in a fishing boat accident that weekend.

The four police officers went every fall, to get in some last-minute weekend fishing, in their speedboat. One of them tried to be slick and outrun a bigger boat, but poor judgment, combined with drugs and alcohol, caused them to crash the boat into the pier, which exploded. These were the type of men who bore the badge, but did not live by it.

One by one, Bryan's enemies ended up dead, and were never able to carry out any threats against him. All this was unknown to Bryan. Amy found out and thought it strange that, somehow, he was protected. She noticed it since the night he came into the church, before he was shot. Amy also knew very well, from that night Bryan's was beat at his own house, the people against him were serious at carrying out the threats and destroying Bryan. Amy knew there were people praying for him too. If anyone needed protection, it was him. Even though, he could very well protect himself, it was because of his love for her, he did not proceed to kill others. His trial would be in a few days and she wondered what would happen.

Amy went to Scotty's house and asked his parents if he could testify in court tomorrow. "Absolutely not," they said. "This is your problem. We have to protect Scotty from any backlash and bullying at school."

Unknown to the parents, Scotty was listening on the stairwell to the details of the time when the court case would be. Scotty was the witness of what was said that day at school and Scotty would tell the truth. Amy thought Scotty was the only hope of proving Bryan's innocence. Her heart sank.

Redemption Has No Limits

Court was set for 9:00 a.m. sharp. Amy wandered in and sat down. Bryan, heavily chained, was escorted in by police and sat down. The parents and the 5 boys that threw the eggs at Bryan were there, and a lawyer began to question them and they told all kinds of lies on Bryan about what he supposedly had done. They had framed him. Bryan wrote down what happened and gave it to the judge. Then it was Amy's turn. "Did Bryan put his hands on that youth over there?" the lawyer asked.

Amy said, "He did it in self-defense, and to protect me. They were throwing eggs at him." Amy could feel her anger rise at the lies and injustice. "Your honor, Bryan has done nothing wrong. He only wanted to protect me as we were taking a walk. They came and were taunting and harassing us."

"The boys provoked him to anger by their mockeries, they egged him, and these boys also egged the house I bought."

"That's irrelevant! The fact that Bryan put his hands on the boy is what stands!" snapped the lawyer.

Amy said, "Bryan has proven he has changed, by not harming anyone and these boys drove him to do it in self-defense!" The court then erupted in protests.

"Order, order!" cried the judge.

"Okay, we heard all sides, and Bryan must be sentenced back to prison for putting his hands on the youth. Andrew Bryan Conners I therefore sentence you to…"

"Your Honor," said a voice from the back of the court.

It was Scotty! Amy gasped, "What in the world?" she thought.

"What is your name, young man?" asked the judge.

"I am Scotty, and I shovel snow, and Miss Amy is one of my customers. I want to tell you something."

"Okay, step up to the stand. I will hear you," said the judge.

Chapter 13

The boy said, "These five boys here, had been plotting to do this for a long time. They would brag about it in school, of how they wanted to cause damage, and set Bryan Conners up, and provoke him to anger so they could get him in trouble. They were planning to egg him and his house, among other things they have not yet done, and was also planning to set fire to his house." The judge listened as Scotty told everything that they said in school. The five boys glared at Scotty.

The judge reviewed the boys' records and indeed, they were all starting on a path to nowhere, from breaking in, to stealing and other misdemeanors. The judge sentenced the five boys to a military school for six months and another six months in a juvenile jail system. In hopes this would give them a chance to re-think what they were doing to hurt others. They could continue school, but in those types of systems.

"Bryan Conners, I hereby release you on this day of October 20th. Release him from his chains." The police unlocked him and Amy sobbed with relief and ran to Bryan and hugged him. Bryan was, too, crying tears of joy through his mask. The five boy's parents scoffed and stormed out in a huff.

Amy hugged Scotty. "How did you?" asked Amy.

"Well, let's just say I skipped school to come to your aid!" beamed Scotty.

"Thank you so much!" cried Amy! "I just hope you don't get in trouble."

Scotty said, "Well, let's just put it this way. I had to come to your aid because my customers are important to me! I also did not want to see you sad and lose your friend."

"A thousand times, thank you" said Amy. Turning to Bryan, she said, "Let me drive you home Sweetheart."

Scotty was still too young to know what love was, but he had a hunch that they would be getting married, just by how they acted towards each other. But Scotty, however, was more interested in making money and that is where all his attention was. Scotty did indeed get grounded. But his parents could not stay angry long, as they knew how responsible Scotty was, and how important his customers were to him. It would be awhile before the five boys would return to a regular school, if at all. Scotty's parents were, in a way, proud of him for standing for what was right. They just did not want him bullied at school, because he took a stand. They had to be okay with Scotty's actions, and were sure that he would handle things when, and if, the time came. Scotty thought beyond his age and was level-headed.

Chapter 14

Amy drove Bryan home and they spent the day together. Bryan seemed so clingy. He just could not keep his hands off her. He wanted to hug her, kiss her cheeks and hold her tight. "Bryan, what is wrong?" He tried to gesture to her, but she said, "Can you write it down?" He took the notebook and wrote. "*I was so afraid to lose you forever, and they would take me away from you, I could not bear that ever! I am so glad those boys got what they deserved, and I am sorry, but I am so in love with you. I don't want to let you go, ever! That is why I want to keep holding you, because I cannot believe this is real, and things are changing for me, that somehow, I have that same protection you did on the night I tried to kill you. I know we are supposed to be together and now I do know that for sure. Normally things never worked out for me. They were ready to lock me up.*"

Amy hugged his big form tight. "Yes, we are meant to be!" she said. They spent time together until the wee hours of the morning. "Well," Amy said, "I must go to my home. You know I have to go to work in the a.m." Bryan was sad but okay with that. He was able to let her go knowing that she would come back the next day. "The wedding is soon approaching and then you can hold me forever, and we will never be apart," Amy said, then she was gone until the evening.

Bryan could not wait for that wedding day. He was not interested in the wedding itself, but just to have her, possess her as all his own. So many times, he wanted her so passionately, but did not know how, because she was so pure. He did not want to violate what was sacred, and fought against his own will to do so. He knew rape would be out of the question, as he was not one to rape people and it would not be right. It was disgusting to him and she would still be pure even after they were married. His own angel. His own beloved. His own. All his and no other men would stand in the way of their love. He knew she must have had many suiters wanting to be with her, because she was so beautiful. She did not choose him, he chose her. He knew from the start some how, he wanted her and make to her his. He only had eyes for her.

He thought and thought about her and drifted off to sleep peacefully in his quiet house. He knew he had enemies, but somehow, each and every one of them were silenced on this new way. He did not have to lift a finger to do anything to them, but things just seemed to take care of themselves. Maybe there were some things unseen after all, that worked behind the scenes. He did not understand it all, but as he read about it, he would eventually understand the reasons how everything worked out in his favor.

Bryan dreamed of being in a dark place that night. A hideous, giant creature, he tried to fight off, was chasing him. Beating him over and over in different places. This "being" took him back to the jail, the state hospital, and other places he had been in his real life to beat him. A creature he had only seen in horror movies pursued him. It was far more hideous, with a brownish black body, sunken blacker than black eyes, super long razor-sharp fangs, claws that could shred him, superhuman strength and worst of all—it stank, a horrible smell of death. Bryan knew that smell very well from his victims, but this was from another realm, or otherworld, or far worse. Bryan was in chains, but could not break free. He screamed over and over in his head in his dream and through it all, he remembered the cross that night at the church. In his thoughts he screamed out, "Jesus save me!"

Chapter 14

These other shining beings, with an appearance of fire, appeared out of nowhere and destroyed the hideous creature with one blow of a long sword. Bryan heard the being call it the sword of the spirit. Bryan woke up shocked and amazed at what just happened. The dream was as if he was awake.

It was not even 6:00 a.m. and Amy was awakened to a frantic pounding sound on her door. She sauntered down the stairs. "Hello Bryan, good morning." Bryan appeared frantic again and rushed in trying to tell her something. "What is it Bryan?" He tried to gesture, and she gave him the notebook.

He wrote: "*I had another bad dream, and this huge ugly creature that must have been 12 foot tall. I tried to fight him off, but he kept taking me back to places where people beat me. He was beating me over and over. The whipping and pain seemed so real, like I was there back in those places. The feelings of shame and humiliation of being beat were coming over and over again, but then something happened. I called on the name of Jesus, and these two, fiery-like beings came, and destroyed the hideous creature. Initially, I was in chains and once the creature was destroyed my chains were gone.*"

Amy knew what the dream meant. Amy said "The big evil creature influenced all those people to beat you without mercy. Those chains were real, and God now has your back. Since the day you said yes to Him, He fights your battles. From this day forward, you will never be beat on again and you were shown that in the doctors…" Before she could finish, Bryan snatched her up, gave her a huge hug, whirled her around, and kissed her through his mask.

"Uuugh Bryan, your strength… my ribcage… your crushing me!" He put her down. He let her go and finally Amy said, "I have to get to work soon, but I will fix you breakfast." So, they had an early breakfast of eggs and toast, and Bryan bid her goodbye and made his way back to his house. "See you tonight," Amy said.

Redemption Has No Limits

Amy got ready for work, but still had plenty of time to spare. She read her devotional before she began her day. She made some strong coffee, because she did not sleep much the night before, she was over at Bryan's house until late. Then he came to wake her up earlier than her usual wake up time.

Bryan thought, *"I can't help my passion. I don't mean to grab her so hard, it's just, I am just so strong,"* and he could not figure it out, why he would always hold her so tightly. His urge to hold her was so strong and overpowering. He was lost in those thoughts, as he made his way back to his house before dawn--but he was so glad to even spend just a few minutes with her.

The early morning pre-dawn reflected off her face as she sleepily said "Hello" at the door. She wore a aqua robe, that covered every inch of her from her neck to her ankles. He came to know aqua was her favorite color, and tropical blues, as well as gold and white. Those colors were her, and they looked perfect on her with her skin color and hair. He went home satisfied just to see her again. Her sweet smile…The dream still bothered him. He had never lost a fight to any victims, but this was different. He could not understand why he could not fight off this thing in his dream, and it made him mad. He would ask Amy about it tonight when she came home.

Amy bounded over to his house after work and he gestured for her to sit down. She could tell he was angry. "What is it?" asked Amy.

He took the notebook and wrote *"I am bothered by that dream. I am so angry. Why I couldn't fight this thing off. I have never feared, or lost a fight, to anyone. It makes me so mad! I have always been the strong one, to overpower people. Help me understand what that thing was!"*

Amy said, "Well, the devil is real and so are the angels who follow him. He was once the most trusted, powerful, musical angel that wanted to take God's place, his name was

Chapter 14

Lucifer. There were several angels that followed him, they became the creatures that you saw in your dream. These fallen angels have been in a battle to destroy and desecrate mankind, who are made in the image of God. Those are demons are strong—creatures, they are not humans like we are. They are evil spirits set to destroy and deceive mankind. I know people have viewed you as a evil creature, but you are not a demon. God spared you more than once, to live again. We cannot fight these things because they are spirits, and we are human; however, the good news is Jesus defeated them when He went to the cross - and we don't have to fear, as ugly as they are.

"Why did that thing smell so bad and why did it look like that?" Bryan wrote.

Amy said, "Once they fell into sin, things got ugly and because the devil was prideful and wanted control over what was God's throne, he wanted to be God. God cast them all out of heaven, and ever since then, they have had the sentence of death on them, that is why they may smell like they do. When someone sins, it's like they die and it was sin that transformed those once beautiful angels into something hideous and something ugly," Amy said.

"You mean like me when I would kill people? I was driven by a force and tormenting thoughts to kill over and over again, and I would listen and do the acts?" Bryan wrote.

"Yes, but we all do things that are bad. I am no different than you are. I am not perfect, and we, in our humanness, all fall short. But God forgives us when we do. It was the devil that tormented you with those voices to kill, and there was no amount of psychiatry that would have helped you silence those voices, because they were from the enemy of our souls. Sometimes medications are needed, but all too often, they are spiritual beings sent to torment and vex people to point they think it's their own thinking. It is not your thoughts, it's the forces behind the scenes," Amy said.

Redemption Has No Limits

Bryan pointed to his heart and wrote, "I love you so much and I will do my best to try not to crush you!"

Amy thought it was cute and laughed. "Okay, you strong, sweet one. I will take you at your word!"

Amy taught him and showed him more from her devotional. He began to understand why things in life worked the way they did, and why people did the things they do. There were forces behind the scenes driving people to do the things they did and in their weakness, they would do the things they did, including murder.

The days flew by, and pretty soon it would be October 31st. Her brother, William, came in by plane, he would be staying with her that Friday night and the wedding would be that Saturday afternoon. Her brother and would fly back that Saturday nigh—taking a cab back to the airport. Amy planned the honeymoon for right after the wedding. She let her brother know about the plans, so he knew he would need to call a cab after the wedding. He would have his things with him at the wedding, if he wanted to leave right after.

She first had to pick him up at the airport. She was very nervous at what he might say, had he met Bryan and about the mask. Amy waited at the airport and she also told Bryan that her brother would be coming in and would be staying with her for the weekend. William looked like Amy, with the same features. He had olive skin and darker features with dark brown eyes, but was much taller than Amy and was always the life of the party.

He loved cracking jokes, and sometimes at the expense of upsetting people, but he was a charmer. Everyone loved him, but his pursuit was money. "Hey William, how have you been?"

"Hi Amy, how have things been? I see you have been on the news and I am sorry I have not called you for a long time." They embraced.

"Yes well…my future spouse is very different from the rest and please try to be sensitive about him," Amy said.

Chapter 14

"Well, what do you mean?" said William.

"When you meet him, you will see." Amy tried to explain his white mask and why Bryan was the way he was.

Her brother said, "Oh sis, you know me. I will try not to say anything wrong. But you know very well I do have a loose tongue."

"Yes, my silly brother, but that is what makes me nervous about you. Please try not to. He was once a serial killer, please don't provoke him," said Amy.

"A serial killer? Amy, how in the world did you end up with that?"

"It's a very long story with a lot of details, and I am not so sure you want to hear everything, but I will fill you in the best way I know how before you meet him," said Amy. Amy tried to fill her brother in on all the details and of how they got involved with each other and how Bryan has changed. The good news is he doesn't kill people anymore.

The drive back was about 45 minutes and Amy had a lot of time to get caught up with her brother on old times, and about Bryan. They conversed, laughed, and goofed off with each other all the way home. Amy turned the key to her house and got her brother settled in her guest room. "You may stay in the guest room across from my room, first let me show you around the house," said Amy.

The hallways were painted in a lighter olive green, and the guest room was a lighter blue neutral color. Nothing too loud for Amy's home. The downstairs kitchen and living room were neutral shades of black, gray, white walls, and flooring and silver accents and silver cone-shaped lights that hung down, giving it a simple, yet elegant look. Topped off with cushy gray furniture, high ceilings, and a wood burning fireplace. A lush, shag-white rug was in front of it. The living room presented a welcoming look to any guests.

Amy said, "Will, please go ahead and get comfortable and I will start dinner." So, she made a special chicken dinner for the three of them, and she chose not to have a rehearsal dinner, because this would be a simple, small wedding and she already knew what to do. She had it all written down step-by-step on how to proceed in this type of wedding.

Her brother was busy taking a big gulp of his soda when Bryan walked in. Will practically chocked on his drink and almost spit it out when he saw Bryan come in with his mask on. "Will!" Amy said sternly. Like her, it did not take much to get Will laughing at something. If given the opportunity, he would have laughed at Bryan. He stifled a laugh that was threatening to come out.

He quickly said, "Excuse me, I'll be right back." He quickly left the house to the outside, far away, where neither of them would hear it, and let his laughter out. When he was done, he came back inside.

Amy looked at him sternly and said, "Bryan, meet Will. Will, meet Bryan." "Uhh well, umm, Bryan… nice to meet you." Will extended a hand and Bryan just nodded at him through the mask. Amy sternly looked at her brother and explained he does not talk much.

"Well… I guess not," chuckled Will.

Amy shot him a threatening glance. "Anyways, let's eat. The chicken is ready," said Amy, trying to smooth the awkward situation over.

"Good, I am famished from the long flight here," said Will.

"Let's dig in and eat," replied Amy. Will and Amy ate, and Bryan ate through his mask. Bryan would pull it up only around Amy, but being she had a guest, he just ate through the mouth hole through his mask. Bryan then would clean off his mask on the inside, and outside, in case there was food left over. He did take care of his mask after he ate.

Will was finding it very difficult to not laugh, as he had to excuse himself from the table more than once, and then made the excuse of needing fresh air and how he was jet lagged.

Chapter 14

Amy knew he was not jet lagged, he was laughing at Bryan, she knew Will very well. After all, they grew up together, and once the joking started, there would be no stopping it. That was how they rolled at the expense of hurting others and provoking them. Goofing off ran deep, and so did laughing, it was their culture and very much a part of them as brother and sister. To live, laugh, and love was an Italian thing, and it ran deep in them both. A lot of laughter they did growing up, and it was hard for Amy to transition out of that once it started. This time however, Amy held her ground and was firm on that. She could not entertain her brother's goofy, provoking ways. She deeply loved her goofy brother. However, as hard as it was, she had to stand firm for Bryan's sake.

Bryan too, was struggling with his thoughts. He felt Will was making fun of him and he could tell from the expression on his face, his eyes, and how he was acting and that was making him angry. Bryan was among people that looked different than him and they were a different ethnic-type and darker people, compared to his paleness and that too, made him uncomfortable. Amy and her brother had a different way of doing things, and they seemed to have a certain bond that made him somewhat jealous. Their laughter and joy made him angry, and jealous of how they related to one another. He knew their culture was different and struggled to be a part of it. Amy was also struggling and torn, between her thoughts of goofing off with her brother, just like old times, and keeping firm to keep Bryan from getting angry. Will was very proud of his culture and Amy was comfortable with who she was, and Bryan seen that in both of them. Amy had wished the night was over. The temptation was becoming too great to start goofing off with her brother, she had not seen in so long. It was getting pretty tense, especially the comments her brother made about powder-white skin, as a reference and inside joke to Bryan's white mask and pale skin.

Redemption Has No Limits

Amy kept changing the subject and bumping her brother with her elbow, to indicate to stop teasing him, because she knew if Will continued, it would be a problem. Amy knew Bryan was at his breaking point, as she seen the anger in his eyes. "Will…I think we need to call it a night," Amy said. "There is a lot to do tomorrow. What do you say?"

"Okay, sure," Will replied. Amy was relieved about that.

"Bryan, I have to get to bed because I have a lot of preparations tomorrow and I must get my beauty sleep. Let me walk you out." Amy hoped inside Bryan would be okay with that. Thankfully he was. Amy said, "I will see you at 1:00 p.m. sharp. Don't be late, and they kissed." Will stifled a laughter, and turned away and bit his tongue, to keep from laughing when Amy kissed Bryan on his masked lips. Bryan then headed home, and Amy breathed a sigh of relief. "Now, we just have to get through the wedding," she said to herself.

Will lost it and doubled over with laughter when Bryan was down the street and the door closed. "Hahahaha!!! Oh my God, are you kidding me? How are you guys going to… you know…?"

"Will, Stop it!!!"

"Of all the guys that like you, you would end up with one like this? How is this possible?"

Amy said, "Stop it! He might hear you! I love him, and yes, he may be different, but he is very sweet!"

"Rubber sweet?" said Will.

"Knock it off!" said Amy "Go to bed already! I love him for him - not anything superficial, or what he can do for me!"

"His skin is white as paper!" laughed Will.

"Will!!! There is much more to a person than his coloring! You need to stop please!" Amy tried hard not to laugh too.

"Okay, Okay! I'll stop," said Will.

Unknown to Amy and her brother, Bryan stood in the bushes listening to everything they had said. He was getting

Chapter 14

angrier by the minute, eyes blazing and knuckles white. He did not like this cocky brother who made fun of him and his mask, but he had to focus on Amy, because she loved him for him, and he should not worry about the brother, who would be flying home tomorrow night. He was glad the brother lived far, far, away, and he did not have to see him often. Amy mentioned that they only talked once in a blue moon, as this brother was always working to achieve the American dream and was career focused, as Amy said. The last thing he wanted to do was ruin the wedding. After hearing all of that conversation, he sauntered home and read her devotional for comfort. She let him keep it months ago. He was so close to snatching up this brother and doing harm to him, because no one make makes fun of him. It was then he noticed how much he realized he had changed. The change was subtle, but it was definitely a far cry of what he would have done a year ago. Will would have been dead already. As for the voices, he no longer heard them regularly, but only when he got angry.

Chapter 15

Amy's yard was decorated for the wedding, and it would be a short and sweet ceremony event. Amy's two friends, Pam and Sheila, helped set all the decorations up and made sure all the details were covered. It was unseasonably warm for so late in the year, about 60 degrees and sunny. The leaves seemed to be turning late that year, so they were in their peak of colors. "Perfect," Amy thought. "I was hoping fall would stretch out this year, just for my wedding."

Amy wore a beautiful stunning, simple, chiffon-layered dress and Bryan waited for her with his tux and mask on in the front. She wandered up the makeshift aisle, as "Here comes the bride" played on a CD player. Bryan could not believe how beautiful she looked! She was glowing, literally! Wedding vows were said, and rings were exchanged and now they were married. This would be perfect! On October 31st…and the mask was perfect for that. Amy was quite sure other couples that got married on this specific day, did other crazy things like this too. So the mask, fit into the fall theme. Bryan was not made to feel uncomfortable, and it all seemed to flow together.

Thankfully, Amy's brother busied himself, flirting with Sheila and Pam, instead of his focus being on Bryan, and making fun of him.

The dinner was a catered, roast beef plate, with all the trimmings. Bryan ate through the hole in his mask and was cordial to everyone, but he still did not like crowds and he did not talk to anyone. He did nod, and greet them quietly. Everyone knew he was mute, and they respected him, and did not try to get him to talk. Thankfully, everyone treated him like a normal human being, at Amy's request. The afternoon wore on, and Amy made her rounds and socialized with everyone. Then it came time for cutting the cake. Photos were taken, and dancing.

Bryan did not dance, he just sat in the shadows under the trees and looked forward to being alone with Amy. He did however, slow dance with Amy. The wedding celebration was drawing to a close and Amy bid everyone "good night."

Pretty soon, Amy and Bryan would be on their way to a rental cabin by the beach. That was their choice for the honeymoon, to enjoy their time together. He seemed to really enjoy that special place near the beach. The only reasonable place to go, would be there, for the week. Even though it would be colder, they could still enjoy each other's company inside the rental, and take walks where there was no one to make fun of Bryan. No one would see them, and it would be safe away from town.

Pretty soon, the crowd dispersed and then it was once again Amy and Bryan alone. "Well, my new hubby…are you ready?" Bryan nodded his head excitedly. "I have a special place for us to go for the week, for our honeymoon." They packed their bags and climbed into Amy's convertible. Amy decided to take the convertible, just in case it may be warm yet. Bryan really seemed to like the car and he loved Amy in it because it was so her. Amy looked at Bryan and could tell he seemed very happy as they drove away and got on the road. Amy was still in her bridal gown because she wanted the moment to be special as they arrived at the cabin. They settled into the car, their drive would take about an hour. Bryan was getting more and more excited by the minute, in anticipation, as the location got closer. She stopped and got a week's supply of groceries for the cabin. They pulled into the gravel driveway of the rental and got out of the car.

Chapter 15

It was no sooner that Amy turned the key to the door of their rental, that Bryan swept her up. This was the time both of them had waited for, as everything became a blur. Wave after wave of ecstasy swept over them, over and over, as two hearts and souls became one. This was the special night they both had waited for, and love would be all right, and the marriage bed undefiled. He gripped her tight over and over again. This would continue for hours, as virgin blood was spilled, and passionate love and desire met, into the early streaks of the morning light. Souls and hearts were unveiled, and bared open, hours through the night and when the early hints of dawn appeared in the sky, they both fell asleep and woke well into the afternoon.

They talked, they rested, they laughed, they ate and they shared. The same activity of the first night, continued night after night, by the fire, on the plush rug, before the fireplace. She was all his and nothing would ever change that. He could never get enough of her, and he could just be there in that place forever. They were now a part of each other forever. A part of him permanently inside of her, and a part of her permanently inside him.

All the anger toward her brother dissolved, as now it did not matter; she would be his one and only, and he would always protect her and cherish her. Some of the time, they spent together with his mask on, and other times, it would be off. He trusted her enough to show his face. "That beloved face," Amy thought.

Amy accidentally knocked his duffel bag off the counter, and out came a large knife. "Oh my God! Bryan were you going to…kill me after the wedding? Oh, please say you were not planning to do so!"

Bryan frantically gestured *"NO! NO! NO!"* He grabbed the notebook and wrote. *"I thought I needed to protect you, and the things your brother was saying about me were hurtful. I was angry, so I brought the knife just in case anyone tried to hurt you! I never understood family or brother-sister relationships. I heard everything through the window that your brother said about me and wanted to kill him. I thought he was hurting you and I knew for sure he was mocking me, and it made me angry. That night, I just had to come back just to see you and make sure you were okay. Amy, I just can't get enough of you. I just have to look at you, and I thought it was odd you ended the night so early."*

Amy said, "I am so very sorry he was being hurtful. I did not want you to lose your cool and hurt my brother. The calling of an early night was for you. I'm sorry I did not explain the way my brother is, to you, and what it's like to have a brother or sister you love. I forgot to do that, and I could've told you how he is, and warned you ahead of time, that he does joke around a lot. Will means no harm he is just like that. Sometimes he can go overboard with his joking, and we come from the same stock."

"You mean... you would make fun of me too?"

"I would of in my old life, and in our family, goofing off and laughing runs deep. It's easy to do so at the expense of others, but I am not like that anymore. I love you Bryan for you, and it's my culture. We love to laugh and have fun, but no, you are my sweetheart and I could never make fun of you now. My love for my brother is different than it is for you. It's a family thing not a spouse thing," said Amy. She fell into his strong arms and buried her face in his broad chest. Amy was relieved he was not going to kill her, and she began to understand that part of him needing to protect her out of his love, and that he was not going to kill her after all.

Bryan held her close to his heart and she laid her head on his chest. She loved to hear his heart beat. He never wanted this time with them together to end, but he also knew he would have the rest of his life with her. He cherished every moment they were together, as they snuggled by the fire, under the blankets, long into the nights, which grew cold. He

Chapter 15

was so happy she had picked this place away from everyone and everything that involved others. He just loved the quiet places of peace and tranquility.

Amy said, "Well, now that we married, what do you want to do with our houses?" Bryan did not understand the question. He cocked his head and seemed puzzled. "No, I mean do you want me to move into your place, or should we keep both homes? I have been living at my home alone for a long time, and wanted to know what you thought?"

Bryan got the notebook and wrote, "*I think I want to keep my own house, because I like how you fixed it up. At first it made me very angry that they sold it out from me. I still want to keep my home…but we can also live at yours too. We can also go back and forth each week.*"

"Okay, no problem Bryan. Anything for you and your happiness too. I was wondering about that, because I could tell you were very tied to your home, and it is in my name. Do you want it in your name? I mean, we can transfer the deed."

 "No, we are together now and whatever you share with me is ours, and my house is yours too."

"Okay," said Amy. Bryan did not want to be bothered by any bureaucracies involving people, and they probably would not take him seriously and he did not want to put Amy through that either. They both have already been through so much, even before they were married, and that was the reason for him leaving things the same.

Bryan was still Bryan, in his unique three to five hours a night sleeping habit. He would be up late, still watching her sleep at night, in the cabin and sleep was not a priority, and he felt he had to protect her. He just adored her face, and would watch her breath in and out, and he could tell she was dreaming by the way her eyes would dart back and forth under closed lids…and those full lips slightly parted.

Redemption Has No Limits

He was a short sleeper because of all he had to endure in his life. Sleep was not a privilege growing up, as Dad would come home many nights drunk and beat him. There was also beatings he received while in prison. He would just stay up and watch her sleep. It was a flight or fight response, so sleep was scarce for him.

He stared and tilted his head through his mask, as he watched her sleep, for hours. He gently traced her full lips with his finger. "*My precious angel,*" he said inside to himself. He stroked her olive face with his white finger tips. Those long, black lashes, feathered and rested on her face--as her eyes darted back and forth beneath closed lids. Her breathing shallow and soft, he wondered what she was dreaming about. Her hair was everywhere on the pillow, as it cascaded in waves. To watch her and stare at her gave him pleasure, as it was so delightful to gaze upon her.

It was his own secret, and he could not tell her how enamored he was with her, watching her sleep each night, because it might scare her. "*I guess it will have to be my little secret,*" he thought, as he traced her lips with his fingers again. He could not resist the view of her sleeping every night next to him. Bryan leaned in to look at her again before heading off to bed. Only this time, he did not have to leave the room. He simply slid into the bed beside her. "*This feels so much better with us together than having us to be apart from each other,*" he thought. He glanced at the clock. It was now 3:30 a.m. "*Time to get some sleep myself,*" he said inside himself, and drifted off. He was so happy she had said yes, as he put his arm around her and held her close. He snuggled up next to her body for warmth. The cabin was cooler, being it was early November and there was a fall chill in the air.

The next morning at breakfast, Amy said, "Our honeymoon is coming to an end, but we can always come back when summer comes if you would like." Bryan nodded yes. "*I would be very happy with that,*" he thought. Amy could tell by the gleam in his eye, he really enjoyed the cabin.

Chapter 15

They packed up the car and drove home. It would be Sunday night by the time they got back. Amy was too tired to cook, so they swung through a burger joint on the way home from the honeymoon. Thankfully it was dark, so no one could see Bryan's mask, and make some nasty comments. They arrived back in town and Amy drove her car through town and she said, "Tonight, will it be my house or yours?" He pointed in the direction of his house and Amy turned the corner in that direction. "First, I have to pull in and get a change of clothes, because it's back to work for me tomorrow, and load the washer with our old clothes," said Amy. They pulled into her driveway and she quickly got out with the bag of dirty clothes, and Bryan followed her. She quickly crammed a new set of clothes in a duffel bag and they both left the house. She realized that now she was doing washing for two people—and not just herself, so she put Bryan's clothes in with hers. She took more clothes over to his house. However, her wedding dress was a mess. It was not on very long after they arrived at the cabin and it was stained with what? It looked as if there was blood on it. A lot of blood from the waist down! Bryan did not stab her, but it was from another source. Everything was a blur that first night, and she figured out why it was stained, and hopefully it would come out. If not, it was so worth it. It was Amy's first time and she was glad she waited for that special one.

She delightfully recalled and cherished that first night, and remembered well, everything that took place, and held the memory close to her heart. Bryan's hands, his face, his pale blue eyes, his heart, his everything! She knew in her heart there would be many more times like that special night. They were both new at this intimate type of life, called marriage, and they would have the rest of their lives to share together. She was delighted, and so was he, as he caught her viewing her wedding dress at his house. She heard the floor creak and quickly shoved the wedding dress behind her. She jumped, "Bryan, you scared me!" Bryan came up to her with a loving gleam of tenderness in his eye, reached behind her, and slowly removed the wedding dress from her hands.

He looked at it as if studying it, and she was embarrassed and put her head down. If someone of her complexion could blush, she was blushing. He tenderly touched her face and held her to him, and put his finger under her chin, as if motioning her to look into his eyes.

"Bryan, I, uhh…just was trying to figure out how to get the blood off the dress to keep it as a keepsake." Amy tried to smooth the awkward situation over. Bryan shook a finger at her and smiled through his mask. "What are you trying to say?" Amy said.

Bryan got the notebook and began to write: "*You don't ever have to be ashamed of your purity. I have cherished every night we were together, and it was my first time too. I could not resist you, the blood spilled and for once, I saw that it was not from a kill, but coming from you. It was special, it was meant for me. You don't have to clean the dress, because it is of great value to me. As wicked as I was as a serial killer, I still value purity in the highest regards. The sight of couples in lust, would make me furious. This is love in its purest form, in marriage, and sacred. PLEASE, PLEASE, DON'T clean the dress!*"

"Uh, okay," Amy said. "I don't understand Bryan, but if it means that much to you, I will not do it. Will the sight of blood stir you up? Like say, what you used to do?"

"*NO!*" wrote Bryan. "*Those kills are nothing compared to this…treasure I have here in my hands. This is a part of you I want to keep and hold dear,*" wrote Bryan.

"Aww, that is so sweet Bryan! Okay, I won't clean it," said Amy. Inside, Amy was roaring with laughter, because she did not know if she should cry, or laugh. Actually she wanted to laugh, and cry, at the same time. But she knew this was a tender moment for him, and she dare not laugh.

Chapter 16

"He DOES have a tender heart after all!" she thought. It was evident in his previous actions, but now more so, it was being shown to her in their brand-new marriage. Responding to those emotions, she threw her arms around him and gave him a kiss. He whirled her around with a big bear hug. "What will I do with you Bryan? You are so intense and unique!" He just smiled and smiled at her through his mask.

That night, long after she was asleep, he cried into the dress, in a room down the hall. He felt the sobs coming, so he quickly headed down the hall and closed the door to one of the other rooms. His sobs could have been heard by her if she had been awake. The walls were well insulated from the remodeling done in the home, so she could not hear him cry. He could not understand why he was crying.

All he ever wanted was love! That was it! He knew God loved him now, by giving him her. His own special treasure and he cherished her dearly. This was no accident they were meant to be together! Everything just fell into place perfectly! He held the wet, tear-stained dress to his heart for the longest time and waited until he had calmed down. Quietly he walked back to her room, sat down and watched her like he did every night by her bedside. The room was faintly light by a dimmer switch, and it was shadowy enough, so she could sleep, but light enough, so he could see her pretty face. More hours passed, and he finally crawled into their bed and fell fast asleep, still clutching the dress.

The alarm went off and Amy arose to get ready for work. "Well Bryan, this is my first day back to work. Will you be okay by yourself?"

He nodded yes.

"I am going to…" Amy felt the laughter again. He sat up upright in the bed, with the dress in his hands, and clutching it to his chest. This time her laughter came out uncontrollably. She began to laugh hysterically, and she was caught off guard by the sight of him clutching the dress. She had not expected that, first thing in the morning.

Bryan looked sad and hurt.

"No! No! No! Please Bryan, I am not laughing at you but your…intensity and passion touches and tickles me deeply on the inside. I cannot help but laugh. It is delightful, exhilarating, and moving! I don't understand it, but I have always responded to things differently than others do! Please don't ever think I am laughing at you, I am just…different!"

Bryan lifted his head up and seemed to understand. She gave him an encouraging hug. Amy thought this was going to be very interesting, being married to Bryan. The thought exhilarated and excited her at the same time. But would they be okay together and have a peaceful life, or would others come to harass them as a couple?

"Bryan, I do have to stop at the grocery store, because we don't have enough food to get through the week. I will be late coming back home, about an hour or so."

Bryan nodded, "*Okay.*" Amy showered and got ready for work.

"I will be back around 4:30ish. Enjoy your day," she said. Bryan took her in his arms. He did not want to let her go. "I know Bryan, but I have duties and I will show you more soon about my life." He let her go, knowing she would be back later that night.

Chapter 16

Thoughts of being harassed as a couple bothered Amy, as she got ready for work, and she made them a quick breakfast and headed out to face the day. That evening she planned to make a big breakfast casserole with the groceries she would buy, and a big bowl of fruit for the mornings, so she would not have to make breakfast every day, so Bryan would have something to eat. The week would be very busy, getting caught up at work, with her being gone, things always piled up.

Amy always like to make sure her bin was empty each night when she left. Pastor Mark was always kind and let her slide at times, but business was business. Amy was continuously faithful to complete the tasks at hand.

"Well Amy, how was everything? The honeymoon?" asked Mary.

"It was so wonderful! We had a wonderful time! He has changed, and God is still not done with him yet, as in all of us. I believe it's going to be a wonderful marriage," replied Amy.

Mary said, "That is so awesome! What about his life outside of marriage, like his spiritual life?"

"Bryan believes there is a God, he does watch inspirational television and he reads my devotionals. But I don't think pushing him to come to church with me would not be right. When he feels ready, I believe he will. I mean, look what happened when he tried to come that night? I guess being attacked inside a church would make anyone leery, even Bryan. Can you blame him?" Amy flatly said.

Pastor Mark came in, overhearing their conversation.

Pastor Mark said, "I believe Bryan was indeed touched deeply that night he tried to come to the spring event. I have a lot of insight into his unique situation, and due to his background, it is best not to push him."

Pastor Mark continued, "He has been horribly abused all his life and when he is ready, he will come…and when he does, we must show him love without hypocrisy and religious judgment. It is religious people that run off the sinner, with self-righteous attitudes. Sometimes, it may take someone a long time to get over abuse. So, lets pray and love him unconditionally, when, and I believe he will. He has Amy for support.

When he comes, I will be here." Amy said within herself, "Go Pastor!" Amy was so happy Pastor had stuck up for Bryan. Mary had the older way of thinking, and sometimes she could be a little religious and self-righteous. But, Amy still loved her like a mother, none-the-less.

Amy went to the grocery store after work and got what was needed for the breakfast casserole, and other things for the week's dinners. It was busy in the store at this time of day. She could not help but notice she was being followed by this blonde older lady. The woman appeared about ten or so years older than her, and she was rough looking, long, tall and lanky. It seemed wherever Amy turned, there was the woman in the same aisles she was in. It was making her nervous. The woman seemed unstable, and Amy quickly paid for her things and got out of there! The woman started following her to her car but got stopped by cars driving down the aisle of the parking lot. This bought Amy enough time to get in her car and get away.

Maybe she was just imagining it, but it was a very strange incidence. Amy dared not tell Bryan, because she did not want to set him off. They just had a wonderful wedding and honeymoon, she did not want to ruin it with any bad news.

Amy looked in her rear view mirror and she noticed she was being followed by another red car. "No, it was not just a coincidence!" she thought. Amy sped up and quickly and made a few twists and turns down some streets. She lost whoever was following her.

As she drove on, she looked again in her rear view mirror, the person was following her again, but far behind, with the

Chapter 16

same red car. She quickly went by the church and swung into the parking lot in the back and cut her lights off. The person slowed down, and drove by slowly, and then was gone. Amy waited for about 20 minutes before venturing out of the parking lot. She wanted to make sure whoever was following her was long gone.

This time, she was afraid for herself and for Bryan. What would he do if he found out his wife was being stalked. She did not want to lose him again, so she did not tell him. Certainly, Bryan would be upset when she got home, it was hours after she got off work and she had to think of something. Amy did not like to lie, but it seemed the only option, due to Bryan's tendency to want to protect her in the way he only knew.

Amy walked in the door with the groceries, and there stood Bryan, waiting for her. He was upset, as she knew he would be.

He wrote, *"How come you're so late? I thought something happened to you! I was about to go out looking for you!"*

"Bryan, I, uh…just got held up at the store. There are a lot of holiday shoppers out, being it's November and there are a lot of early Black Friday sales out there."

"Held up WHO? Let me put my hands on them!"

"No Bryan, not THAT kind of held up. The kind where there are long lines and it takes a while to shop."

"OH, now I get it. You know how I feel, should anyone put their hands on you. Your all mine. I don't ever want anyone to hurt you," wrote Bryan.

"I know my dear. I so love and appreciate you." The store was indeed busy, but Amy did not tell him the whole truth. She busied herself by making the casserole and dinner. She had hoped he would not ask any more questions about her day. He helped with the casserole by layering it, as she cut up potatoes, veggies, and the fruit. They worked in silence to get the week's meals prepared. "We are going to have some good dishes this week," Amy said. Bryan enjoyed her cooking, and

Redemption Has No Limits

he was glad he no longer had to steal things just to eat. She had helped him survive and she noticed he had put on a little weight because of it. He was tall, big and stocky. She noticed a little thickness around his belly, but not fatter, just thicker and it looked good on him.

Chapter 17

Amy drove to work each day, because it was now cold. She nervously ventured out to work. After that night of being stalked by that woman, she was more gun shy, and would nervously look over her shoulder, to see if she saw that weird lady again. Amy did not know her and hoped she would never run into her again. Bryan also knew of the nights she would have practice for dance and plays, being the holidays were coming up soon. He knew she had things to do that involved the arts, and he learned to be okay with it.

One night after work, she decided to stop at the bakery. She wanted to surprise Bryan with a cake, just because of who he was. She did not even know when his birthday was. With all the things that happened, it never came up in conversations they had or perhaps his family never even celebrated his birthday. So, she just figured she would celebrate him. He liked chocolate, by the way he always seemed to want it. She went in and got the cake and picked the prettiest one. It was thick, with decorative frosting, and had candy corn accents on the bottom. Amy said, "Can you write 'Because of who you are' inside a heart on it, and put three roses on the top?"

The baker said, "Sure thing, I will have that ready in a jiffy!" He put it in a box, Amy paid for it and headed out to her car.

Redemption Has No Limits

Amy unlocked her car and put the cake in the backseat.

She was then startled by, "Ma'am, I need to talk to you!" Amy turned around, stunned like a deer in headlights.

"It was that crazy woman! The woman who had been following me!" she thought. "Can I help you?" asked Amy.

"I see you married Bryan Conners, the well known serial killer. How dare he have a normal life like nothing happened and you!"

"Look, I don't even know who you are and what your purpose is for coming at me like this. Why?" asked Amy.

"My name is Laureen, and that monster killed some of my family and my cousins. Why did you marry him? He is evil, and he should have died in prison by death penalty! I wanted him dead. Why is he not dead yet? Laureen said with an evil sneer, shaking from head to foot."

Amy said sternly, "You leave my husband alone! Don't you realize people can change?"

Laureen said, "He will never change, just watch and see! He used to be infatuated with me, and you are his little pawn! How does it feel to know he killed people that are related to me? And you are prancing around town with this monster like nothing happened? How dare you?"

Amy said, "I don't have to listen to this, and you need to leave me alone!

Aren't you married to him?" Laureen demanded.

"What does that have to do with anything?" Amy fired back.

"People have said to me that I lost my mind because of him, and that I have never been able to get on with my life. Shame on you for being with him…and I hope he dies a horrible death and rots in hell!" Laureen yelled.

"Leave us alone!" Amy yelled back. She quickly got in her car, and Laureen tried to get in the car with her, as Amy sped off.

Chapter 17

Amy was shook up as she drove home. She dared not tell Bryan, for fear of what he would do to this lady. He surely would know who she was and go after her. She shook off the thoughts and focused on surprising Bryan. She walked in with the cake and said, "Surprise!" Bryan knew she was late again, and Amy said, "I got this gift for you to celebrate you, and let you know I appreciate you. That's why I am late!" She said sheepishly." Amy hoped this surprise would deter him from asking any questions. The run in with this crazy lady bothered her thoughts. He kissed her, as if to say, "Thank you," and smiled brightly through his mask at her.

Amy did not know what drove this woman and why she could not let this go. It had been several years ago when the crimes were committed. Amy knew losing people was hard. But was it madness, jealousy, hate or a little of all three? Amy certainly did not want to make enemies, but she had to tell someone she was being stalked by one of Bryan's haters and her life and Bryan's might be in danger once again.

"Pastor Mark, can I talk to you in the sanctuary?" Amy asked, at work the next day. She did not want Mary to hear her.

"Sure," Pastor Mark said.

"Do you know, by chance, an older lady named Laureen?" said Amy.

Pastor Mark said, "Yes, in fact I do. She was never the same since Bryan murdered some of her family members."

"She approached me and has been following me around. She almost got in my car. She is also threatening me with physical harm, because I married Bryan," said Amy.

Pastor Mark said, "Please be careful, she was in the mental ward for a while, and claims Bryan is in love with her, he never was." Amy told him everything.

"I will be praying for you," said Pastor Mark. "You can also go down to the police station and file a restraining order against her too."

Redemption Has No Limits

Amy said "I think I will do that. What is her last name?"

"Waller--and believe me, everyone knows about her in this town. She never got over the deaths. It's sad how people react when they have no hope or forgiveness and can't move on. As hard as it is to forgive, bitterness is like a cancer," said Pastor.

Amy immediately went after work to the police station to file a restraining order against Laureen. The chief of police, Tim, happened to be there. "Hello Sir, I need to file a restraining order against a stalking and threatening individual."

"Who is it?' Officer Tim asked.

"It's a woman named Laureen Waller, and she has threatened me."

"Oh, was it about Bryan?"

"Yes," Amy said.

"Don't mind her, she lost her mind and was not able to bounce back and has been locked up, claiming Bryan loved her. He killed some of her family many years ago. Nevertheless, we will file a police report and restraining order to keep her from stalking you. She cannot come within 100 feet of you and she has to obey that law," said the officer.

Amy was relieved that she filed the restraining order, but she did not know if this would stop the woman from coming after her again. Amy came home from work and asked Bryan if it would be okay to install a security system in his house. Her house had one, but Bryan's house certainly needed one. He could well protect himself, but she needed evidence if anything was to happen.

"*Why do you think we need one*?" Bryan wrote. "It is to protect your house from break ins when we are not here… you know how we spend time between our homes. I mean, my house already has one, and its only right that yours should have one too. I will pay for it." Bryan agreed to it. Amy once again, was struggling by not telling him everything. She was

Chapter 17

torn between telling him and not tell him. She also knew the risk and what may happen if she did.

That weekend, the security people came out and put up cameras, and an alarm system on Bryan's house, while he stayed at Amy's home. Amy handled the affairs of the security camera set up. She was at Bryan's house during the installation, set up, signing the papers and paying the bill. She knew how to monitor the tapes, and she would make sure to keep an eye out, in case this woman would come around their properties.

Several days had passed, and Amy did not see the woman on the streets or on the tapes. "It was better to be safe than sorry, and Bryan would be safe from getting in trouble with this woman, Amy thought to herself.

It was Wednesday, and Mary said, "Do you want to go out to lunch?"

"Sure, where are we going today?" "Let's go up to the burger joint down the street! They have the best burgers and fries," said Mary.

Amy said, "Sure thing! I could use a little extra protein today."

"Consider it a date!" said Mary.

The burger place was within walking distance, and it was a cold, late November afternoon, the wind was whipping leaves everywhere. The snow would fly soon, and this time Bryan and she would be together, safe and sound. No matter what storm would come their way, they would be home-nice, warm, and snuggling together. She smiled at the tender thought. She hoped for snow days, so they would be snowed in.

Mary and Amy made their way to the burger joint laughing, joking and talking about holiday plans. That's when Amy saw Laureen again, about 20 feet away. She knew it was her, staring and glaring at her with rage. "Geez, I must be a stalking target or something," Amy thought humorously to herself, but was still nervous. Amy played it off like it was nothing.

Certainly, Laureen would not attack, being it was daytime, and Amy was with other people from work. The restraining order did the trick. Amy tried to forget about this woman during their lunch and focus on Mary.

After lunch, they headed back to the office and after work, Amy made sure she viewed the tapes at her own house, to not cause suspicion in Bryan. She purposely had it rigged were she could view the tapes from her own house, and watch his house through the system, in a secret place in the attic, so Bryan did not know about it. "Why am I being so secretive?" Amy wondered. She did not want to betray his trust, but she was so afraid he would do something to her. Or maybe would run away and hide again. "Where is my faith to trust everything will be okay?" She prayed, everything would turn out somehow. She still could not get Laureen's crazed face out of her head.

From her own home in the attic, she had viewed the tapes from the cameras on both of their homes and sure enough, Laureen had been hanging around both of their houses, across the street. It was her, clearly, in the tapes, watching and waiting. Laureen must have known that both houses were taping her from the cameras, so she did not want to get any closer to either of them. That must have been why she stayed a distance away. The tapes showed the dates and times. Amy kept the tapes as evidence in case something more would come of it. She quickly headed to Bryan' house, so he would not be suspicious of her being late again. He was very protective of her, and he knew how the streets were in their cruelness, small town or not. He just wanted her safe and sound and always at his side.

Another week had passed, and Amy had dance practice the next Wednesday. The whole rest of that week, there had not been any sign of the woman. Amy felt, maybe Laureen

Chapter 17

had given up or gone somewhere to pester someone else. She breezed joyfully through her day and focused on the holiday dance she and her girls would be doing and what songs they perform in the town square, Christmas week and Christmas eve.

She raced home and fixed dinner for herself and Bryan. It was a quick handmade pizza, before she headed out the door again for practice. She put on her dance outfit. Bryan loved her angelic dance outfits.

He had, however, noticed she was not acting like herself lately. As if she was almost hiding something from him in her goings and comings. She was also not as talkative and he could not put his finger on it. But he was determined to find out. Bryan was very street smart and could easily figure out people.

As she prepared to head out the door, he blocked the door and nodded his head "No."

"What is it Bryan?"

"*Please, don't go to practice*," he wrote in the notepad. "Bryan, please understand my dancers need me and Christmas is only a few weeks away. I am the one who teaches them the dance they are to perform."

"*Okay, that is fine. I am going with you then. I feel I must go with you. Something is telling me to do go. I will wait in the car for you, till after practice*," he wrote.

"Okay, sure, you can come," Amy said, sounding puzzled, because she had never seen him act like this and she did not understand why he would want to come with her.

Amy made her way inside the church, and Pastor Mark happened to be staying late with Matt the church janitor, working on some special projects. The girls were already in position and stretching out, to do the moves they had been working on. This would be a short practice, because most of the dance the girls already knew. Amy breezed through the practice and she released everyone early. Amy met Bryan

Redemption Has No Limits

outside in the car, and Pastor Mark and Matt were busy unloading some pieces and backdrops for the Christmas play that would take place. The men and the dancers came outside and talked a bit before departing.

Pastor Mark said, "Oh, hello Bryan. Remember me? I am the one who married you two." Pastor extended his hand and Bryan nodded and shook it.

"Who's this?" Matt asked.

"Matt, this is my husband Bryan." Matt sheepishly waved hello.

Bryan nodded through his mask and put his arm around Amy.

"Well, now I won't have a chance with her. I should have jumped when I had the chance," Matt thought to himself, dejected. Just then, there was a rustle in the bushes next to him, a blur of blonde hair and a flash of silver.

"DIE, you evil S.O.B." screamed a female voice. It was Laureen. She missed Bryan's shoulder as he turned around, but stabbed Amy in the arm.

"NOOOO!" Everyone screamed. "I told you, I was coming for you…you little tramp! Bryan does not deserve any happiness, and I am here to end his source of happiness here and now!"

Laureen screamed insanely. Amy winced in pain, as Bryan grabbed Laureen by the throat in a death grip. He threw her violently, through the air and she landed about 15 feet away. Laureen jumped up and rushed again at Amy. Before Bryan could grab her and finish her off, because he was planning to, in the way he knew how to, there was another flash of silver. Amy quickly moved out of the way, and Laureen stumbled over the curb and plunged the knife into her own stomach. Pastor Mark and Matt quickly jumped into action. They wrestled the knife away from Laureen and tied her hands together so she could not hurt anyone else. "NO! THEY BOTH HAVE TO DIE!" Laureen screamed hysterically.

Chapter 17

Pastor Mark called 911 and police were quickly dispatched. Laureen was taken away in an ambulance. Amy was taken to the hospital, as well and her arm was stitched up. Bryan would not leave her side no matter what. Many of the member of the church came to visit her, and soon it would be, all around town, what a hero Bryan was for trying to protect his wife. There were witnesses who saw him protect her, and slowly, over time, people's opinions of Bryan changed. There would always be those few who never got over things…and Amy and Bryan knew very well, that would be the case, but love would conquer all things.

Laureen was immediately taken to the state hospital, locked up for the rest of her life, as she was unfit for society, never to be heard from again. Amy told the officers she had tapes for evidence, of Laureen's stalking. A new problem she had to deal with was Bryan's intense anger at her for not telling him everything.

In the ambulance, on the way to the hospital, Bryan sat by her side, as Amy winced in pain. Bryan's eyes were smoldering with threatening anger, through his mask, as to why she did not tell him. "Bryan… I can explain." He abruptly turned away, his back to her. He was very upset, she hid things from him. The paramedic applied pressure to her arm. "Ouch, that really hurts!"

"Ma'am, the wound is deep. We will have to stitch you up." Bryan briefly turned back to her and hated to see her in pain, but she hurt him deeply by hiding things. Things, that he could have solved. He would not have killed Laureen, but just would have scared her off. There was too much at risk with his marriage had he killed her. They would send him back to prison without reserve.

"*That Laureen!*" he hissed inside. "*How dare she hurt my wife! My precious wife!*" He never loved Laureen. He had never loved any women, except Amy. Amy did not stay overnight at the hospital, and they would release her with instructions on how to take care of her wound. Amy and Bryan got a taxi home, and immediately, Bryan grabbed and pressed Amy against the wall. With his mask puffing in and out, he demanded an answer as to why she did not tell him. He was careful not to touch her arm, but he was furious.

"Please Bryan, I can explain. It was to protect you. I so don't want to lose you. Please try to understand, why I did, what I did, to protect you! I love you so much, and never wanted to see you put back in prison for killing someone else!" There, it was out in the open-her confession. Had she been thinking that all along? Had she not trusted in what he said about the change in him, or was that her fears that he may snap again? Yes, he was putting his thumb on her greatest fears. What if he had not changed? What if it was just a front, just to get her in marriage, and he was waiting to snap again? All the what-ifs were too much to bear, and she hid those too.

He released her and angrily wrote, "*Do you not see that I have changed? In the last year? I would not have killed Laureen, but only did something enough to scare her, where she would not hurt you. Why do you not trust me. Why do you view me as still the same way? I know I can be very intense in my ways, in scaring others, as what they call the Boogeyman, I have been a long time out of society…detached from society, and all I knew was killing; but you hurt me very much by hiding all this from me. You also kept things inside of you that you felt about me. I know your life was in danger and I could have helped prevent her from harming you at all. The cameras, the security system on my house, the chocolate cake? It all makes sense now. You knew about this for weeks and yet you did not tell me your life was in danger! Amy, all I want to do is make sure you are safe. God, I love you so much! Do you not see that? Why?*" The angry words on his notepad cut her deep in her heart.

Chapter 17

She broke down and cried, "I am so very sorry, sometimes my fears are so much more then I can handle and yes, I was thinking those very things. I judged you according to what you were, and that blinded me to seeing what you are now. I am so very sorry I judged you so wrong. Please forgive me. I am not perfect, by any means. It's just, you know, kidnapped, and all I have been though with others trying to kill you, had been so much for me!"

Amy continued, "I am not used to being stalked and stabbed, and anything else." Amy bawled and sobbed gut-wrenching sobs. "I-I never wanted to hurt you. Please, you've got to believe me! PLEASE, if I tell you everything now, please promise not to get angry."

"*It's very hard for me not to get angry about this matter, but I will try,*" Bryan wrote.

"Laureen had followed me out to my car the day I went to the grocery store and was harassing me there. She then proceeded to follow me in her car, I zigzagged quickly down some streets. Then I went and hid behind the church and waited till she was long gone. She stalked me at work, even after I got a restraining order. Then I went to the bakery to get your cake and she confronted me again with threatening words and tried to get in my car. She was babbling on about why you should not be happy in this life and said hateful things to me for being married to you! Bryan, it scared me so much, and I was afraid for you too, because I was terrified I would lose you again! I was torn, on whether to tell you or not. I didn't feel I knew you well enough to make an accurate judgment on what you would do, so I did not tell you. They say marriage is a lifetime, to get to know someone, and we just got married a month or so ago. I guess it will take time. I wanted to protect you and have the tapes of the security cameras as evidence, so the police can see what she was doing. Let's go to my house, so I can show you the place where the cameras keep track of activity around our houses."

Redemption Has No Limits

So off they went. Bryan was much calmer after she shared with him her heart.

He wrote, "*I know I have done many things wrong, even to you. I had not planned to fall in love with you. I could not help myself, I saw your beauty that day, the way you looked at me, as I hid in the bushes and when you bought my house. Yes, I was very angry, but that gave me more of a reason to pursue you. I did not know love, or what it was, but I am trying to change. A lot of my ways are still rough. That night I came to your church, all my wrongs were laid out before me. I wept and meant every tear, and every word in my heart. Love washed over me before that cross. I have never been the same since then. I know God's forgiveness is real. For you to judge me, my sweet Amy, was very hurtful and when you do that, you are no different than those who can't forgive me.*" Those words cut her deep.

"You know Bryan, you are absolutely right and if God forgives you, we humans should do the same to each other. I am so very sorry. I was wrong, and fell into fear and not trusting," Amy responded.

Chapter 18

He took the notebook and wrote, "*I forgive you. Please, please, please, don't do it again. It's so painful when you hide things from me. I just want to be trusted.*" He was trembling and near tears, as he took her into his arms and kissed her passionately. She felt small compared to his size. He could not stay angry for long because of his love for her. He stroked her face and looked deep into her eyes for the longest time. He could not take his eyes off of hers, as if he was transfixed. He saw the light in her eyes as it always has been, especially when she confessed the hidden things. It seemed the light was back in her eyes, and that purity he so loved!

They went into the attic where all the equipment was, at her house, and she showed Bryan how to work the cameras. "This is the monitor, and you can hit this button with rewind and see all the activity of the day, and it will show everything," Amy said. Bryan was intrigued by the cameras and he recalled many a camera with prying eyes, that would be watching him when he was in the hospital, and in the prison. This invasion of privacy made him angry, and now it felt good to be on the other side behind the monitor, instead of the one being viewed. He hit rewind, and sure enough, he could see what time and day things happened when people came home from work and also animals scurrying about, like dogs, cats, and squirrels. He could see when Amy would be walking home to his or her house.

Redemption Has No Limits

Bryan became like a kid in the candy store with the cameras. He loved them (hopefully not too much, Amy smiled and thought), he just could not get over the fact that he was no longer the one being viewed, now he was the one doing the viewing. He played on the monitor to sharpen images, hone the color of the things outside and even turn the screen to a black and white color. This new thing was very intriguing to him and he seemed to catch on quickly.

"Well Bryan, it looks like you have a hobby. Do you like the cameras?"

Bryan nodded his head *yes*.

"The cameras see everything, including anyone coming up to the house." Bryan just kept pressing this or that button, and it was clear he was having fun. Amy liked to see him happy.

"It was so cute to see him like this. A playful side she had never seen," she said to herself. She giggled inside. "He was so cute with all those cameras."

Amy checked her calendar, and realized she had a doctor's appointment on December 18th, right before Christmas. "Just a routine check," she said to herself and also thought it strange she was not pregnant. They had been very active in their private time, in their new marriage. She would find out some things about her health. She was not one, that desperately had to have a baby. She knew some woman were, but Amy was different, it did not matter to her whether she had kids or not. In fact, she was more focused on her spirituality, her marriage, her job, their life together and somehow, a baby just did not seem to fit into the equation, right now. Amy was happy and content and did not need a baby to fit into her life to make her complete.

Amy waited in the waiting room and pretty soon she was called into the doctor's office. Dr. Sam said, "Oh, I see you changed your name and just got married."

Amy said, "Yes I did."

Chapter 18

"Well, congratulations!"

Amy said, "Thank you, it has been quite a journey."

He said, "Marriage always is." He checked her blood pressure and all other things through blood work and then did the routine check that women go through every year to see if things were normal. Amy then went on to work that morning, wondering what they would find if anything. She had been kind of tired lately from everything that had gone on in the last few months, and even the year.

A few days later, her tests came back. Her iron was a little low, and the tests showed some problems with her ovaries, and she needed to call the doctor's office right away. She called and inquired what was going on. "Hello, this is Amy Angelo Conners. I got my test results in the mail and I need to talk to the doctor.

The nurse said, "Hold on, I will get the doctor."

There was a pause and Dr. Sam came on the phone, "Hello, Amy, I had you call my office because I have some news for you. Your iron is low, but you can get supplements over the counter to combat that. The other news is, Amy, I am sorry to say, but your test results are showing there is a chance you may be infertile.

I am going to recommend you see a specialist regarding this matter."

Amy was saddened by the news, but she was okay. But how would Bryan respond? She could not hide it from him. She knew now, he would not like if he did not know about it. With him, marriage had to be an open book.

Amy struggled with these thoughts on the drive home. "How would I tell Bryan, and how would he react?" She figured she would wait until after dinner to tell him there may be a possibility she was be infertile. She pulled up, and he greeted her at the door, as he always did. She had made him a key to her house, so he could easily let himself in whenever he would like. So, he was waiting at her house when she came home that night. He pulled her into his arms and he automatically could tell something was wrong. She hung her head and burst into tears.

He tilted his head and he was puzzled as to why she was crying. He put his fingers under her chin and inquired with his eyes, out of genuine concern, as to what was going on - and demanded an answer.

Amy said, "I…don't know how to say this but… I may be infertile."

Bryan became angry, and she could tell his frustration from his eyes through the mask. He took his fist and slammed it on the table in anger.

Amy jumped, startled, and said, "No Bryan, it's not you it's me. Things inside me are not working right and they are going to send me to a specialist to verify the tests, so there may be hope. Please don't be angry—its me."

Bryan angrily grabbed the pad and wrote, "*I KNEW IT! I KNEW! I was cursed in some way because of all I did wring in my life!*"

Amy said, "No! No! Bryan you are not cursed, these things happen all the time to women. I am okay. I really am, and if you want to, we can adopt."

"*I don't even know the first thing about parenting and I would have liked to have had a child. If it's not meant to be, I guess I will have to accept my fate as someone who is unable to produce anything in life.*"

Amy said, "No sweetheart, you are NOT defective and it's my body they have ran tests on. Please don't take it personally. I am quite sure you are fine on your end." Bryan calmed down, but he was very sad. He appeared like he was going to cry, so Amy held him tight and they cried together.

Amy went to the specialist for further testing, and the tests came back the same, a few days later, that she was indeed infertile. Bryan was waiting at the door when she came come. He had the test in his hands from the mail. He was very sad.

Chapter 18

Amy said, "I guess you now know the news. We will get through all of this and everything life throws at us together. I love you just the way you are, and nothing will ever change that…baby or no baby." Bryan hugged and held her tight, and they cried again together, yet again.

Amy was careful not to say anything more, about any babies, because she did not want to upset him more. She realized he knew very little about everyday life, and had a hard time learning how to respond, when life throws curve balls at you. She doubted he had ever experienced domestic things like this. The only way he knew to respond was in anger, when things did not go his way, or for unexpected things, but Amy had to take it in stride. Up to this point, he had never hit her and he just did not know how to deal with his feelings about things in the way that is proper. She would take this time to show him life things, and how to function. Instead of grieving over the news, this would give her and Bryan time to grow more together in their marriage. She could teach him a lot about everyday life, and in many ways, he was just like a child in a man's body. Yet, he was very intelligent—especially, the day he came to her aid when she got stabbed. How had he known? She also knew, with Bryan, timing was everything, so, to talk to him about certain things, she would have to take it slow on some things, and be sensitive about life skills. Not that she feared him, but she knew he had such a tender heart and the wounds of the past were so deep. The last thing she would want to do is upset him. To go from being someone with no, or repressed, emotions as a cold-blooded killer, to having a super tender heart, was beyond what she could understand, but she was sure everything would level out over time.

Christmas was days away. Amy put up her tree at her house and Bryan came over to help. They both were trying to enjoy the holiday season despite the news of her being infertile. Based on Bryan's lack of knowing where things went, she doubted if he had ever celebrated anything Christmas.

"Bryan, do you know and understand what Christmas is about? Have you ever celebrated it?" asked Amy.

Bryan scratched his masked head and nodded *"No."*

"Can you tell me what you think it is about and write it down?"

Bryan wrote, *"I never understood Christmas, because we never celebrated it in our home, growing up. My dad used to get stone drunk and beat me horribly, especially during this time of the year. I had bruises and welts from the back down, of whippings from his belt. He did not use the belt, he used a hanger, or anything he could get his hands on just to beat me. I hated this time of the year, and was so angry seeing everyone else happy, at school and around town. I could not understand why people were so happy in their lives at this time of the year— singing, for what? I did not understand all the decorations. I was never given any gifts. I don't even know why people give gifts?"*

Amy said with tears in her eyes, "I am so very sorry you went through all of that. You never had a chance to enjoy things that were happy. Can I read to you what it means?" She picked up her devotional and read, so he could understand why Christmas is special.

After reading, Amy said, "I know you have been reading my devotional, and maybe you did not see this part, but different sources have proven this story to be true." Bryan pointed to his heart as if to say, *"I believe."*

Amy hugged him and said, "I know you do."

Bryan wrote, *"No one ever told me about this story. I never understood, when all I knew was getting beat until I could not sit, and the drunkenness in my home during this time of the year. We never put up a tree or had any decorations, but there was plenty of alcohol in the house."*

Amy held his face in her hands, looked deep into his eyes and said, "I will show you that there is so much love this time of the year, and God can heal all that, down to the memories.

Chapter 18

It's not your fault people did that to you. I am so sorry your heart hurts from the memories of all of that. The bitter waters can be made sweet, and that is why I am in your life. It was not an accident that we ended up together.

She suddenly remembered the last word of her grandmother's prayer the last time she saw her. "Send her someone that she will love her always and forever. She has so much love in her. Send her someone who deserves what she has in her." She then smiled at Bryan and said you are an answer to prayer and you deserve to be loved. I will show you how beautiful Christmas can be. You don't have to be sad ever again during this time of the year. There is a lot of catching up to do and we will truly enjoy this season together. I will show you how to do it. Tomorrow I will go Christmas shopping, and I will be home later than normal after work, so please don't worry about me."

Bryan shook his head, "*NO*" He wrote, "*Please, I don't want nothing to happen to you. Remember the last time you said you would be late? That Laureen girl went after you and almost killed you.*"

"Bryan, please, this time it won't happen. All of the people that came after you and I are locked up or dead because of the choices they made. Can you trust me that I will be home? I will even call you, and I know you will pick up the phone but not say anything, if that will make you feel better."

He nodded his head as if to say "*Okay.*" He took her into his strong arms and hugged her, and they proceeded to decorate the house.

"Okay, these are lights and bulbs, they go on the tree. The lights go first on the tree, then the tinsel and bulbs." She showed Bryan step by step what to do. She was patient with him due to his situation that he had no idea. Once they got the tree done, they both wrapped the banister in greenery, and decorated the fireplace. Amy liked the white bulbs, and how they looked on the tree when all the lights were off.

Then they unwrapped the Nativity scene. Bryan tilted his head, pointed to the figurines, seemed puzzled, and looked at Amy for an explanation.

Amy said, "This is called a Nativity set, and this is based on the story of baby Jesus. Do you remember what I read to you earlier?"

Bryan nodded "*Yes.*"

"This is a set symbolically that is set out, as a reminder, that Jesus was born and came to save the world then later died on the cross for you, me, and everyone."

Bryan pointed to himself and wrote, "*Do you mean like me?*"

Amy said, "Yes, of course. He died for everyone who would ever be born; but loves each of us so much!"

Bryan's eyes teared up. He was just so happy to be forgiven and held his hands to his heart and thought, "*perhaps this Christmas might be special after all.*" He had looked forward to what Christmas may bring. Bryan gestured to Amy about all the decorations and wrote on his notepad, "*I would really like some of these decorations for my own house because they are so pretty and it would also be another way to forget about the past and to start again!*"

Amy smiled at him and said, "You got it! Sure, that can be arranged." This happened to be the week they stayed at Amy's house, so Amy would surprise him with Christmas furnishings at his house.

The next day, after work, Amy went shopping. She bought Bryan a few more jump suits, since he liked them so well, two special hooks for both homes, he could hang his mask on, when he showered. She also bought him a camcorder. Since he liked cameras so much, she might as well support what he loved and that was cameras and filming (which was his new-found hobby). He had a lot of surprises coming, some T-shirts, socks, shoes, and underwear. Amy shopped for Bryan, Mary, her Pastor, and his wife, for Christmas. She

Chapter 18

also sent her brother a gift card in the mail, for one of his favorite stores. She made sure Bryan would be spoiled for the Holidays. Unknown to Bryan, she snuck in the back door to his home, and decorated his house, as a surprise, after she got back from shopping. Her shopping list was not that big, and she made sure she hit the number one places for all of her needs, to save time. She brought him a prefabricated six ft tree with all the trimmings and white lights, so she could get back home quickly. It was a tree that was a more rustic style tree, with rustic style decorations, such as pine cones and other ornaments. She got another Nativity scene and decorated his stair well with tinsel and greenery. She was amazed at how it took so little time to decorate everything and all his gifts were wrapped and under the tree, so he would come home to a surprise.

She wanted to make sure he would have the best Christmas ever, to make up for all the bad ones. She phoned Bryan to let him know she was okay. After she was done, she quickly rushed home. It was only 7:00 p.m. "Not bad after all," she said, as she unloaded the rest of the gifts and put them under her own tree. She had bought enough gifts for both places, and he would be pleasantly surprised when he got to his own house. She was so excited for him to receive something good for a change. She thought it was more blessed to give then to receive. Bryan helped her unload the car. He was very happy, she was home.

Amy had always had her pastor and his wife over on Christmas eve. They did not have family in town and would be staying in town this year. "Bryan, what do you think about having my pastor and his wife over for dinner, Christmas eve? It's kind of like a tradition that I do almost every year, unless they go out of town to visit family." All of Amy's other friends would be out of town, or with their own families, and Bryan seemed to be okay with having a few guests over.

Redemption Has No Limits

That year, Christmas eve fell on a Friday and Christmas day would be on a Saturday. So, service would be during the day, about 12 noon and she would have them over for dinner, Christmas eve, around 3 p.m.

On Christmas eve, Amy arose early to start cooking up a feast with ham, turkey and all the trimmings, pumpkin pie and chocolate cake, which was Bryan's favorite. She had finished the Christmas cookies the night before. There would be plenty for everyone to eat.

At about 11:45 a.m., she got ready and went to church. Earlier that morning, she had asked Bryan if he wanted to come.

"I am not just ready to come yet, and face the people, after that night of being shot, but I need to make sure you're okay, so I will wait outside in the car," he wrote.

"Okay, no problem. When you are ready you will come. No pressure," Amy said. She knew not to pressure him about that, because, now twice, they both had been assaulted in the church. She knew he was very sensitive about that, when it came to other people besides the people she knew, that were her close friends. As Bryan waited, he heard the music they sang, and it warmed his heart, he so wanted to go inside, but felt he needed to wait until the right time. He just was not ready. He practiced his faith at home and would sometimes stand next to the church to hear the music and message, but would not go inside at this point. Something was pricking his heart though.

Chapter 19

Yet he stayed, listened, and watched through the bushes on days her desired to go to church with Amy. He just did not want any trouble for them. When church let out, he quickly went to the car, to not be seen by anyone and waited for Amy. She quickly came out and they left rapidly, so she could finish cooking. Pretty soon it would be time for her guests. The table was set, and they were ready, the doorbell rang. It was Pastor Mark and his wife Crissy. "Welcome to our home Pastor and Crissy," Amy said. They all embraced and greeted. Bryan was not sure how to take the embrace, and Amy said, "This is what we normally do when we are at church. We embrace each other, and it's kind of like a family." Bryan seemed okay with that, and relaxed. Pastor and Crissy unloaded their gifts and put them under the tree.

"Wow! Everything smells delicious!" said Pastor Mark.

"It's almost ready. Please excuse me while I put all the fixings on the table. Help yourselves to some crackers and the cheese ball over on the counter," Amy replied.

Soon dinner was ready, and everyone sat down. "Pastor Mark, would you like to say Grace?" asked Amy.

"Sure thing!" said Pastor Mark. Everyone bowed their heads including Bryan. He wore his mask at the dinner table and they ate. Bryan ate through the mouth hole in his mask. "Amy, I want to discuss some new things coming for the next year, with you, and some events we are going to plan. Are you game?" Pastor Mark said.

"Of course!" said Amy.

"We will have more outreaches, and we are looking into someone who can videotape our services to put them on TV and more national programs, so more local people can see what we do as a church."

"Sounds exciting!" said Amy.

"I will let you know more about next year, we are in planning stages for this," said Pastor Mark.

"Okay no problem," said Amy.

"By the way everything is delicious! I am so full, I am about to pop," said Pastor Mark.

"Well, there is still plenty to go around, and it looks like you will be taking some leftovers home," replied Amy.

"We could use them, we did not shop yet for the week."

"Okay, I will get you fixed up when you are ready to leave, but first, let us open gifts, then have some dessert," said Amy.

They all went in the living room. Amy stoked the fire in the fireplace. Bryan had started the fire earlier, but it needed more logs. He helped her to add more logs. They all sat down on the couches in the living room. "Bryan, would you like to open one of your gifts first?" asked Amy. Bryan was very happy to be able to open his gifts. He opened the ones that had coveralls in the boxes and was very happy to receive them. Amy could tell by the sparkle in his eyes, he was thrilled to receive gifts.

Pastor Mark said, "Oh, I have one for you Bryan. This is from my wife and I. Bryan opened it and it was a devotional just for him. So now he would not have to borrow Amy's.

He was happy to receive it, held it to his heart, and nodded to say, *Thank you.*"

Amy gave Pastor and his wife their gift certificates, to restaurants for Sundays, when they did not feel like cooking after church and matching sweaters. "Amy, here these two are for you," said Crissy.

Chapter 19

Amy opened the gifts, and they were a gold cross with four red rubies and perfumes. "Thank you so much!" Amy cried, "this is beautiful!" Amy had not thought of getting Bryan a devotional, even though that could be one thing he needed. She was glad her pastor thought of it even though she didn't. She had planned to, but it always slipped her mind in her busyness, and he always read hers. He did in fact, need one for himself, so she could now have her own back.

They talked over dessert as the night drew to a close. Amy would soon be alone with Bryan again, as they always had been at night. Bryan had a lot more gifts to unwrap, but they could wait till Christmas morning and he still had more surprises at his other house as well. Amy fixed pastor and Crissy some leftovers to take home. Before Pastor Mark and Crissy left, they made small talk at the door.

"Well, good night," said Pastor and Crissy. "Thank you so much for having us over. We enjoyed Bryan and your company very much!"

"We enjoyed having you, and it's always a pleasure anytime!" replied Amy. The door closed and off went Pastor Mark and Crissy. Bryan's back turned to her. He was shaking and trembling. He was sobbing.

"What is it?" Amy said.

"*In all my years of existence, I have never been shown such love, like you all have. Usually, I was laughed at, judged, or treated as less then. But, you all treat me as… like one of the family like others I seen growing up, who had happy families. How they embraced, hugged, and showed each other love. Is this what its really like at your church?*" Brian said.

Amy said, "No family is perfect, and church people are not either. We do try. There are issues that do happen, but it's God's love that keeps everyone together and going. Like when I lost my job and then they did not want me back. Then some rallied for me to get my job back. You know, things like that." Bryan seemed to understand what she was talking about.

"*You're so special to me and I never want to lose you. It's just I-I, did not get you anything,*" wrote Bryan.

"Don't worry Bryan, it is not a big deal, and you will never loose me. I will always be here. We have much more to do tomorrow. You don't have to perform to earn my love, because you already have it. I love you for who you are, not what you can do," she said. "We have some more things to do tomorrow," she replied, and smiled with a gleam in her eye.

Amy was off the next few days and her Pastor closed the church down for the week, for his staff, so Amy got to spend more time with Bryan. She made him a special breakfast, and he opened up the rest of his gifts, and everything else he received. He treasured each gift. He really liked the special hooks to hang his mask up when he showered and he was moved of how she even thought of that little detail.

"Bryan, I am off for the week and we have somewhere to go. Can you get ready and come with me?" Amy asked.

Bryan nodded his head "Yes" and went upstairs to shower. He took his mask off and hung it on the hook she gave him. He cleaned it, and as he did, he noticed how scarred his back was, down to his legs, from his childhood, adult beatings, and stabbings. He was so white, and those scars stood out starkly against his creamy white skin. He knew they would never go away and were permanent.

He wondered if Amy noticed them, and if she had, she certainly did not say anything about them. She had noticed, the night of their honeymoon, and he felt shame. She in fact did have plenty of opportunities to see them, as nothing was hidden those nights and subsequent times with her. The thoughts really bothered him, and he would ask her about it. Amy got herself ready in the other bathroom downstairs. They finished at the same time, but Bryan was bothered by those thoughts of his scarred back and legs. Why did these thoughts bother him now? They never bothered him before. She did not seem to be ashamed of the way she looked and

Chapter 19

was confident of her appearance. He could not see any shame. Was it because of her background? The thoughts bothered him as they got in the car.

"Is everything okay Bryan? You seem troubled by something."

Bryan wrote as they drove, "*Did you see the scars?*"

"What scars?" asked Amy.

"*The ones all over my back, all the way down to the back of my lower legs. The ones you cannot miss…the red welts and knife scars. I am permanently scarred, and they will never go away.*"

"Aww, Bryan, so what if you are scarred, that could never change anything. The fact is, I love you sweetheart, and your scarred back and legs don't matter to me. If our marriage was based on superficial things like that, then it would not be worth much, but our marriage is not superficial. We all have wounds and scars, and some are just not visible but here," Amy pointed to her heart.

"*I understand, kind of like memories and hurts from the past,*" wrote Bryan.

"Yes, that's exactly it," said Amy. Amy asked, "Is that why you wear the coveralls, black pants and long sleeves?"

Bryan wrote, "*Yes, so people cannot see the ugliness of the scars. The coveralls hide a lot, even in the summer.*"

Amy said, "I love you just the way you are, no matter what you are dressed in." He grabbed her hand and held it tight.

They pulled into his driveway and got out. Amy said, "Now close your eyes and cover your mask…don't look. Don't peek!" Amy led him by the hand into his house and into the living room.

"Okay, now you can look."

He uncovered his eyes. His eyes widened in shock!! "*Y-You did All THIS FOR ME?*" He scribbled on the pad of paper, he almost always carried with him. He was so shocked he did not know what to say.

"Yes," said Amy, "because you are worth it, and I wanted you to have to best Christmas ever!" He swept her into his arms and kissed her for the longest time. He then unwrapped his gifts. The biggest surprise of all, was a camcorder she had gotten him. He immediately put it to use by filming her smiling, and her laugh.

"*Her infectious laugh!*" he thought, and how he wished he could laugh more and be more like her.

They spent the day together, and the night, having a quiet time, watching the snow fall. Certainly, this was the best Christmas ever, for both of them. "Compared to last year, this truly was a joy just to have him here. No more of him missing for months or being beat up like last year," Amy thought, as they snuggled in for a long winters nap.

That week she was off, Amy decided to spend the week beginning to teach life skills to Bryan. How to clean. How to cook and other life skills. She knew it would be trial and error. The first afternoon, he overflowed the washing machine three times, and they spent the rest of the afternoon cleaning up all the soapsuds that ran onto the floor, all over the basement.

Bryan hung his head in shame.

"Oh Bryan! It happens! No biggie. Don't worry. You are learning how to do new things. You will never learn if no one gives you a chance to," Amy said reassuringly, as they mopped the floor up. Thankfully, it was hard tile and not carpet. She knew he suffered severe punishment growing up, if he had done something wrong and he just needed a chance to learn, and do it correctly, without being whipped and abused.

The next wash, she marked the cup on how much soap to use. It was a success, and they dried the clothes, and Amy taught him how to fold everything and put it away. "Well, I guess that's enough laundry for today," she said.

Bryan agreed, as he jokingly wiped his brow.

Amy said, "You're so silly." Bryan grabbed her and kissed her as if to say, "Thank you." The laundry was piling up and

Chapter 19

this would be a perfect time to show him how to do it. They eventually got it all finished, dried, folded and put away.

"Today, I will show you how to bake some things. We can start with cookies and then go from there," Amy said. They both mixed the ingredients with the dough and placed the cookies onto the cookie sheet. In the first two attempts, Bryan almost burned the house down, by not seeing that the cookies were already ready. When he went to take them out, they looked like smoldering lumps of coal. Bryan again hung his head in shame. Amy was trying not to laugh and reassured Bryan that it was okay. The next day, they went to the store to get a timer.

Amy had the day already planned out. They would try the cookies again and then eventually move onto a dish. They tried it again, Bryan heard when the timer went off and he pulled the cookies out. The cookies were a success! They cooked different things throughout the days she was off, and just had a fun time together. Bryan eventually got the hang of it, it was trial and error. Amy was patient with him, and he responded to her love, and became confident in doing the new things she showed him.

Amy also noticed that week they were doing chores together, he took his mask off more often, but would keep it firmly on his face when others were around. Either he was hot from working, or he was slowly coming out of his shell.

"Such a sweet face!" Amy thought. His face was very white…but sweet, as he was pale, like a delicate flower; but oh, so handsome! She wondered why he continued to hide behind that mask. Why it was so slow to come out of his shell? She had believed he would in time and if he did not, she was okay with that. Maybe he was slow to get comfortable with her, and she would wait. She would be patient, and she knew he needed a lot of love in his life. She let him choose to wear the mask, or not wear it whatever he was comfortable with. Amy would be okay with whatever he chose to do about the mask.

Chapter 20

One-night, Amy came home from work, and Bryan had prepared a complete spaghetti dinner, complete with salad and garlic bread for her. He and beckoned her to sit down. He had lit the candles for a romantic setting and the table had already been set. "Aww, Bryan, that is so sweet! Thank you! You are learning so fast!"

Bryan wrote in his notepad, "*I wanted to surprise you when you came home from a day's work. I noticed sometimes you are tired. So, I took the initiative to cook something for you tonight before you got here.*"

"Aww, thank you again. That means so much," said Amy.

The suddenly, without warning, crash! Went a rock through the window of Bryan's house.

The had a note tied to it that said, "YOUR DEAD MEAT!" Amy and Bryan jumped. Bryan quickly grabbed a knife off the counter. He was enraged, as an effigy of himself had been put up and set on fire in his front lawn. He went out to see if he could find out who had done this. He was furious. He saw some teens quickly speed off in a car. He started after them but did not catch up.

"Bryan, wait, WAIT!!! We can see who did it on the cameras! Remember?" Amy cried out! Bryan walked back to the house. He went inside, and was pacing back and forth.

You could see how heavily he was breathing as the mask blew in and out. His eyes were crazy with rage. He once again looked like a madman. Bryan in the midst of his anger, forgot all about the cameras. "Let's go to my house, Bryan, and view the cameras. If they were foolish enough to come around and start trouble, they are foolish enough to get caught. They must not have seen the cameras. Now we will know who did it! Let's handle this the right way," Amy said.

Amy and Bryan immediately went to her house and viewed the tapes, it was some boys she did not recognize. Then they both went to the police station, so the police could view the tapes. This time Bryan went inside with her. "Ma'am, could you view these tapes? Our home was vandalized, and we want you to view them," stated Amy. Jane, the woman police officer was there, she said, "Oh, sure…umm, is that Bryan Conners with you?"

"Yes, but he is with me," said Amy.

"Well, where did you say it happened?" continued Jane.

"On his property," said Amy. "Well ma'am, we can't do much, being it's his property and not yours," Jane flatly said.

Amy protested, "Well, I own the property, and the deed is in my name. I bought it before Bryan came back! We came to press charges on whoever these youths were," said Amy, becoming irritated.

Jane fired back, "Well, I'm sorry, you will have to come back in the morning. We are busy tonight."

"No, I will not! You need to know that Bryan is just like any other citizen in this town, and you all need to stop discriminating against him. As you recall, he did save my life when Laureen Waller tried to stab me in the arm! Look for yourself it is in the report! If it was not for Bryan, she would have stabbed me in the heart and killed me!" Amy protested again. Jane went through the files and sure enough found it in the system.

Chapter 20

Jane's eyes widened in shock. "Oh, Ma'am, I…did not know that he saved your life. We will view the videos immediately," she said, stunned. After viewing them, Officer Jane continued, "These youths are the cousins of Laureen Waller. Yes, we will dispatch a police officer to their parents' homes, and you may get the paper work started to press charges. Here is the paperwork to fill out."

Amy and Bryan filled out the paperwork with the details of what happened and Jane did the police report. "Oh… I did not know he could write," smirked Jane.

"Of course, he can! He just does not talk. He is not an animal. He is a human being," Amy defended.

"Well…" said Jane, "being the house is in your name, you will have to fill out the paperwork to press charges. Here is the new paperwork."

"Okay fine," said Amy, with abject annoyance. "Why do they have to treat him like this?" she thought. She would be glad to get out of there and not have to deal with this female officer. Bryan was beaming under his mask at his wife the whole time she stood up for him. If she had not been so upset, she would have noticed the tender way he was looking at her.

The following week Amy and Bryan had to go to court. Amy said, "Please write down everything you know and saw and then we can give it to the judge."

Bryan wrote, "*There were three youths who threw a rock through my window and then set an effigy of me on fire, then got in a car and sped off. I tried to go aft…*"

Amy stopped him and said, "Please don't put that last part in there, because they will look at you as suspect, and people are slow to understand you have changed. Less is better. So, he rewrote the statement and ended it at "off." Amy was relieved that he changed the statement. They both went in and testified against the teens. The tapes were played. Amy testified, and Bryan's statement was read. The parents of course, were for their sons, who they thought did not do anything wrong. One of the dad's said, "He deserved the death penalty. Why is he is still alive?"

The protests began, and the judge said, "Order, ORDER! It has been also brought to my attention that Amy, as we all know, is an upstanding pillar of society here. She is in charge of the art events here in town and new information states Bryan also saved her life from an assault, when Laureen Waller, who is a known mental patient!"

The court gasped and were shocked. The judge said, "I hereby sentence you three boys to clean up the mess. You parents, must pay for the damages to his house. Also, the boys will receive six months in the juvenile system and the families must pay $1,200.00." The parents grumbled in disgust as they walked out. The window was replaced the next day. Amy took time off work to deal with the situation at hand, as Pastor Mark understood she needed to be there for Bryan.

Word spread quickly around town, that Amy and Bryan's houses were rigged with cameras all over both properties. So, no kids or teens ever tried to mess with their homes, or them again. Amy purposely had put the cameras at every angle of the houses, so nothing was missed. Now she was very glad she did, because after the incident with Laureen, she had a feeling more people would try to cause a problem for them both.

"I guess those cameras came in handy after all," said Amy.

Bryan took his notepad and wrote, *"Yes, and I'm so glad you're my wife! Let's go home because I so want to love you right here and right now!"* Amy knew what that meant, as she giggled in her silly, teasing laugh, which he loved. He put his arm around her and back home they went for a beautiful time together.

Over time, Bryan learned to drive a car at Amy's instruction, and learned other life skills as well. Amy was

Chapter 20

amazed at how quickly he learned to be able to do things. On a Friday, they went down to the Social Security Administration building and got him set up with a monthly Social Security check. So, he could somewhat be independent financially. He was only set up for $800 a month, but Amy was amazed when they set him up to receive a monthly check for $1,100.00 a month.

"God keeps moving things in the right direction for Bryan," Amy said to herself.

It was Monday and Amy walked into work. Pastor Mark said, "Come in my office, I need to talk to you."

"Okay, sure thing," Amy replied.

"Have a seat," said Pastor Mark.

Amy thought, "Oh no, what is it this time? Things are starting to go well for us," Amy thought.

Pastor Mark said, "How is Bryan, really? Like, living with him. Does he treat you well, and how does he function?"

Amy was relieved the conversation would not be anything bad and said, "Well, I have been teaching him life skills and he is catching on pretty quickly."

Pastor Mark said, "That is great! I knew in an unusual way, somehow, you would be the right one for him. Everyone deserves love."

"As for treating me well, he is learning how to function like the rest of us. He loves me…a lot and he is very jealous, and protective, as you seen in the incident with Laureen."

Pastor Mark said, "Those are good qualities to have. That means he cares for you. That brings me to another thing. Did you say you bought him a cam recorder for Christmas?"

"Yes!" said Amy, "and he absolutely loves it! He is always filming me off guard. He likes to stalk and sneak up on me, to film me when I am singing or just watching TV! I guess that's his sense of humor! The stalking never left him, he just stalks in a different way now!" said Amy.

Pastor Mark roared with laughter. "That is so funny! Well, Amy do you remember what we talked about at Christmas. About the new things we were going to do this year at the church?"

"Yes," Amy said.

"Well," said Pastor Mark. "I know, maybe, I am stretching my faith a little here but…how would Bryan like a job on Sundays?"

"What would you want him to do?" replied Amy.

"I would like him to be our audio-visual guy in the church. No one else can do it or wants to."

"Oh Pastor, he would love that! He told me, he has been wanting to come to church, but every time he tried, bad things would happen and he has shied away from it."

Pastor Mark replied, "That is totally understandable. We are building a booth in the church that is a special booth, where he won't have to interact with a lot of people if he is not comfortable with that. Let me show you something. Follow me into the sanctuary."

Amy followed him into the sanctuary. "I want to show you this booth I had specifically designed for a higher view so no one can look inside. The audio-visual guy can look out. The booth is high enough. Also, the glass is tinted. There is a little square hole cut out of the glass, were the camera lens protrudes out, to be able to film and another slot to slip tapes or CDs in, for him to play. I figured audio-visual is an art, and they need to work alone in seclusion. The booth is almost complete, and I would like to have Bryan up there if he is willing. Also…these steps lead down to the outside of the church where no one can see him exit," said Pastor Mark.

"This is so perfect!" said Amy. "How can we ever thank you enough? I think he would love this!"

Pastor Mark responded back, "If he is interested, can you bring him by tomorrow night? I would like to talk to him and show him the ropes if he would like that."

Chapter 20

"Sure thing," Amy said. "By the way, he drives now, too! I showed him how!"

"That's awesome!" said Pastor Mark. "Okay, how does 5:00 p.m. sound?"

"Sure! If it's a go, we will be here then! Thank you so much! I really think he would love this!" replied Amy, excitedly.

Amy rushed home. Bryan always greeted her at the door. "I have a surprise for you," said Amy. "Please sit down, I think you're going to like this." Bryan sat down. "Pastor Mark has been looking for an audio-visual guy for his booth at church and wanted me to ask you if you would like the job," beamed Amy.

Bryan looked at her intently and fearfully shook his head "No."

"Why would you not like the job?" Amy sadly responded.

Bryan grabbed his notebook and wrote, "*I don't trust myself around other people, and I don't know how I would react, or they would react to me if I don't so something right. No one has ever offered me a job before, and it's hard for me to respond to kindness from others unless they are you.*"

Amy said, "The booth was meant to be yours and it was designed specifically for seclusion, so no one can see you, but you can see out and it has steps leading right to the outdoors of the church, so you would never be seen."

Bryan wrote, "*Really? It was designed for me?*"

"When Pastor Mark designed it, he did have you in mind, but was not sure if you would want the job."

"*Okay, yes, I will come to the meeting!*"

Amy threw her arms around his neck and said, "I love you and you will love it!" That was all Bryan could take as he swept her up in his arms and carried her upstairs for a night of love and pleasure.

"*My sweet Amy.*" Bryan thought, "*She is always thinking of me, and I have finally found value to someone, and a group of others. My life has changed so much since I met her, and I never want it to stop,"* he thought as he passionately loved her all that night. It was her love and care for him that stirred his passion. It was her pure heart that stirred him to react like he always did. He would never hurt her or let anyone else hurt her as long as he lived. He would always be there for her until the end of time, no matter what they faced. He would never leave her again. He knew he was loved. He knew there was security in their home. He knew they were under a canopy of God's love and it gave him great peace and joy, he never felt before.

He always watched her through the night and could not get enough of her face. Those full lips, her dark curly hair and eyes. It was always the same. He would caress her face. He would trace her lips with his fingertips. He had her face firmly pictured in his mind and when she was gone at work, he would remember every night his little secret of staring and gazing upon her as she slept. That part of him would never change because it was who he was, to stare, watch and stalk. But this time, it was for love, passion, and desire.

Amy quickly finished the workday and headed home, so they could get to the appointment at 5:00 p.m. When they got there, Pastor Mark was there, waiting by himself. He wanted to make sure that Bryan would be okay, and the less people around, the better. He gave Mary the rest of the day off with pay.

Unknown to Amy and Pastor Mark, Bryan had been wrestling inside himself about taking his knife. He wanted to make sure Amy would be okay. He want to come prepared to strike anyone that would harm her. He hid the knife inside his coveralls. He had made the same mistake the last two times, of coming around or inside the church and he was not been prepared to strike back at anyone who wanted to harm Amy or himself. He wanted to make sure he was ready this time, in case anything would happen. *"I will not let anything happen to my precious Amy, so I will take my knife,"* he thought, as she

Chapter 20

pulled up in the driveway. He quickly tucked the huge knife in his coveralls. They were loose and hid the knife well. They sat down to eat a quick dinner of leftovers from the night before, then swiftly headed to the church.

"Hello Bryan, welcome to my office," said Pastor Mark, who greeted him warmly and shook Bryan's hand. "Please, the both of you sit down, and help yourselves to some coffee over there." Amy sat down with a masked Bryan, and she got up and made some coffee for the both of them.

"Bryan, I spoke with Amy here, and I am interested in offering you a job as an audio-visual worker. You would be alone in the booth, so you would be more than comfortable. I would put out a list of songs every Sunday for you to put up on the screen.

We usually do about 3-4 songs every Sunday. The people sing to the lyrics on the screen. At the same time, the camera would be filming the service. The service will be taped automatically to the local TV stations to be broadcast as soon as you are trained. Are you up for the job?"

Bryan nodded his head "*Yes.*"

"Awesome deal!" said Pastor, "Would you like to start this Sunday?"

Bryan nodded "Yes."

"Also, there is one more thing. You will be paid a monthly stipend of $200, so it does not interfere with your SSI income. How does that sound?" Proposed Pastor Mark. Bryan wrote in his notepad and gave it to Pastor.

"*I am pleased and excited to start.*"

Good deal," responded Pastor. "Let me show you some things in the booth today, but can you be here a half hour early Sunday, just to go over some things?"

Bryan nodded "*Yes.*"

"Come upstairs and let me show you some things," instructed Pastor Mark. Amy and Bryan went up inside the booth. "Okay," Pastor Mark said, "This is your spot where you can sit. Here are the switches to operate the equipment. This button switches everything on and this switch is for the screen that lights up to show the words of the songs. For the filming, all you have to do is hit this switch on the camera and everything starts to film. The service is then pipped to the local TV stations so people who can't to go to church, like the elderly or sick, can view the program. Let's see you work with the switches."

Bryan sat in the comfy chair. He turned the switches on and off, just as he was instructed Pastor Mark was amazed how he was such a quick learner. Bryan most certainly would do a good job. "Okay, the job is yours. We will see you Sunday." Bryan and Pastor Mark shook hands.

Amy said, "Thank you so much for giving Bryan a chance."

"It is always my pleasure, and I see value in everyone," Pastor Mark said. Bryan nodded his head and Amy and he went home for the evening.

Bryan could hardly contain himself that Sunday, as he got up hours earlier than Sunday service. He woke Amy up very early. "Uggghmmph," Amy said, rolling over. "Sweetheart, its 6:30 in the morning…can you let me sleep a little longer?"

Bryan could hardly contain his excitement as he woke her up 15 minutes later. "Okay, I am up now," said Amy. She got up and said, "10:00 is not going to come enough any faster. I guess, I can make you breakfast now." Amy was amused at how excited Bryan was. "He is so childlike and innocent. I can't be mad at him because someone cared enough to give him a chance to do what he loves!" She said to herself amusingly.

She grabbed her clothes and got ready. She took a long hot shower which seemed to perk her up. She heard something crash and turned around quickly and there was Bryan's eager face peering inside the shower. "AAAAAAGH! You scared me! Let me finish my shower," said Amy, laughing. Bryan's

Chapter 20

eager face went out of the shower and out of the bathroom. She began to laugh hysterically. "Oh my God! When he gets excited about something, he gets excited!" Then in came his face again. "Bryan, you silly man! What am I going to do with you? STOP… ahahaha!!"

It was then she realized he was playing with her, combined with his zeal for his new audio-visual job. She was laughing, and he was enjoying it. Making her laugh even more by popping in and out of the bathroom shower. "Bryan…are you even ready yet?" she said, as she got dressed.

He shook his head "*No.*"

"Well, funny one, I might suggest you get ready. You will need your shower, and other things we do, like brush your teeth, when we get ready to go somewhere."

Bryan nodded "*Okay.*" Amy was going to turn the tables on him. When he was well into his showering, and the mask off, she popped her head in and said "SURPRISE!!" She took off running full blast. He grabbed a towel and set off after her, caught up and grabbed her. They both fell down on the ground, laughing hysterically. Bryan with his quiet laughs and Amy with her hysterical laugh, that he loved so much. He stopped and smothered her with kisses. "Uhh…Bryan we have to get ready remember?"

"*Oh yeah, that's right!*" Bryan gestured in agreement, and then went back to showering. He grabbed the notebook and wrote, "*But wait till tonight though.*" Amy giggled with delight and smiled within herself. She was so glad to be married to him.

In all its craziness, she still had great joy in her marriage. The trials they have gone through together made them get closer. They both could let their hair down more, but she still wondered what would come next. It was just a slight thought, but it was still there. Small and nagging, like a small stone in a shoe. She quickly dismissed it and hoped for the best.

Redemption Has No Limits

They arrived at the church a half hour early as promised, and Pastor Mark welcomed them in before others could get there. He ushered Bryan upstairs and Amy sat near the sound booth, so she could be there just in case Bryan was uncomfortable, he knew she would be nearby. A few minutes later, people started to file into the sanctuary, and soon service would start. Amy bounded up the stairs and came into the sound booth. "Bryan are you okay?" He gave a thumbs up, as if to say he was okay.

Pastor Mark said, "I think he has it down pat. He is a natural. I will check on him before I come up to speak."

"Awesome!" Amy said, and then she went back downstairs and waited near the booth.

The service started, the songs were put up according to what pastor wanted, and everything seemed to be going well. Pastor Mark went upstairs mid-service to check on Bryan. "Hey Bryan, how are you d...?" Pastor gasped at the sight and ran away downstairs.

"Amy, you need to come upstairs right now!" Pastor Mark was white as a ghost, and in shock.

"W-What is going on?" Amy inquired nervously.

"Bryan has the biggest knife I have ever seen in his hands, and is playing with it, and I don't know why he brought it in here! He won't communicate to me why he brought it, and I did not want to question him, and I thought you could help him understand, we don't bring things like that to church. Can you, uuugh, help me here?" Pastor Mark responded.

Amy ran up the stairs and went inside the sound booth, and Pastor Mark behind her. "Bryan, oh no, no! Why did you bring that in here? Can you please tell me, because it is scaring Pastor, and it may scare others if they see it, and they all want to be okay? Can you write and explain why?"

Bryan grabbed his notebook and wrote, "*I only wanted to protect Amy from anyone else who would try to hurt her. I meant no harm...I just wanted to protect my wife. I have been shot, and my wife stabbed, the last two times I was here and I*

Chapter 20

wanted to bring the knife to make sure she was not harmed. I am sorry if it scared anyone. I am not trying to scare anyone. This is all I know to protect my wife. I mean no harm, really I don't. I want to be here, but I want to make sure we are going to be safe."

Pastor Mark said, "I am sorry, I did not understand you. I just thought you were going to harm someone and I am sorry again. I don't want you to go, but I was just caught off guard. I understand where you are coming from." Amy was embarrassed because she was wondering what Pastor Mark would think of him now, but he was patient and said, "I know sometimes hard habits take time to die. We all have them and we all have different backgrounds. I can reassure you, Bryan, that all of you and Amy's enemies, are all gone, or locked up. There are no more people who mean you harm here. We all love you very much, and some here, deem you as a hero, the night you saved your wife from that crazed woman who stabbed Amy."

Bryan wrote, "*Thank you, but I don't see myself as a hero or much of anything. I only want my wife to be safe here. I feel it was being married to me that caused trouble for her, because she never had enemies before. I also don't want to ever loose her, and that is why I feel I have to protect her at all costs.*" He handed Pastor the notebook.

Pastor Mark read it and gently said, "Bryan, I really can assure you that you are both safe here. We don't believe in violence here, and those people could not help themselves, as they let the sin and darkness of their heart consume them, to do those acts. Those things they did caused them to meet their end, whether it was jail, or even death." Pastor continued, "I am also sorry you had to see that happen in a place like this, where it should never happen. The world is cruel enough, but to have it happen in a place that is supposed to be a place of God and peace…it should not have. I am so sorry, because of what all the others have done to you Bryan…I really am. You

ARE truly a hero, and don't you ever forget it. You are always welcome here anytime!!"

Bryan began to cry through his mask.

Pastor said, "Is it okay if I give you a hug?" Bryan nodded yes, and all three embraced. That was what Bryan needed—to hear it from someone else who truly cared about him and that all people were not bad, and out to get him. Pastor Mark said, "I am late for my sermon. Let me get down there, and we can always talk another time if you would like." Amy stayed behind, upstairs with him, to comfort him as he did his job. The service ended on a high note, Bryan was encouraged and they drove home. He refused to let Amy go, as he drove with his arm around her all the way home. Bryan's heart swelled with a happiness he never knew, and he was also going to get Amy back for the shower incident earlier. And, he did. As soon as they got home, he pinned her against the wall, a gleam of delight in his eyes, and carried her upstairs to have an afternoon of intimacy.

Many hours later, Amy came downstairs to cook dinner. "Hmm, I think I will cook some cheesy potato soup, and sandwiches." She began cutting up veggies, when she felt him standing there in the room, his breath, hot on her neck, as he snaked his arms around her. She jumped. "Geez you scared me! You know I love your stalk—you seem to pop out of nowhere—but it's not safe when I have a knife in my hand. I don't want to cut myself or you." His eyes told a different story…they gleamed with love. He loved her dearly, and embraced her again, and traced her lips with his fingertips then, gave her a long passionate kiss through his mask. "Hun, you are so passionate! You never stop stalking me, even in marriage, and that is what is so special about you! I think of a story I read about this beloved man, who is white and ruddy like yourself and he always stalks the one he loves. I just read it the other day and it so reminds me of you." Bryan gestured to her devotional and pointed to his throat. "Yes, it's in there. Do you want me to read it to you?"

Chapter 20

Bryan nodded "*Yes.*"

"Can we eat dinner first? I am starving, but I can read it after dinner."

Bryan nodded "*Yes.*" He was very eager to know more about this person, who was like himself.

Chapter 21

Amy read the Song of Solomon to him, starting with Chapter 1, but when she got to the part, she smiled and said, "and this part is what reminds me of you!" Song of Solomon 2:9-10 "*My beloved is like a roe or young hart, he stands behind our wall, looking through the windows and showing himself through the lattice.*" Also, she showed him Song of Solomon 5:10, "*My beloved is white and ruddy.*"

Bryan eyes widened, and he wrote, "*I guess I am not the only one who knows a good thing when they see it. Wow! The man is white and ruddy like me? The woman is dark like you? Wow and Wow! The man in this story sounds just like ME! I did not know that was in there either! I have just been reading the book of John. I love stalking because it stirs me. It makes me desirous of you, and in my old days, I stalked for different reasons, which I did not understand. But now I stalk you because I love you!*"

"Oh, dear one! You are too much, baby, you can stalk me anytime," cried Amy, with teasing, joking and in amazement. Bryan took his mask off, set it aside and kissed her. It was too much for him to just hold back, and before Amy knew it, they were continuing the earlier activities of the afternoon after reading her devotional. That night she laughed and laughed in amazement, as she did not know how to react to Bryan's passion. He had learned to accept her and her culture of live, laugh, and love. Her laugh was another thing that stirred his passions. It was teasing, tantalizing, and delightful to him. It only encouraged him to pursue her in ways that led into the early hours of the morning. When they were together, time stood still. It was as if hours would pass as they never could get enough of each other.

Amy glanced at the clock, "Oh dear! It is 4 a.m. Bryan, I really, really have to get some sleep. Yesterday was Sunday and now it's Monday. I will have to be getting up for work soon. I need some sleep." Bryan nodded and understood. He kissed her goodnight. Only he did not go to sleep. He watched her again and was amazed at how quickly she fell asleep.

Within minutes she was fast asleep. *All day and night activities must of wore her out. Now I get to watch her,*" he thought. He so loved watching her sleep. Watching her face also stirred him with delight and desire and it would only build up to when they could be together again.

Any desire to kill was now far away from his mind. It did not even enter as an afterthought, now that he knew what love was and he was thoroughly loved by Someone much bigger then himself. That's all he really wanted was to be loved, free and complete. "*I guess this must be a part of heaven here on this side, because it surely feels like it, and I love it!*" he thought.

That morning Amy dragged herself out of bed to face the day. "I guess I better make myself some very strong coffee, espresso style," Amy said. She showered and got ready for work. "Bryan, I love you and will be home soon. See you later." He kissed her at the door and saw her off. Amy drove to work, shaking her head. "Wow, Bryan is something else," and she wondered if all men were as he was. He was the only one she had ever been with and she was the only one he had ever been with. "I guess if any of this makes sense, as to why he was almost normal, he just needed someone to show him

Chapter 21

some love. Not sexual, but just unconditionally." She came up with a resolution, "That's it! It was love that had changed him so much, from being a cold-hearted killer, to someone who is able to love and love passionately, in more ways than one." Amy was so happy for Bryan that Love had changed him for the better. Amy was so happy to know she was part of Bryan' transformation, as well as her Pastor too, and if anyone needed love, it was truly Bryan. Joy filled her heart as she faced the work day.

Amy came home from work that day and realized she had not had the chance to ask Bryan how he liked his new job yesterday. They sat down on the couch together and snuggled. He was so happy to see her after a long day at work. He held her close. "Bryan, you are so clingy, and I don't mind. What is it that drives you?"

He wrote, *"Ever since I met you…it is you that drives me. I had no feelings at all and did not care about the people I killed. But you…you gave me a chance to be loved, a chance to change, a chance to have a shot at a normal life. A loving secure home was all I ever wanted, and now I found it. When everyone else abused, rejected me, and made fun of me, you were there. I thought you were like all the rest of people in the crowd that night at the bonfire that hated me, but you were different. I had been watching you for weeks. Your comings and goings. Places you would go; and I could not forget about you. I now know not all people hate me, and this has changed me. I cannot believe how blessed I am to have you. I never thought, almost two years ago, it would come to this. I guess that's what happens when one as cold-hearted as I was, comes in contact with someone who is true and has His light of Love in their heart."*

Amy hugged him and said, "I do try, but I am not perfect either. It's God."

Bryan nodded "Yes" in agreement.

"By the way, how did you like your first day on the job yesterday?"

Bryan wrote, "*It's a perfect fit for me and I really like it. No one will come upstairs will they? I don't want anyone to see me because I don't want to frighten anyone, with my appearance… you know, with my mask and all.*"

Amy said, "If anyone is frightened, they have not learned to love. Its love that casts fear out of one's heart, and everyone is at different stages in their life, in this walk. It may be best they don't see you. Just lock the door. This will stop anyone else from coming up to the booth except Pastor Mark or I, if that is more comfortable for you. The pastor may announce in the near future, the church has a new sound man. He knows how to in a tactful way, not bring attention to you."

"*I would really like to not have any attention brought on me right now. I am now ready yet,*" Bryan wrote.

"Maybe, I could talk to Pastor Mark tomorrow about that. We will see what he says. He is sensitive to your situation and is not going to embarrass or make you feel bad," Amy said.

The next day, Amy went to work and thought ahead of time how she would approach this situation. "Pastor, can I talk to you?"

Pastor Mark said, "Sure, what is it?"

"Bryan is very uncomfortable in bringing attention to himself, regarding his audio-visual position and is wondering if you were going to announce his position to the church."

"Of course not, I will say it in a very tactful way—that he does not like to be disturbed when doing his job. How would he feel if I called him 'sound man M,' or no announcement at all?"

Amy said, "I think he may like that, and is it okay if he locks the door, so no one can barge in the room?"

"Once he is trained he may lock the door, but not until then. This is just between you, my wife and I and because of what happened with the knife, lets approach this slowly. If

Chapter 21

you can stay by the sound booth to make sure no one goes up there, I would really appreciate that. Just until we get him trained and more comfortable. I will also install a peephole in the door…that way, he can see who is out there, and he can decide who he will let in or not."

"Okay." Amy said.

"Okay, I have the latest scoop on what is going to happen up in sound booth," Amy said, as she got home. Bryan was all ears as he greeted her at the door. "Pastor Mark is either going to call you 'sound man M,' or, he is not going to announce it at all."

Bryan gestured to her number two and wrote, "*I think the less people know about me being there the better…and I feel more comfortable if no one knows I am there.*"

"Okay," said Amy. "I will talk to him tomorrow to see if he will just keep it to himself. I am sure he will honor your request, considering all that has happened." Bryan nodded and gave a thumbs up. "Okay, its settled then. The less they know the better."

The next day, Amy talked to her pastor about the sensitivity of the issue. Pastor Mark made the choice that he would not announce it to anyone. It would be just something he, his wife, and Amy knew about. Amy was relieved, and that day she came home and told Bryan of the plan. He was happy about it as well.

Amy and Bryan were up very late the Saturday night into next Sunday, enjoying each other's company and before they knew, it was time for church. Bryan had to be on the job. Only this time, he did not sleep, but watched her through the night. He was so lost in her, he lost track of the time. Now this time, it was him that was dragging himself out of bed. They were running behind schedule, as Amy tried to get him out of bed. She quickly showered, and she knew they had to be there by 9:30 a.m. "Please Bryan, time to rise and shine, remember you have a job to get to today."

Redemption Has No Limits

Bryan rose out of bed and was so tired he put his shirt on backwards and stumbled out of bed. "Sweetie, your shirt is on backwards," Amy said with a smile. He fixed his shirt and did not shower. There simply was not enough time, so he freshened up the best way he could. He washed up, brushed his teeth, and out the door they went. Bryan was so tired, he tripped up the stairs to the sound booth. Amy stifled a laugh, because she knew he was so tired from being up nearly all night. "Now he kind of knows what it's like for me to have to go to work so tired, when he keeps me up some nights very late." Amy wondered if he went to sleep or stayed up doing who knows what? He was a man of mystery, and there was a lot more she did not know about him. What he did at night when she would be asleep? It sometimes was hard for him to fall right to sleep, so he would leave the room, to not keep her up. His sleeping habits were different from hers.

Up in the sound booth, Bryan got ready for his day. He put his headphones on to monitor the service, and to know which slides to put up for each song. He was ready, and Amy exited the booth and stayed nearby, to make sure no one would go up there. Today the team would sing four songs. Once the first song was finished, the next slide was supposed to be up. It did not go up. Amy thought "What is he doing up there?" Pretty soon they were singing the third song, and Pastor quickly went to the back and noticed the slides were not being put up on time. The slide was still up from the first song, and people in the pews began to look around, they too, noticed there was no change in the slides.

Pastor Mark said to Amy, "We have to get up there right now to see what is going on." They raced upstairs to the booth. "Bryan? Bryan?" They both knocked on the door in haste and jiggled the handle. It was locked. Pastor Mark noticed that Bryan locked the door by mistake and thankfully, he had a key to open the door.

Chapter 21

To their amazement, they found Bryan fast asleep with his masked head down on the counter and Pastor Mark quickly switched the slide to the current song. "Bryan, wake up!" Amy and Pastor Mark nudged him.

He stirred and looked at them like "*Where am I?*" Then his eyes widened, and he realized he fell asleep on the job!!

Amy said, "I am sorry, he had a very late-night last night, and he is not used to working yet, and must be excited for his new job."

Pastor said, "It's okay. Its only his second week. Bryan please make sure you get more sleep on Saturday night, so you can be fresh for Sunday. Are you okay?" Pastor Mark said and smiled.

Bryan nodded "*Yes*" and wrote, "*I am sorry I am such a sleepy head today.*" Bryan rubbed his masked neck and head to keep himself awake.

Pastor Mark and Amy laughed. "Oh no, it's okay," Pastor Mark said. "We all learn new things in different ways." Pastor Mark exited saying he had to get downstairs to deliver the sermon.

Amy loved that Pastor Mark was so patient with Bryan, but Amy stifled more laughter, because it was so funny to see him fast asleep on the job, and the scene was quite comical. Amy said between chuckles, "I will be downstairs if you need me." Once downstairs, she had to step outside the church because she doubled over in laughter. It was just too much "Poor guy! He was so cute, endearing and innocent," she said to herself. She was quite sure others had to hear her laughing. Once she calmed herself, she quickly went back inside the church and sat down near the booth.

Once the song ended, and before Pastor Mark started to preach, he said, "Sorry for the technical difficulty, as we are just getting bugs worked out in the new sound booth." Amy was positioned in the back to make it look like she was the one running the sound booth, when in fact, she was making sure no one went up there.

When people looked in the back they would see Amy, so no questions would be asked about the sound man... and the sensitivity of Bryan's situation of not wanting to be seen. This was at Pastor's request. Pastor started Bryan on the songs, but, if anything else needed to be up there on the screen, Bryan would eventually run that too. Each service was recorded at the start of the button on the camera. All Bryan had to do was turn it on, but it would be several more weeks before it went to the television stations and he needed to be comfortable with the job.

Pastor Mark wanted to make sure Bryan was okay with each step first, before running the whole booth by himself. He was a quick learner, but it was a matter of getting him on a good schedule of sleep Saturday night to prepare for Sunday morning.

After church Amy said, "How do you feel about taking a walk in the park?" Bryan hung his head and was sad. "What is wrong?" Amy said.

Bryan wrote, "*The last time we walked in the park, there was trouble from those kids that harassed us.*"

Amy said, "I can honestly reassure you there won't be any more trouble because, Scotty, my lawn care guy, told me all the kids in the area know not to mess with you anymore, or our homes. It will be okay. Scotty knows a lot of people and no one will be bothering us anytime soon." Bryan reluctantly shrugged his shoulders and nodded. "Deal! I will make some flavored coffee!" Amy said. So, they went for a walk.

The leaves were beginning to change and fall off the trees, and Bryan and Amy trudged through them. It was a beautiful cool fall day, and the sun was shining. The leaves went crunch, crunch under their feet. "Bryan, you are a man, a mystery and I just love being with you." Bryan nodded and held her close as they walked. Bryan was still nervous about any kids that would mess with them as they tried to have a normal life. They saw kids at the park, but the kids avoided them now, or

Chapter 21

ran away, teens included. Word got around town and schools that they were no longer to be harassed.

Bryan thought, "*Maybe it's just me, being everything that happened, and I am just acting paranoid.*" His suspicions were right when some of the parents of the youths that had to fix his window, from them vandalizing his house, came up and wanted to have some words with him. They were on an outing at the park with their kids. Bryan and Amy turned quickly to walk away.

"Hey where are you going?"

Amy said, "Just ignore them Bryan please."

The parents caught up to them and said, "He should have never been let out of jail!"

Amy said, "Look, we are trying to have a normal life! Leave us alone please!"

"Why are you with him? You know, guilt by association."

Amy said, "He paid his dues, leave him alone!" "He is the scum of this community and we want him gone. He doesn't deserve to live!"

Amy could tell Bryan was getting angry because his fists were white and clenched. "Oh no, I need to get him out of here now and do something quick before he does something to them!" Amy thought. "Stop harassing us! We have done nothing to you. We're trying to enjoy ourselves here! YOU ALL NEED TO LEAVE HIM ALONE NOW!" Amy yelled. "Let's go please, Bryan." They quickly left before Bryan could react. Once in the car, Bryan slammed his fist hard in a stabbing motion on the dash, cracking it.

Amy quickly responded, "Bryan, Bryan! It's okay, people are just mean and ignorant. Do you remember a long time ago, that I said some people don't want to let things go?"

Bryan nodded, "*yes*".

"Well, these are those people, and we will go down at once and file a restraining order against them." They immediately went down to the police station and filed a report.

Once back in the car, Bryan appeared upset and wrote, "*I told you, I did not want to go to the park and I wished you had responded to my wishes, because this is the result every time we go out in public to places where there are other people. They harass me, and I just want to try to forget the past and live a normal life.*"

"I am so sorry," said Amy. "It is very sad that people just can't leave you alone, and hopefully one day it will pass. Can you forgive me for wanting a normal life, to where we can have a walk in the park? I love the outdoors and just wanted to enjoy a date with you."

Bryan wrote, "*I would love to have a normal life too, without being harassed and made fun of, and this is why I don't want people to see me at church, or anywhere around here if possible. I do forgive you. You know the real reason I wear the mask? It hides the hideous scars on my face, and I still am tormented with the things I once did, and I am still ashamed.*"

Amy said, "I completely understand Hun. I love you, and nothing will ever change that. But just know this, God has forgiven you, and sometimes we have to forgive ourselves too. Tell you what, we will make sure we go somewhere else, a good drive away from here, the next time we are on an outing. Maybe next Sunday, if the weather is still nice." He smiled through his mask and hugged her close.

The next Sunday the weather would be perfect again, and Amy had another plan. They would take a Sunday drive to their favorite secluded place and do a picnic and hiking. It was an hour drive, but it would be fun. Amy said that morning, "Bryan, what do you think of going to our favorite place an hour away, by the water?" Bryan was eager to do so as he swept her up and excitedly whirled her around.

He nodded "Yes."

Amy said, "Ugggh, ribcage! Bryan you're so strong!" Amy laughed hysterically and said, "Put me down! Bryan, Bryan! Okay, I take that as a yes. I will get some food

Chapter 21

together. We can do a picnic," she said, tweaking the nose of his mask. "Remember, we have to do church first. So please, don't forget to get some sleep tonight."

Bryan nodded, but he knew he would not go right to sleep, as watching her at night was a part of his plan and secret.

That Sunday, Bryan was dressed, ready to go to his job early. He wanted to surprise Amy with breakfast, so he made breakfast this time. It was a breakfast of eggs, sausage, and toast. Amy said, "Aww, thank you Bryan! This makes things easier, getting ready for Sunday and all. I also got our picnic lunch ready too." She opened the refrigerator and pulled out the package. It was bologna sandwiches, chips, and fruit. "I will put it in the cooler. This will be ready to go once we are done with service. We can then hit the road."

They arrived at church and talked in the car before going in. It was around 9:30. Amy said, "Well, we better get inside and…" But before she could finish her sentence, she saw a car coming to the church. It was a distance away, but she knew it was headed their way, and it was the Joneses. They were the nosy kind, and always in folk's business. Amy thought, "Oh no! Of all people, it had to be them! Bryan, Quick! Get inside, hurry!" Amy said, as he trailed behind her. Bryan was a slow mover, but he followed her. They raced around to the back of the church and quickly went up the stairs to the sound booth. Amy was hoping they would not be seen.

"What a relief!" Amy said, as they went inside the sound booth. "Are you okay Bryan?"

Bryan nodded "*Yes*."

"The Joneses, I love them dearly, but they are the biggest gossipers in town and I just don't want you to be in the middle of anything they have to say. It will for sure be around town. They really do have good hearts, but I cannot tell them anything without it getting around, and they are not perfect, it is just something they struggle with." Bryan eyes widened.

Chapter 21

He did not want to be seen. "Don't worry, I have a plan if I am asked anything by them," said Amy.

Bryan prepared the booth for his duties for the service, but everything was in a disarray. The slides where everywhere and not neatly stacked. Bryan stacked them up in one pile, hoping they would be the slides Pastor wanted up. Unknown to Bryan or Amy, the janitor knocked everything over when he cleaned the night before, scattering the slides everywhere on the counter, so Bryan in his utter frustration scooped them up into one pile. Pastor Mark could not make it till 10.00 when service started. He was late that day because he had an emergency with one of the members that morning. So, Bryan was on his own in the booth.

"Oh my gosh! We don't even know what slides to put up, and Pastor Mark usually gives the order of what slides to put up. There must be about 100 of these slides."

"No worries, I think I can do this. I will just listen to what they are singing and put it up. I got this," Bryan wrote.

"Okay. I will be downstairs by the booth if you need me," Amy said.

The Joneses were already scouting around the church for Amy, and Amy knew the questions would be coming. "I will play dumb," Amy thought. She remembered a story that she read in her devotional about a man who would play dumb or insane to avert his enemies in order to avoid getting killed. Amy sat down by the edge of the stairs and waited.

"Oh Hello," Emily and Matt Jones said. "Hello, how is your day going?"

Amy replied. "Fine,"

Emily said. "Who was that man trailing behind you?"

Amy faking puzzlement, "What man?"

"The one we saw you with going around the church," Emily inquired.

"I don't recall any man. All I know, I have to be here early to assist Pastor with anything he is needing as part of my job, so I come early. I don't know, probably the maintenance man or janitor," Amy responded.

Emily continued, "Well, we saw someone one following you from a distance, as we were driving in. He had brown or black hair and Matt the maintenance man has blond hair."

Amy struggled, "I don't know, must be the janitor then. I don't know what he looks like and all I know is I get here early and my focus is what Pastor wants me to do. I get a salary. My job is never done." Amy turned the attention to herself on purpose.

Emily said, "Okay, well, I just was curious."

"Curiosity killed the cat," Amy thought. Emily was always fishing for information, but Amy, who was smart beyond her years, was not going to let her precious Bryan be the subject of gossip. Emily seemed satisfied with Amy's response, and she and her husband walked off.

Service began a little late, as the choir filed in and began to sing. Bryan, in the meantime, was frantically shuffling the slides to get the right one onto the screen. He could not find the right ones. Shaking his head, *"Oh heck! I will just put up what I know are my favorite songs about the blood!"* They sang about the Kingdom, but the blood slides went up on the screen. One after one, the lyrics about the blood where put up on the screen. The members of the congregation looked puzzled at Amy. Amy was shocked, and when no one was looking at her, she quickly went upstairs to the booth.

"Bryan, what's wrong?" The pastor came bounding up the stairs as well. He was already late. Pastor Mark said, "What's going on here? The slides on the screen were all wrong. Someone, with good intentions I am sure, told me this as I came in. I am so sorry I was late. I had an emergency I could not get out of. It was one of the members whose husband had a heart attack, so I had to be there at the hospital. I am very sorry I was not here to help set things in motion."

Bryan wrote, *"The slides are all disorganized, and they were all over the place when I came in, and not organized, so I had to put up what I knew to do; and tried to keep up!"*

Chapter 22

Bryan eyes had a crazed look of frustration, as Pastor comforted him, and Amy said, "Pastor, the slides were indeed everywhere, all over the counter here, and we think someone knocked them over and just picked them up and put them anywhere."

"It must have been the janitor because he cleans up here too. Are you okay Bryan? I never intended to frustrate you and I would like you to stay. We will get you a file bin, so they will be organized from A to Z, and I can reassure you this will not happen again. Again, I am sorry I was not here to help you get started today," Pastor said. Bryan extended his hand to shake…he understood why.

Pastor Mark shook it and said, "I have to figure a way out of this one. I mean, I was the one late, and I will do the explaining. No worries Bryan." Pastor smiled and walked out the door.

At service, Pastor Mark said, "I am sorry I was not here earlier. I had an emergency, I could not get out of. Amanda's husband, Scott is in the hospital and I needed to pray for them. We are still working out the bugs in the audio-visual room, so please be patient with us as we transition to the slides. Amy is helping me do that. I want to thank you all for being so patient," he tactfully explained without exposing Bryan. Amy was so happy that he was wise with his words.

After service, Bryan quickly went to the car and made sure he was not seen. Amy soon followed right at the end of service, and they quickly drove off. She always made sure they parked on the side of the church, to be able to get out early, and not been seen as they were leaving. "What an eventful day!" Amy said.

Bryan nodded in agreement. They drove off to get to their designated place by the beach. It was still cool, but warm enough yet, by the water. They both enjoyed a peaceful drive in Amy's convertible, and drove on until they reached their spot. Amy got out of the car and said, "Let's eat." They immediately set out to that spot where no one would be there to harass them. They laid the blanket down and unpacked their lunch from the cooler.

"*Did those people ask you about me? The ones you were telling me about?*" Bryan wrote.

"Yes, indeed they did, and I told them that I knew nothing in a nutshell." Bryan was puzzled. "I played dumb, like I did not know what they were referring to and explained that I am there early to help Pastor get stuff in order, and I am salary employee, so my job is never done. They seemed satisfied with that," Amy said.

He wrote on his tablet, he carried with him most of the time, "*Good, I am so glad you are my wife! I just want to love you all over again.*"

He grabbed her and began to touch her face and caress it. "Bryan, please not here. We are still in a public place. I want to, but can we do this tonight?"

"*I thought this place was secluded and no one was here?*" Bryan wrote.

Amy said, "Well it is, however, there are still rentals up that way, and people can still come this way to…shhh! I hear voices!" They were the voices of some teens and a mother and father. "Hide quick! They must not see you!"

Chapter 22

They both went to hide behind some large trees. The group came across their blanket and food. "Gee, I wonder who else is here too? Where did they go?" said the father, with his eyes scanning the area. They paused for the longest time.

"Well, maybe they went for a quick walk, and I am sure they will be back," said the mother. "Leave their stuff alone Brian…and you too Doug!" she shouted.

The family turned around the walked the other way. Bryan and Amy breathed a quick sigh of relief and went back to the blanket when they knew the family was far away. Amy and Bryan went back to finishing their lunch, then went hiking. As evening approached, they drove home. The sun was setting. It was the most beautiful fall sunset. Amy said, "Look, how beautiful! I wonder if that is what heaven looks like? How lovely!" Bryan treasured the moment as well. He had never taken the time to view such a beautiful sight. He had rarely seen sunsets. Most of his time was spent indoors, which is what he was used to. The sunset displayed every artistic color one could imagine. There were pinks, reds, greens, oranges, yellows, and purples, that faded into night as they drove home. Amy had never seen anything so beautiful. The sight of the sunset made Amy hum with thankfulness.

Bryan stared at her, and he loved her angelic hum, and her glow. He just could not take his eyes off of her. He waited till they got home and then he would plan and plot to make his move. As soon as they walked in, he swept her up and threw her over his shoulder and carried her upstairs, so they could be alone. He had waited all day, and it was building up. It was all he could take of his desire towards her. She was laughing hysterically with amazement as he carried her upstairs. She knew what was going to come, after he had carried her upstairs. The night was young, there would be plenty of hours ahead, as desire was met. Amy would be dragging herself to work again that Monday. But with her, that was okay. That was her Bryan, all would be well as long as she had her coffee.

Amy went to work that morning, tired, but very happy, because of the wonderful weekend she had with Bryan. "You look tired. Bryan must be keeping you up at night again," Mary said, with a sparkle in her eyes.

"Well," Amy said, "Let's just say it like this…Being married to Bryan is rather interesting." Both women laughed and went into their daily routines.

Throughout the weeks of Amy's dance practice, the practices were getting more and more demanding, as they were striving for more excellence, because they realized now, they would be on camera an different flags would be used. Now, crown and pillows were also being incorporated into the dances. Amy knew inside, somehow it would not be anything local, but would become national. She was feeling things were different at her church, and in the dance team she put together.

Weeks went by, and Bryan perfected his audio-visual skills. Which is good, because the services would soon be on TV Months went by, and calls started to come in and requests for Amy and her team to travel and come to different places for different events. They were day trips, but it was so hard for Bryan to see her go. "I have to go Bryan. I really do. This is what I do, and it's part of my job. These places pay for us to come." Bryan was very sad that she had to leave for the day. It would cause a problem, and Amy had to think of something soon, because she knew that one-day events would turn into more than one day. It would only be a day, but that day was like an eternity for him. She had never been gone before that long and he would be alone in the house. He motioned a gesture to please call me. "I sure will, to let you know we got there safely. Don't be sad Sweetie, I will return soon." So, he waited. After a few hours, she called as promised, and she

Chapter 22

knew he answered the phone by his heavy breathing. "Hello Bryan. I am here safe darling. I love you and will see you soon. Bye bye."

He loved the sound of her voice. He could not wait till things slowed down again, and he just wanted things to be back to normal again, and he was conflicted. "What if they don't? I will lose her forever, and I don't understand why we cannot go back to the way things were. I liked the little once in a while event." He sat there and turned on the TV and watched and waited for her. She finally did come home, and he took her in his arms again, and was so happy to see her home.

She was dreading another event two weeks from then, because of Bryan. He simply did not understand why she had to be on the road, when there was plenty to do locally. She knew this would be a change, and a time to grow in their marriage, and she needed to talk to someone.

"Pastor Mark, can I please talk to you?" Amy asked.

"Sure thing. Come in and sit down," Pastor Mark said.

"It's Bryan, he is really struggling with us being on the road. He does not understand why we are gone a lot. I fear it might cause a problem in our marriage. I don't know what to do," Amy replied.

"Well, can you ask him, would he feel comfortable coming with you as you do the events?" said Pastor Mark.

Amy said, "It's the mask. What will we even tell them, and would they know him from the past?"

Pastor Mark said, "I would not worry about that. He does have a scar on his face doesn't he?"

Amy responded, "Well, yes he does."

The pastor said, "I know he got it either from his dad beating him, or his injuries came from when he killed people and the fights with them, but I know it came from somewhere. That's it! You can tell them he wears it because of that!"

"That's a brilliant idea! Thank you so much Pastor Mark. But now the question is, will he even come?"

"We shall soon see. Hopefully he will. Don't you guys go in the church van?" asked Pastor Mark.

"Yes, we do," said Amy.

"Well, maybe you guys could drive separate."

"Pastor, your awesome!" Amy said.

"God's wisdom," said Pastor, as he pointed upwards to the ceiling.

The event and Amy's departure was getting closer, but she was having a hard time of how to communicate it to Bryan. So, She stalled until a few days before. Finally, it was time to break the news to him. "Bryan, I have something to tell you. Would you mind if I went out of town again the weekend of the 7th?"

Bryan viciously shook his head. "*No!*"

"Bryan, please I have to…I must go, and I was wondering if you would like to come with me."

Bryan grabbed the notebook and wrote, "*I don't want you to go, and I understand that they are paying for you to come. But what if something happens to you? I did not mind it being an event here or there, but now it's a few times a month. How is it that now you have all these engagements, and less time with me? I feel like I am losing you to this…whatever it is you do!*"

"Please Bryan, you don't understand. I…"

Bryan viciously slammed his hand down on the counter, shook his head and wrote, "*No! Please don't go! I want you to be with me! It's not fair to me! I miss you terribly when you are gone!*"

"Bryan please, you are being unreasonable. Why are you doing this? I thought we had an understanding…I would call you when I got there."

Chapter 22

Bryan continued and wrote, "*It's just I have enemies out there who still hate both of us, and we have been through so much together. It's my fault I brought all this in your life, when you did not need this. I am so afraid if something would happen to you I could not go on with my life alone. I must have you in my life! I don't want you to go.*"

Amy said, "Do you not trust God to bring me back safe? It's not like I am cheating on you! I have always been there for you, and supportive! The least you could do is support me in this new chapter of our lives, with my dance team!" Amy became angry and stormed out in tears. She went to her room and slammed the door and cried in her pillow. Bryan did not come up after her. He was very upset that she would even want to be away from him. He did not understand why she was leaving him. It was night time, so Bryan went out and took a very long walk, so he could cool off. But he was still careful that no one would see him. Amy had prayed and cried herself to sleep.

Bryan had been gone most of the night and into the morning and Amy had noticed he had not come home yet, and she had to go to work. "Bryan, Bryan? Where are you?" Amy searched the house and then she went to his house and yet nothing. "Oh no, not again!" She had no choice but to leave for work. She left early, without eating breakfast, and hopefully she would find him, when she searched for him around town, before work. There was no sign of him anywhere. "Where could he possibly be?" Amy was in tears from the argument, and now Bryan was gone again.

"Pastor Mark, I cannot find Bryan. We had an argument last night about me taking these trips to various events. He does not want me to take them, and now Bryan has been gone all night. I am so worried about him!" Amy burst into tears so that Mary heard it.

"Are you okay?" Mary asked, coming into the room.

"Please pray for Bryan. He has been missing all night."

Pastor Mark said, "Please close the door Mary. I need to speak with Amy." Mary closed the door and went back to work. "Okay, so he did not want to come with you on the trips?" Pastor Mark asked.

"No, he just jumped to the conclusions that I was cheating on him and thought something would happen to me while I was on the road. He did not want to listen, and he was also concerned about all of his enemies. Now my enemies. Because of everything we have been through, he was worried."

Pastor Mark said, "That is a reasonable cause for concern, but not reasonable enough to stop you from going to these events. Maybe I could talk to him."

"I don't know, he is obsessed with me being away from him for too long, and he was pretty upset," Amy said.

Pastor said, "Sometimes marriage in the first few years is like that, and trust is built. It does take time, so be patient with him. This is probably how he deals with things. Maybe he will have a change of heart…and I am sure he will be okay."

Amy said, "I sure hope so. Thanks Pastor." Amy excused herself and went back to work.

Bryan, in the meantime, was struggling with his own thoughts, as he made his way back home. *"How dare she leave me! I don't understand it at all, and I don't want her to be with no one else, or any other guys! She is priceless to me and I cannot lose her. Anything can happen when she is on the road. Why now?"* On and on the thoughts came. He went deep into the woods, and had to think, because he was so upset, and needed to cool down. He lost track of time. He finally fell asleep in the woods, where his makeshift shelter was, from a few years back, that he stayed in after the three men beat him.

As Amy was at work, he went back to his house and fixed himself something to eat. It was lunch time, and he figured he would watch TV and wondered what it would be like when

Chapter 22

she came home. Perhaps she would just go to her house and not bother to come looking for him. "*She was pretty upset,*" he reasoned within himself. He switched on the TV.

Chapter 23

"Each person has a God given destiny, and you only have one life to live. Before you were on this earth, God put eternity in your heart to live with a full purpose that can only be accomplished through the cross. Not everyone is called to the pulpit. Some are just called to the background, or to specific careers. Don't rob anyone of their destiny, or even rob yourself from your God given purpose. Some are janitors at the church or sound men. Every single human being has a purpose, because it is what you do for eternity that matters." Bryan was shocked, and he felt the person on TV was speaking directly to him. He broke down in tears.

He took his mask off and wiped his tear stained face. He realized how wrong he was at hurting Amy. He was unknowingly blocking her from her destiny by being selfish, and realized she was not just his, but she was special to God. He realized he could not stand in her way, because he knew at that instant, he had a purpose too. As he rubbed his hair he thought, "*Oh my gosh I was so wrong! I hurt this precious treasure and delicate flower so badly…will she forgive me? I have been so selfish thinking she was only mine, but she needs to share her gift with others, so all can see what a treasure she is. She will always be mine. I just did not see the bigger picture here!*"

Redemption Has No Limits

He wrote in his journal, "*Amy, I am so sorry. I did not realize I was being selfish. You do have a purpose and destiny. I am so sorry I fought you on this. I know you belong to God, and I was keeping you from your purpose and did not realize it. I was just afraid, and you're right, I did not trust you or myself. I have not had much to trust in growing up. I have had a lot of betrayal in my life. I am learning to trust. I ask that you would be patient with me as I grow to trust. I am sorry if I worried you by leaving last night. I am so very sorry, sorry, sorry!*" He then drew a sad face with tears pouring out of the eyes.

Amy came to her own house and fixed herself some dinner. She decided after dinner, she would go looking for him again afterwards. But she was tired, and needed to unwind from the workday, and the worry about him. She was cutting up some veggies and she felt the familiar stare and turned around. He was there with a tear stained masked face and held out his notepad.

She said, "Oh my gosh! Where have you been? I was worried sick about you. I was about to come looking for you!" He gestured for her to read his note. She read it and responded "Aww, sweetie, of course I forgive you! I am just so glad you are not hurt or worse!" He swept her up again and kissed her.

He wrote, "*Thank you so much for forgiving me. No human being has ever said they forgive me, and that means so much!*"

Amy said, "Bryan, I treasure our relationship and marriage, and we cannot let anything get in the way...if you are not wanting me to go, I won't."

Bryan gestured "*No!*" and wrote, "*That's not what I meant. I know you have to fulfill the call on your destiny. I watched someone speak of this on TV and it pierced my heart. I also realized I have a purpose too. I was being selfish by not letting you go. I just have to trust everything will be okay.*"

Amy said, "Really Bryan? Oh, thank you so much!!! Are you sure you don't want to go? You can, any time, and we can drive separate.

Chapter 23

"No, *you go ahead and enjoy yourself. I will be okay,*" Bryan wrote.

"Let's eat dinner. Are you hungry?" Amy said.

Bryan nodded "*Yes.*" So, they sat down to a nice taco salad.

Several years went by, Bryan and Amy got closer together, as their marriage deepened, an trust was built. Bryan eventually let go of most of his insecurities. But letting go of the past was not easy. The thoughts from his past still haunted him, it was always God, and Amy, that reassured him he was forgiven. He became a pro at the audio-visual job at the church. Filming productions, and many other special things, was his passion. He did it with excellence and he grew in his own faith, as Amy had.

Amy and her team would go on day trips to do productions, but there was a time coming when they would be away for more than one day. Bryan still struggled with that, but he knew he had to let her go.

"Are you okay Bryan?" Amy asked.

"*I am just having a hard time with you being gone now three days for this event coming up in Texas. I really miss you when you are gone. My love for you has not changed. Its actually deepened. Its just… so hard at night when I don't get to see you sleep in the bed,*" Bryan wrote.

Amy said, "What do you mean?"

Bryan realized he slipped, by accidentally telling her he watched her sleep. "*Well I…watch you sleep through the night because I still am standing guard over you, and I love your face, and it stirs me so much. I cannot get enough of you and your beautiful face. I have watched you, ever since I kidnapped you, through the night and I can't stop. You mean the world to me, and I would die all over again just for you. Just to protect you. You are such a rare treasure, and any guy would be happy to have you. But you will always be mine, always and forever. I know God is there, but I must guard you at all costs.*"

"Bryan, what do you mean? Are you saying…you have been watching me all this time at night, and through the night, hardly getting sleep for yourself?"

"*Yes, I have,*" wrote Bryan. Amy marveled, and she started to laugh hysterically.

"Oh my Gosh! Oh my gosh! All this time?" Amy commented.

Bryan hung his head in shame and nodded "*Yes.*"

"No, no Bryan, you don't ever, ever have to be ashamed of who you are. I just cannot believe you are so sweet and passionate for me! It tickles my heart so much, and I feel so loved and protected when I am with you. Just so you know that always. Don't ever be ashamed of your passion for me, my beloved. This is part of marriage and I know you have been so touched by God. This is who you really are, it's just your passions where misdirected at one point, and now they are in the right place. So, no…don't ever be ashamed. You can watch me anytime, as long as you can be up for Sunday morning service, she laughed lightly. When you get a chance, read the whole book of The Song of Solomon. It is a love story about a couple who can never get enough of each other." He nodded with a gleam in his eyes, as if to indicate he had read it.

Amy's egging him on to watch her was too much. That was all it took. Bryan swept her up in his arms and carried her upstairs, Amy laughing hysterically the whole time he carried her upstairs. Her laugh always stirred him even more, to have her as his own, and so they went upstairs for a time of intimacy. Amy wondered what it would be like after she was gone for three days. She may never come out of the bedroom. She thought about it and laughed inside herself. Bryan was just so passionate with her, and she wondered if other marriages were just like hers. They have had many ups and downs and challenges, but they hung on, and others now hardly bothered them or their homes anymore, they almost had a normal life.

Chapter 23

The kids and teens that once harassed them grew up and moved away to college or other cities, and all was quiet. Bryan had marveled at how far he had come, from living a useless life of darkness and terror, to almost becoming a part of society. He still liked being alone with his wife and did not like a lot of crowds, Amy was okay with that. The only other people he liked to be around, was her pastor and his wife. These were the only people that mattered to him, and they were the first ones that showed him love without judgment. These people were an example of what it was to be a Christian. Though they were imperfect, they did know how to love. That love and acceptance was what changed him for the better. Bryan would never forget that as long as he lived. He was very happy in his life now, and that happiness would carry him for the rest of his life. He knew he had come so far, and one day he would get the courage to go on the road with her, but right now, was not the time…yet.

"Okay, let's take our places," Amy said. "We must be ready for the Easter production, and we must do this with excellence. Remember we are being filmed for TV. Thank you all for coming and practicing in your garments you will wear that day. You all are beautiful. I needed to see how all this would play out. Each of you get a flag, and Sheila and Pam, you can get the bigger banners to carry down the aisle, because you are the veteran dancers here. The newer dancers can get the smaller ones. Okay, let's position and take it from the top." Amy turned the CD on and they ran through the song.

Unknown to Amy, during their practice, Bryan snuck upstairs to film them, as they practiced, on his cam-recorder, and the church's camera. Just in case one or the other film did not turn out, he had a back-up. Thankfully, the church's back door had been unlocked, and it was dark out. So, no one saw him go upstairs. He had walked to the church on foot. Earlier that day, as Amy was at work, Bryan saw a TV ad, advertising a talent show contest, for all talents. He made a plan to support and surprise Amy and her team, by planning to send the tapped performance to them and if they won, they would be on the next plane to Houston, Texas. The contest would be May 30th of that year. So, he had plenty of time to send the video in.

She had been so supportive of him, in all he did, and now he wanted repay the favor, by showing her how much he loved her, by doing this for her. He had still hoped to stay hidden from the rest of the congregation on Sundays, because he still wore his mask in public. Pastor did a very good job at hiding him away and honoring his request. But he still wondered for how long? The mask still gave him security, and he was ashamed of that scar down the side of his face, and the other scar on the other side of his head from the lobotomy. He still struggled at times with his dark past. Even though he felt forgiven, sometimes the past did not always let him go so easily, in his thoughts and in dreams. Yet, he trusted it would be well with him, as more time went on. He was now settled in his marriage, and in his mind. Yet, he was never tired of being with her, and each day was a new day for him, as the first time he met her. He still watched her at night, but now she knew that he did. He loved sneaking up on her and filming her, and she enjoyed who he was, as he stalked her.

Stalking her excited him now, and it was thrilling for both of them. They enjoyed the cat and mouse games they would play with each other. She would run away, grab her and kiss her. He knew now, how to grab her not so hard. He would always remind himself, that she was more delicate and much smaller than he was. She ran, but in some way, he always would catch up to her.

Sometimes, he would still slip into the old way of grabbing her…but he was learning. It was just his way. He never knew he could have this much fun and be able to love someone like this.

Chapter 23

"*Amy, can I talk to you?*" Bryan wrote.

"Sure thing, what is it?"

"*I just cannot believe how blessed I am! My life is normal, and I am so happy here with you, and my journey in faith. I don't hear the voices anymore, and I don't even have a desire to kill anyone. In all the years I was locked up and getting shock treatments and lobotomies, nothing helped. They made me worse. But you…and this journey I have been on, has truly changed me. Changed my heart, and my mind is completely different. I am amazed at how wonderful life really can be. I am just totally in awe, and I truly thank God for you! I do believe in love!*" Bryan wrote and held her close to his heart.

Amy said tenderly, "I thank God for you. You know, during the day before that night of the bonfire and hayride, I had made a comment to my co-worker Mary, and I remember it plain as day…

I wonder if I would meet Mr. Right tonight? She told me, I had plenty of time, and there were a lot of guys who were interested in me. But in the most unusual way, I met Mr. Right, and he is sitting right here with me! I am so grateful, and love you very much!" Bryan hugged her and held her close to his heart again and would not let go. He began to cry tears of joy.

"*I am so very sorry I scared you that night. I never meant to do that. I realize now, I was in love, but did not know how to deal with my intense feelings or understand any of it. Over time the extreme feelings that I called hate were actually love, in the most unique way. At the time, all I knew was hate. I am so glad this is how it worked out. It was somehow meant to be. Even through all my dark, twisted thinking, I gained salvation, a new chance at life and a treasure sitting in front of me,*" he wrote.

Amy said, "That was the time to put my faith to the test, to trust God and He brought me through. Now, I never want to be apart from you, ever! Even though I have to leave to go on these trips, you are with me always, in my heart. Eventually, I would love if you could come with me sometimes…but, I won't push you to do so." Bryan hung his head.

"Are you okay with me going on the three-day trip?"

Bryan reluctantly nodded yes. He knew he had to let her go.

"I promise I will call you." He knew she would.

Amy had been pondering if she should get all her financial affairs in order. Being she was married now. Just in case anything would ever happen to her. But, she did not know how to explain it to Bryan, about her wealth and of course, the will had to include both of them, just in case she would pass away first. She had not planned to tell him about her millions, but now she was faced with the struggle to tell him or not. At breakfast that day, she realized she had to, because he did not like secrets.

She knew and learned that from the incident with Laureen. However, at the time of her Grandmother's passing, she was not married and she knew inside that Bryan was not a deceitful, greedy, or materialistic kind of guy who would steal from her. So, she decided she would tell him everything because he may have to go down to the office to sign the will too. She chose Saturday as the day to tell him. She cooked up a five-course breakfast and made the morning special by making all his favorite dishes.

Amy was nervous because she did not know how Bryan would react, or if he would treat her any different if he knew she was wealthy. "Bryan, there is something I have to tell you. You know how you don't like me to hide anything from you?"

Bryan nodded *"Yes."*

"Well…what would you do or how would you react if I told you we never have to worry about money for the rest of our lives?" Bryan looked puzzled and cocked his head. "I did not know how to tell you, but my Grandmother, at the time of her passing, left a will. You know how we are married now.

Chapter 23

At the time I was not married and I made a promise to never tell anyone as she wanted and I wanted to honor her with that promise. But, now that I am married, I feel I must tell you about It…just in case anything would happen to me.

Bryan stared at her and nodded to go ahead.

Amy said, "I am going to be getting my financial affairs in order, and getting a will done and being we are married now, we may both have to sign it. I am not sure how to say this…or how you would treat me…but my Grandmother left 50 million to me as a trust, but only I can touch it. Bryan eyes widened in shock!

"*You mean to tell me I married a millionaire and you never told me? Okay, I get it now. How easily it was to pay for everything…the security systems, my hospital bill and all the gifts. Money never seemed to be a struggle for you. I have noticed you never stress about money or having to pay bills.*"

Amy said, "Are you upset with me? I was only honoring my grandmother, and I did not know how you would treat me once you knew about it."

Bryan wrote, "*No, not at all. I will never treat you any different. I know you are not very materialistic and live wisely. How then, do you avoid the temptation to do so? I mean, you could leave me at the drop of the hat and yet you…chose to love and stay with me? I cannot believe this! You stayed with me, knowing this, and you never left?! I love you and that will never change, for richer or for poorer, I am still committed to you, and I am so glad for you! I have never been materialistic, and I have not had much in my life. It does not matter to me, and money is fleeting to me. Just the fact you stayed with me, and I was the one who had nothing to offer you…and yet you stayed!?*"

Amy said, "That is so awesome! Thanks for understanding. I have always been frugal and still continue to do so. I get everything on sales and use coupons and as you know, I am not flashy. The only thing I really wanted was my convertible and I even bought that used.

I do like flowers and jewelry, but nothing is really meant to last. I will tell you though, we both may have to go down and sign that will." Bryan seemed okay with that. "By the way…" Amy snickered, "You did not give me much of a choice to leave you… remember?"

Bryan smiled and wrote, "*Indeed, I did not give you much of a choice and I am glad I did not.*" The next Friday they went and signed the will. If Amy passed away, Bryan would get everything and if they both passed away, the church would get everything. They had no children, and Amy did not want to leave it to her brother, who lived large and irresponsibly. So, the next best thing was the church. Amy felt the church could use it to better the community, help the poor even more, and fix up the aging building. She knew pastor would do what was right with it.

Pastor Mark and his wife had blessed her in more ways than one and was always there for her in times of all the crises she had gone through. So, she wanted to give all of it to him and his wife. "Okay, the will is drawn up," said Mr. Evens, the lawyer who did the will. They both signed their names on the line, and each one got a copy and left his office. Bryan proved in the next few weeks, and over time, his attitude did not change, or his love diminish for Amy. His heart was still the same towards her, and she could trust him to not do anything underhandedly. He knew he had to trust her, as she left for the three-day event and she called him more than once a day to make sure he was okay. Amy came back safely from her trip and Bryan was waiting to see her at the door. He scooped her up and hugged her tight. Amy was right about Bryan, as he loved her that night, and throughout the night. He so missed her, and he showed it in his actions of love. His passions never diminished since the honeymoon. It was just Bryan and who he was.

Chapter 23

That Monday while Amy was at work, Bryan put the tape of Amy and her dance team in the mail, and sent it in to the contest. He had been inadvertently collecting stamps, so that he had enough postage for the tape to get to where it needed to go and he had hoped she would win. It's the least he could do for her. "There, it's finished and ready to go," he thought, as he raised the bar on the mailbox to indicate to the mailman there was mail to pick up. He went back inside and read his devotional.

Bryan kept himself busy during the day watching TV, cooking and monitoring the houses through the camera security system. He thought, "This security system no longer seems to be needed anymore, but I will keep it running for Amy's sake." So, he messed with it, changing the colors, resolution, and lighting. "Maybe I really should go on some trips with Amy. It would make sense. I feel kind of lonely, and maybe she would need some company. It would be a good way to see the country, since I never did this growing up," he thought. He had noticed he seemed to be getting restless while at home and needed something more to do. That evening he needed to talk to her about this matter.

Bryan wrote, "*You know, I have been sitting here thinking. Yes, I would like to go with you on some of those trips, but can we drive separate, and as long as I can stay in the hotel room, I am willing to go. I have been getting restless here at home during the day, and never been anywhere else but in this town. I am just wondering, if on the road, some people may recognize me… you know, from my past?*"

Amy said, "I would not worry about that, and the past is the past. I absolutely would love if you came! It would be an honor! We have a two-day Friday into Saturday event in a few weeks and you are welcome!" She hugged him. Bryan gave her the thumbs up.

Amy broke the news to the dance team she would be traveling separate with her husband, and they can ride in the van by themselves.

"Why are you going separate?" asked one of the younger dancers. Sheila and Pam understood, but Amy knew the younger dancers would not.

Amy explained, "My hubby is disfigured and does not want people to see him. He wants to, however, come as my support…he wears a mask."

"Oh, okay," said one of the dancers, shrugging her shoulders. Amy had hoped that the other dancers would not see Bryan. She figured she could bring him in the hotel at the right time. They purposely left an hour before the van did, strategically, to avoid being seen by the other dancers. "Bryan, are you excited? Your first road trip and all."

Bryan nodded "*Yes.*"

"It will be fun!" said Amy.

Once at the hotel, Amy checked in and snuck Bryan in the back door, so he would not be seen by her team. Amy and Bryan settled in the room.

Bryan walked around and inspected everything, and he wanted to make sure he was not dreaming, because it was such a wonderful place and the beds were comfortable. This was a privilege he never had growing up. Amy found it almost amusing. About an hour passed, and Cathy, one of the younger dancers, was frantically pounding at the door. "What's wrong?" Amy said, forgetting about Bryan, who was sitting there in plain view as she opened the door.

"Rhoda sprained her ankle and I came to tell you that she… ahhhh!!!" Cathy widened her eyes in fear and terror. "Oh my gosh! Who, and what, is that??"

Amy said, "Wait! This is my husband Bryan. I am sorry you were not properly introduced. He wears a mask because he is disfigured on one side of his face, so please try to understand."

Cathy burst into laughter and said, "Really?"

"Cathy, I will talk to the team later, but now you must go back to your room."

Chapter 23

Amy shut the door as Bryan hung his head. "Bryan, I am so sorry. I did not expect she would come banging at the door and you were sitting there. Please forgive me. I will have a meeting with my team to explain some things right away. I am so sorry. Don't be ashamed. From now on, we will tell them anytime they have an issue with your mask, you are disfigured. Will that be okay?"

Bryan was encouraged and nodded "*Yes*."

Amy got her team together at a table in the lobby and said, "I called you girls together and I want to explain one thing. My husband's name is Bryan and he is really trying to come out of his shell. So, to be able to travel with us as we go on trips is a huge step for him. He wears a mask that some of you may find funny or frightening. Please do not laugh at him, should you see him, because he is very sensitive about this. He has come a long way in his faith. This is a very BIG step for him to venture out, so please try to be sensitive toward him and accept him as one of the group. He does not like to be seen, people often laugh at him or are scared of him; but if you all do see him, please consider being sensitive." They all nodded in agreement. "Now team, let's get ready for our event. Rhoda, how is your ankle?"

"I have it on ice," Rhoda replied.

"Good," said Amy.

"Hey…isn't he the one that committed those murders and kidnapped you a few years back?" said another dancer in her team.

"Yes, but he has truly changed and it's a very long story of how I ended up married to him. God forgives even him."

The young dancer said, "Yes, for sure He does." They all dispersed and got ready for the event that day.

Amy showered and dressed in her white chiffon and gold outfit, with her ballet slippers. She looked stunning, glowing, and angelic. Bryan simply could not keep his hands off of her. "Bryan…Bryan! We may have to wait until tonight. Remember, I have to be downstairs to perform in a half an hour."

Redemption Has No Limits

Bryan shrugged his shoulders and motioned okay.

"Tonight, I will be back, and we can continue…" she giggled and tweaked his masked nose. Bryan was stirred, but he would wait patiently, then it would be their time together.

He heard the music and opened the door when he saw no one was around. He wanted to see them dance. They were rooming on the second story, Amy and her team would perform in the wide-open area, where he would be able to see. There were rooms all the way around the square. The area was large and open for all to see them dance. The music was loud, and it echoed all around the lobby square. He loved the inspirational music. The crowd cheered them on, as they brought the flags in, and waved the banners. The sight of them doing this made his heart soar. It was so heavenly, and he still could not wait until she came back. She ordered carryout, because she knew Bryan would be hungry, and she also knew he was just hungry for her.

Once she came back, she was scarcely in the door, when Bryan had her in his arms. "I brought some carryout, and I have to hang my outfit up, because we have to dance again in the same clothes tomorrow and they can't get them wrinkled. Hold on sweetie," Amy said. Bryan could afford five minutes, but nothing more. Once she was done hanging her outfit, it was their time together.

Hours later, Amy said, "We have to do this all over again tomorrow at 11:00 a.m. and then head home. This is what we do." Bryan was okay with that and happy as long as he was with her. They both ate the carryout food she brought in from earlier. The performance was even better then yesterday as they checked out and headed home. They stopped and went to the drive -through for lunch. Amy wanted to make sure they would be home with enough time to get ready for Sunday's service.

Chapter 24

Once they arrived home Saturday evening, Amy checked the mail because they had been gone for the two days, and she was sure some miscellaneous bills had come in, or any other information about the will. She thumbed through the mail and came across a letter indicating, "You Won." Amy went to go throw it away and Bryan frantically gestured to her not to. "It's probably just some offer wanting us to spend something to get something," she said.

Bryan wrote, "*No! This is very important, and I really want you to read this. It is not what you think.*"

Amy said, "Okay, I will."

Amy opened the letter and read it. "Oh my God! You didn't! You did this??"

Bryan nodded "*Yes.*" He wrote, "*I did this because I want the best for you—to fulfill your dreams. They will pay for it all too. Just respond back of how many can come. It's the least I could do for you.*"

Amy said, "Thank you SOOO much! I don't know what to say. But I will have to talk to my team tomorrow after church!" She hugged him. "Bryan, this is excellent news, however, can you wait around after service? I will park in an area where they won't see you and then I will come to drive us home."

Bryan nodded, "*okay.*"

The next day they arrived at church a half hour earlier for the usual routine and Pastor Mark went over the songs he wanted to be put up on the screen. Bryan sat down and was positioned himself for his job and was ready to go. "You ready?" Pastor Mark said.

Bryan gave a thumbs up. *"Okay."*

Pastor said, "roll em." Bryan positioned the camera and started to film the service for the TV stations. Everything went well during the service and as Pastor Mark did the message. But Bryan was uneasy. He wondered how much longer Pastor Mark would keep him hidden and if it ever came out, would he be accepted?

He had been struggling with those thoughts for the last month, but never told Amy. His fears would be exposed that day as he tripped over a cord by the door, trying to make his way quickly out of the sound booth at the end of service. He fell all the way down the stairs with a loud crash! Amy had been distracted, talking to another couple, when everyone heard the noise and stopped to look to the back of the church. Thankfully, it was after the service when the cameras were off. Amy was absolutely horrified! She ran to him to see if he was okay and Bryan was exposed, mask on and all. He covered his face, but could not get up. He was laying there on his back physically hurt, embarrassed, and humiliated.

The whole crowd gasped with terror and fear, and Pastor Mark shouted "Wait! Wait!! PLEASE Hold up everyone! DON'T run away or go out of the building! There is something I must tell all of you before you all jump to conclusions! Please hear me out! Look, I have been working with Bryan for the last few years and helping him along in his journey. I never wanted to let anyone know, because Bryan was very afraid you all would not understand, judge him, and would be afraid of him. He has come a very long way, and everyone should accept him because he is our audio-visual sound man. He is here to stay. Please hear me out! Redemption is

Chapter 24

for everyone and there are no limits to what God can do. Will you all please forgive me for anything I have done by hiding him. I was only honoring his request, because he knew you may or may not all accept him. He wanted so much to be here. If it were Jesus, what do you think He would do with Bryan in this very situation? He is disfigured, so he wears the mask. So please, let's try to look past what he has done in his past and accept who he is now. Forgiveness is for all. We have all done bad things. Let us do and act in love here."

The crowd was convicted and began to relax. But they still did not know how to respond. They all stood in silence, speechlessly staring at Bryan as he slowly stood up, totally mortified and hung his head in shame.

He said within himself, "*You clumsy idiot! How did you not see the cord*?" But then to his surprise one by one, they extended hugs to Bryan, and he reluctantly hugged them back. They gathered around him and began to clap and cheer. They all patted him on the back. Pastor Mark knew there may be a few who would be offended and leave his church. That was okay, as long as Bryan would be lovingly accepted as one of the crowd. Pastor Mark did not care and was willing to risk it all, because that was God's heart towards all people.

Bryan was so relieved that he began to cry, and they all embraced him again as one of the them. That was what he wanted all along—to be loved and a part of the group. "Bryan, we love and appreciate all that you do. We want you to stay with us and you can continue to work the audio-visual booth, there is nothing to be afraid of. No one is going to laugh or make fun of you here," said Pastor Mark. Bryan grabbed Amy, held her tight, and kissed her. The crowd roared with applause, and everyone knew how much he loved his wife. Pastor was right. There were those few that left the church because they could not get over the "freak" in the sound booth being there. To them he was a "freak," but to Pastor Mark he was a soul that needed love and forgiveness.

It was perfectly okay with Pastor Mark. Those who chose to leave could go on their merry way if they did not like it. He was going to stand his ground this time. Those that left were more concerned with what people thought, than what God thought of Bryan.

Amy was overcome with joy, as it was such a relief that her pastor stuck up for Bryan. He was willing to risk his pastoral position for her husband and for that, she would always be appreciative of her church. Amy met with her team and told them about the contest, and soon they would be on the plane to go there in about a month.

While Amy met with her team, Pastor Mark said to Bryan, "Come upstairs—let's see what happened." They went upstairs and examined the cord. "Bryan, you sure did a number on the socket as you tripped over the cord," said Pastor Mark. The socket was torn from the wall with the cord intact and still plugged in it.

"Was this what caused you to fall?" asked the pastor.

Bryan nodded, "yes" and hung his head.

"It's fine," Pastor Mark said. "We can replace it…no big deal. Be encouraged. We will also put a rug over the area or tape the cord down." He patted Bryan on the shoulder. Pastor Mark was trying not to laugh, as indeed, it was funny. "Are you okay Bryan? Are you bruised?"

Bryan felt his back as if to indicate he was bruised and nodded "*Yes*."

"We can get you some ice. Can you move your back. What about your ribs?

Bryan nodded "*yes*." Pastor went downstairs to the church refrigerator and wrapped some ice in a towel and gave it to him. Bryan turned and put it on his back. He did not want anyone seeing his scarred back. He positioned his back away and against the chair from the others who were still there.

Back home, Amy examined his back and sure enough, it was bruised and was turning black and blue. She ran her

Chapter 24

finger tips over his white scarred back. "Does it hurt anywhere else?" she asked.

Bryan wrote, "*Just in the areas that are bruised, but I can still move my back. I don't think any of my ribs are cracked. You have to remember. I have been through much worse than this. So, I am one tough guy. No pun intended.*"

Amy smiled and chuckled and she rested the palms of her hands on his bruises for a moment and said, "Yes you are, and I am so glad nothing was broken, or your ribs cracked. So how do you also feel about what happened today at church?"

Bryan wrote, "*I am so happy! I can finally be a part of a group that is loving and accepting me for me and that means so much to me!*"

Amy said, "I am so glad you are too, and I am so happy for you! This is exciting! We can even go to fun things together, when they have events too and you now don't have to worry about hiding ever again!"

Bryan wrote, "*Yes and I cannot wait to be a part of the group. I am excited*!

Amy said, "I am excited for you to come."

"Bryan, are you sure you don't want to come to Houston with us?"

Bryan nodded "*no*" and wrote, "*I will catch it on the TV and watch from home. You know me…with crowds and everything. I will come with you on other events though, that are closer. Please call me when you get there. You know I love the sound of your voice.*"

"Okay, no problem," Amy said. "I will be glad to call you and always am." With that, Amy drove off to the airport.

Amy and her team arrived in Houston, she called him as she promised. They performed and won an award. All the local TV stations picked up the event. Amy knew this was the big time, as they had been working for months on some new songs. It paid off as Amy and her dance team flew home, and Amy was very happy Bryan had done this for her. She knew that Bryan and her, would need a vacation soon. So, when she got home, he swept her up as usual, in the hardy welcome, the Bryan way. He had a warm dinner prepared for her and they sat down. Then she told him all about how they won an award, and the events of the trip. She showed him the award. He was just so happy for her, but even more happy she was home to be with him.

Amy said, "I know I just got back and everything, but I have been thinking about a vacation. My vacation time is coming up and you and I have not gone anywhere by ourselves for a long time. So…what do you think of us spending a week at our favorite spot alone? I can rent a cabin by the water—you know, the one with a privacy fence that is totally enclosed? We will have it all to ourselves and it will be summer. What do you think?"

Bryan wrote, "*I would love that very much and I love that place!! It takes me back to our honeymoon and I want to go again to be there with you!*"

Amy said, "Okay, that settles it. We will do it. I will book the cabin for the second week in June. Hopefully, it's not booked already." Amy got on the phone, called and asked if it was available for that week. Sure enough, it was booked, however, the reservation desk told her the family who booked it had to cancel the plans at the last minute, due to an emergency. So, Amy booked it immediately. "Bryan, it is reserved for us. We got it!" Bryan got up, grabbed her, and whirled her around. He was so glad for them to be going somewhere as a couple. Amy could not wait, as the workdays slowly inched their way toward the time they could get away. She loved her job, but loved being with Bryan more.

"Bryan, you ready to hit the road?"

Bryan eagerly nodded *yes*.

"Let's get out of town!" said Amy, as they pulled out of the driveway. This time Bryan drove. He was driving them more often to church and back, now that everyone knew he was

Chapter 24

there. Amy said, "It will be so good to get back to our favorite place. I cannot wait to feel the sun and the water. Bryan, just a reminder, it is all secluded—so in other words, we will have our own personal beach, because the fence goes all the way out into the water. Bryan do you think you are going try to get outside? I know you prefer the indoors."

Bryan shrugged his shoulders, because he just did not know what he was going to do when having to face the outdoors. He still wondered if anyone would see him. Amy said, "Don't forget, we have to stop for groceries on the way there, so we can put the food in the fridge that is in the cabin." Bryan pulled into the local country store. Amy went in and bought hot dogs, hamburgers, and many other things they both liked for the trip.

They would be doing a lot of cooking out in the backyard, because the rental included a gas grill. Amy preferred a campfire, she thought everything tasted better over an open fire. Bryan knew how to make a good fire, easily, as she had seen him do many a times at home.

The sun was blistering hot, Amy quickly put everything away and headed to change into her aqua colored swimsuit. She was ready to go for a swim. She noticed she put on a little weight—it was a little tighter on her, and she thought, "I guess married life will do that to you. I better nip this in the bud before this extra weight gets out of control. Not till after vacation though," Amy said to herself. She was blessed with a good metabolism, but she did not want to take it for granted. The extra weight fell in all the right places, and it made her hips and legs a little fuller then before. She also knew she was getting a little older and sometimes those changes can take place. Bryan too, was putting on weight, but not too much. He had not aged much in his face since they met and was still gorgeous.

She wondered if Bryan would even come outside…or take his mask off. Only time would tell. The cabin was two stories high and Amy had to walk downstairs and go out the sliding doors to the backyard that led to the beach. The view over the water was breathtaking and invited her to come. Amy set up two chairs down by their own private beach and put some suntan lotion on. Amy did not worry about burning in the sun, but if Bryan went out in the sun, that may be a problem. He would probably fry in the sun. He was so white.

Amy stood up and gazed out over the water, and watched as sea birds flew by. Sail boats slowly inched their way across the lake. Her dark curls were waving in the breeze, as she pondered and took in the beauty. All of the sudden, she was grabbed from behind and held tight. "Ahhh! Bryan, you scared me! How long have you been standing there?" Amy giggled, as she was used to him stalking her.

He was not dressed for the beach, and had his mask and jumpsuit on, and it was very hot out. Bryan wrote in his pad, "I could not help myself! I just had to watch you on the beach for awhile before I made my move to grab you. Wow! This indeed, is the most beautiful view I have ever seen!"

Amy said, "Bryan, do you want to come in the water, and be on the beach? It is very hot out. I bought you some swimming trunks. Black, which is your favorite color. They are in the bathroom upstairs." Bryan hung his head. "What is it?" Amy said.

Bryan wrote, "*I have never been on a beach, or outside in the sun, and I am embarrassed. What if anyone sees me?*"

"Sweetheart," Amy gently said, "No one will see you at all. Remember?   It's enclosed and private." Bryan scanned the area with his eyes and nodded he would be right back.

"Don't forget your sunscreen," Amy said. However, Bryan was already gone. Amy hoped he heard her. He came back out in his black trunks. They were starkly black, against his milk-white skin, that was scarred with welts and marks of his past. His arms, stomach, and legs were thick with muscles that bulged sharply through his skin. His feet were perfectly shaped and flawless as he wrapped his arms around her and

Chapter 24

they enjoyed the day in the sun and water. They slow danced on the beach to Amy's portable radio. Bryan loved to slow dance and he held her close to his big form. Amy could spend all day in the sun and not burn, as the hours ticked away. He had removed his mask because it had gotten too hot for him to wear it.

Bryan, on the other hand, turned red. By sundown he was bright red and in pain from head to toe.

"Oh no!" Amy said. "What are we going to do? Did you use your sunscreen? Oh my! You must have not heard me when you went to get changed, and I bought some for you, knowing your skin type. Aww, sweetheart, I am so sorry you got burned so bad in the sun. I brought this Aloe Vera gel, and we will see if that helps you. Amy bit her tongue and was trying very hard not to laugh but felt so sorry for him.

Does this feel better?" Bryan nodded *yes*. He was somewhat jealous of Amy, of how she was able to brown so easily in the sun, and he ended up a lobster.

Bryan wrote, "*I don't get this. You go out in the sun and you just get darker and me on the other hand, end up red like a blood red lobster. How is that possible when I should tan like you?*"

Amy said, "Well, it's my culture. I am of a different ethnic background than you are. I am southern Italian and Sicilian. Some people just have whiter skin than others. I love you for you, and your skin and scars, which are a part of you. Please don't be ashamed of it." Bryan hugged her close.

The aloe vera gel made him feel better indeed—along with some aspirin he took. So, he made the fire so they could cook out, and was very careful the rest of the week, not to go out in the sun without his sunscreen. Amy knew he would badly peel, with a sunburn that bad, but as long as he felt better, she was happy. They could enjoy the rest of the week together. She was also glad he was given a chance to express himself freely there, out in the open, by the beach. On the last day of her vacation, she had marveled at how time flies, and how close they had become. It was six years, already into the marriage and Amy marveled at how quickly those years had flown by.

Amy pondered those thoughts and said, "Bryan, do you realize it has already been almost six years since we were married? It is so interesting how life is a mystery, and how quickly time flies. Life itself is so fleeting."

Bryan nodded and wrote. "*I know, it sure is, and I still love you since the day we met, and now that love has deepened. I hope for many more years together and for us to grow old together.*"

"Me too," Amy said, and laid her head on his chest and listened to his heart beat. To her every beat of his heart said I love you and she knew this as his love enveloped her over and over that night. They could never get enough of each other.

That Saturday evening, they arrived home, so Bryan could be ready for tomorrow's service. Amy and Bryan were both exhausted, so they went to bed early. Bryan, however, got up in the middle of the night and sat by the bed, watching her, as he had done many nights. She was once again, in a deep sleep. It was 4:30 a.m. and he figured he would stay up. He was wide awake. He had his usual 3-5 hours of sleep already. He went downstairs, as the morning dawned, to make coffee and breakfast for her. He got himself ready for his job.

Chapter 25

Bryan went to many more events in the months ahead with Amy and her dancers. They got used to having him around as one of the group. He would film their dances on the cam-recorder she had bought him a few Christmases ago. He did not know what he was going to do with the tapes, but he kept them for another time. He wasn't sure why, but he did it non-the-less. They were treasures to him of his beloved wife and her team.

He had gotten used to coming to all the church functions and it was so much fun for him to go. It kept him busy during the day. He liked to help out. They truly appreciated his help for all the things he did, and he was glad to help in whatever capacity they needed him to do so. Sometimes, it would be during the day when they would have the food and clothing giveaways. That was a special place in his heart for those people, because he had been there once. He recalled the time he was let out of prison and was grateful at how much his life had changed for the better. He wondered how many out there would be in the same situation he was once in. Some were still intimidated by his mask when he wore it at the events, but eventually, all came to know him as one of the group.

Redemption Has No Limits

Bryan and Amy's sixth wedding anniversary was coming up and they wanted to do something special, so they stayed in this time. It was going to be cold and rainy that night. Amy had a special dinner catered to her house and invited some guests over to celebrate with them. Sheila and Pam were the first to arrive, then Pastor Mark and his wife, they just had a wonderful time all together.

"Six years? Where does the time go?" Pastor Mark asked. Amy had been wondering that same thing herself. She was nearing 40 in a few years and so much has happened already, she thought to herself. The night ended quickly and soon Amy and Bryan would be alone. They spent the remainder of the evening together reminiscing about their years together. Amy pulled out an album of pictures she had taken of them over the years at their places alone together, and said, "Surprise! Here is six years of beauty, adventure and wonder!

You know Bryan, I really love being married to you!" Bryan looked at her with tenderness in his eyes through his mask. She noticed they started to wrinkle at the corners slightly, he was getting older as well.

He wrote, "*My life has been forever changed and I feel almost complete. You have been a wonderful help and for that I will forever be grateful to you, and I love you so much! This is the life I only dreamed about! Thank you so much for your unconditional love towards me.*" Bryan treasured the album and held it to his heart as if to say, "*Thank you.*"

Bryan gestured for her to look behind the couch.

"What is it?" Amy asked.

Bryan kept gesturing to her indicating to "Look behind there." Amy put her hand behind the couch and pulled out a gift. He then gestured for her to open it. She did, and it was a glass crystal dancer that looked like Amy with her olive complexion, forever planted in place on a mount under her feet. The dancer had one foot up in the air and was dressed in a sea green dress.

Chapter 25

"Oh, Bryan you should not have! I know this was not cheap!"

"Aww, I love it! Thank you so much! This is such a treasure! How did you get it?"

Bryan wrote, "*I went out when you were away on your trip and bought it. I drove myself, and I had been saving some money from my Social Security for a long time. I had it custom-made to look like you.*"

"How sweet! I will treasure this always! This means so much to me," and she kissed him. Amy put it in the glass cabinet she had with all her other treasures.

Soon it would be Christmas time again and Amy and her group would perform in the open square downtown. This time Bryan would accompany her to her event openly and publicly. He still wore his mask, but it was no longer a big deal or a threat to people, because they got used to seeing him out and about in this little town. He watched her in the crowd as they danced and performed the Christmas special.

After performing, Amy quickly put her coat on because it was already cold out and went to meet Bryan. Bryan just stood there with his arms open wide and embraced her. He was so happy to be out and about. The lights of the Christmas season decorated the town in full holiday spirit. Bryan and Amy decided they were going to take a walk. Amy said, "Let's take a walk Bryan." They grabbed some hot chocolate off from one of the stands and off they went for a long walk. Bryan marveled at how beautiful the lights were. He held her close to his side. Amy was thinking the same thing too. She wondered and said, "I wonder if heaven is like Christmas— all joyful and happy. From what I read, it is a very beautiful place where it's never night and no sadness anymore, or death, ever." Bryan intently listened to her.

He took out his pad and wrote, "*Is heaven really as beautiful as people say it is? I do remember watching something on TV about someone that died and came back. I used to think* once dead you are dead and that's it. Do you know anyone who ever came back from the dead? I was very close to dying many a times when I was shot at or stabbed, but never did. I would always came back, even though they thought I did die and wanted me to die."

Amy said, "Yes, in fact, I remember someone at my church had a heart attack, she flat lined and died. When she did, she said she instantly left her body and went through a tunnel. Before she knew it, her feet were on grass. She said it was the most vivid shade of green she had ever seen. She also said indescribable colors of flowers were everywhere along with streets of gold. The homes down here don't even compare to what is there. Everything was beautiful and flawless. She felt more alive there, than she was would be here. You see Bryan, it's your spirit that lives forever. The real you. She shared her story one Sunday, and it was amazing!"

Bryan wrote, *"Really? Will I go there too? I have done many terrible, bad things, as you know. I still struggle with them in my head. I still feel the shame from it. What about those I killed? Where are they at?"*

Amy said gently, "Do you remember what you did that night when you came in the church…you know, the night Tom shot you? You knelt down in front of the cross and were crying? At that moment, God washed all your sins away. He forgave you of everything you had ever done that was not right in His eyes. Yes, you are going to heaven. It takes God to change the heart of man, and for any one of us forgiveness is there—we just have to accept it. In you, the change has been real."

Bryan grabbed her and whirled her around, and quickly wrote, *"You mean it?"*

"Yes," Amy said, "it's the enemy who reminds and shames us of our past—we have to forgive ourselves too. Each person, while they are here on earth, has a chance to ask to be forgiven of their wrongs and God is always willing

Chapter 25

to forgive." He continued whirling her around in so much joy! "Ugggh, ribcage," Amy said. They both laughed. Bryan laughed a silent laugh that shook his large frame, and Amy was laughing hysterically. Bryan picked her up and carried her home. "Put me down Bryan, you silly man. Put me down!" she said teasingly. She knew he was too strong to resist. He did not put her down until they were upstairs in their bedroom for a night of love.

Almost every night, as Amy got home, they would spend a lot of time in the bedroom, growing closer in their marriage. The older age in Bryan did not affect him, it only enhanced him. He seemed to have more energy than ever before to do those things that men did. Amy marveled at this, as she was used to it, but what was it that drove him? She knew she was the world to him, and to be there in that place with her, was a little piece of heaven to him. A few nights a week together in intimacy, turned into almost every night. It did not seem normal, but soon it would be spring again. Amy thought maybe it was the winter…and being cooped up so much. It was a hard winter with a lot of snow, after all.

One night in late March, after Amy got home from work, she went to get the mail. "Hmm, what is this?" It was a letter that invited them for an interview from a television show out west, which would be a far-reaching broadcast to the nations. They were inviting her to come, to interview her about what she does in the dance. "Bryan, what do you think of this?" He gave the thumbs up to her and smiled.

So, she called them and told them she would. The interview was set for April 30th and they were paying for her to fly out west. Her dance events were getting well known, and now people were wanting to know more of her story. "Bryan, would you like to go with me on the plane?"

He gestured and wrote, "*No, I am not used to crowds and I've never flown before. You can go by yourself, and this will be a very big step in what you do. I am so happy for you!*" As soon as Bryan communicated that to her, he was beginning to feel uneasy, but he just shook it off like it was nothing.

In the weeks coming up, he began to feel more and more uneasy. He felt like perhaps, he needed to go with her. He had never been on a plane before, so he felt he must face his fears of being ridiculed or questioned. It would be well worth it. That night at dinner Bryan wrote, *"Amy, I think I need to go with you on this trip out west. I feel God wants me there for you. I must come with you. I really don't care…if they laugh at me, they laugh at me. Sometimes, we have to face things, even if it does not feel good. I just feel I need to be with you."*

"Wooow!" Amy said, "I am so proud of you. You have overcome a lot of things in your life and I am so proud of you for stepping out of your comfort zone." Bryan hugged her tightly.

The day arrived for them to board the plane, and they quickly fastened themselves in the seats. "Oh Bryan, I am so excited to go! This is our best life ever!" Bryan just smiled at her and ignored the stares of other people. He just kept his eyes on her the whole time they were in the air. Within a few hours they were at their destination. As the plane touched down, a limo was ready to take them to the television program.

The chauffeur said, "what is he doing here?"

Amy replied, "Sir, this is my husband who is disfigured and that is why he wears a mask, if you were wondering that."

"Oh, okay no problem. I will take you to the program," he said.

On the set, they made Amy's face up, for the television cameras, as Bryan waited outside. When she came out, Amy looked like a movie star. She was indeed beautiful and ravishing. Bryan was happy for her, but as usual, he just wanted to be back home with her, in their home town—doing the simple things in life, like snuggling and cuddling together by the fire. The flight would be early the next morning, and Bryan could not wait. He was done with all the publicity.

Chapter 25

"Okay Amy, we are ready to do the interview in 5,4,3,2,1," said the director. The questions started, like, how Amy got started in dance? What helped her get to where she was at today?

Amy said, "Hold on, I just want to announce that it was my precious husband, Bryan Conners, who has been such an encouragement to me, to pursue my dreams. I would like to honor him. He has not had much honor in his life."

Amy continued, "This is a story of God's transformation, and a walking miracle! Bryan, if you are okay with this, please come out of the shadows. The audience gasped with shock.

The host said, "Wait a minute, isn't that the serial killer from ten years back who wore that mask?"

Amy said, "Yes it is, and he has completely changed. Please honor and welcome him. He wears the mask due to a disfigurement on his face…and he is mute, so he communicates through writing notes." Amy stood up and walked with him out to the center stage, as the audience gasped again. "Besides God, this is the man who made it happen. He has become the most selfless, loving person I have ever met. Please don't judge him. He is a new person." The interview took much longer than expected. They had to break it into a 2-part series. During the interview Amy pondered if Bryan would ever actually talk to her outloud. She could not get the thought out of her head. She could not shake it. "I would do anything to hear his voice just once, but if he does not, I will still love him forever no matter what. I wonder if he has a very deep voice or a higher pitch voice." Amy thought to herself as she listened to the interviewer.

The interviewer asked, "Bryan, what is it that changed you from doing what you once did, into this?" Bryan drew a big heart with the words in big letters: GOD, LOVE, AND ACCEPTANCE on a piece of paper and showed it to the cameras. The audience was very moved by the interview on the set, and there was not a dry eye in that place, or in the nations it was broadcast to. At that instant, all knew what Bryan once was, and how much he had changed. Love had changed him. Bryan and Amy went to their hotel and settled in.

Bryan wrote, "*I want to thank you for honoring me. I have never been honored in my whole life. Initially, I was afraid to come out to the audience. I am moved by it very deeply.*" He started to cry.

Amy said, "You are so worth it! From here to eternity, I will forever be grateful for you!" They cried together and cherished the best life they were having that night…as they made love again and again throughout the evening.

"Hurry Bryan, we have to catch our plane!" Amy said. They got ready and they rushed to the waiting limo with their luggage, to whisk them off to the airport. They caught their plane in the nick of time. They sat in the seats and strapped themselves down. Pretty soon they were in the air. It was a beautiful spring day and the sun was coming up. The clouds were like thin wisps—almost like vapor. Amy marveled at how beautiful they were. She said, "Bryan, look at that beautiful sunrise and those beautiful clouds. They look like vapors, and I read somewhere in the Bible, where our lives are like a vapor—today here, gone tomorrow."

Bryan wrote, "*I just read that the other day in the devotional you gave me and it just kind of stuck with me. It was in James 4:14, "Whereas ye know not what shall be on the morrow. For what is your life? It is even a vapour, that appeareth for a little time, and then vanisheth away."* I could not forget about it."

A few hours later, while in the air, there was an explosion. One of the engines had caught fire. The pilot came on the air and said, "Fasten your seat belts. We are in for a rough ride. I will try my best to land this plane." He then cried, "Mayday! Mayday!" The plane started to quickly drop dangerously and took a nosedive. At 30,000 feet in the air, Bryan knew he would not get out of this one. He cheated death many of times, but this would be it. He grabbed Amy tight, and they held onto each other. The plane began to shake from the violent

Chapter 25

plummet. Bryan's lips began to tremble uncontrollably, Amy thought it was out of fear. But it was much more than fear. As he started to move his lips, to her amazement—*a sound came out*. Amy had never heard his voice before. She was shocked and said, "Di...Did you say something?"

"Yes, Amy...I want you to know, I will love you always, and forever," said Bryan in a deep, husky voice as he looked into her eyes. Amy wept. It was what she always wanted to hear from his lips. They embraced tightly. A giant fireball headed toward them…but never felt it, they were gone in an instant.

They spent their last moments gazing deeply into each other's eyes. They never let go—or took their gaze off each other. They exited this realm locked in an eternal embrace. Their ears and eyes were closed forever to this place, as their souls entered into an entirely new dimension…a place where it is never night, no poverty, no crime, nothing missing, nothing broken and all are healed. All things are made complete and all will never be separated by time or space. Death would never touch them again.

This heavenly dimension is what they had put their faith in and they were there together forever. They would forever be locked in an embrace of two souls for eternity. Now they were complete in heaven and in peace—no more pain, shame, suffering, tears, or sorrow.

The plane crashed near their hometown in a blazing heap in a field. The bodies that were left had to be identified by dental records. In going through the wreckage, the team made a chilling and unique discovery. In the midst of the wreckage, were two bodies locked in an eternal embrace. Fused together at the torso and chests and legs intertwined from the intense heat of the plane's explosion. Upon closer observation, they saw and realized, the fireball must have fused them both together in such a way, they were melted together as one. At first, the women rescuers began to cry, then even the grown men began to weep.

Chapter 26

Medical experts tried to separate them, but they decided it would be best to keep them fused together and bury them both in the same casket. They said, "It was nothing short of a miracle, they died in this manner and that says a lot about selfless love."

The nations mourned over the death. The were deemed a story of selfless love for each other, and some called it a "Romeo and Juliet," type of story, in the news stories. Both Bryan and Amy were honored as one, at their funeral. People came from far and near to honor them. The church was packed out and there was a long line that stretched for several miles, just to attend the service. It was broadcast at many major and minor network news stations. Everyone knew about Bryan's transformation, from a brutal heartless killer, to lover and beloved spouse. There would always be the critics of Bryan, but that did not matter anymore—he was in a much better place.

Their story and lives touched many across the globe. Amy and Bryan would never see that, here on this side of eternity, but it was recorded in heaven. How much they loved one another and how many lives were touched by their story. The funeral would be a closed casket. Bryan and Amy's pictures were displayed near the casket. The procession started and Pastor Mark began to speak. "Ladies and gentlemen, good afternoon. Never in my whole life have a I witnessed such lives of love and devotion to one another. They were married about seven precious years."

Pastor Mark started to cry as he spoke, "Bryan's life was a testimony to many out there, who are now sitting in jails, that there is a second chance for all of you listening to me here today. His story is a story of hope and restoration. You all know him as he was once—a major serial killer in this town. I saw with my own eyes. How he changed, as Amy loved him, and was devoted to him unconditionally, just as God did, in a state of complete forgiveness. I have never seen such a selfless, loving person as she was. Most people would have kicked him to the curb and not given him a chance. She loved him very much. He loved her so much, and I saw it in their eyes when we would go over to their house for many events. I watched Bryan come out of his shell slowly, but you all cannot forget the day he tripped over the cord, up in the sound booth."

The crowd laughed. "He brought me much joy, and It was such an honor to work with this broken man, who was slowly put back together by love. This goes to show you that redemption is without limits." Amy and Bryan, we all will love you forever! You are forever in our hearts and missed dearly. We also know, what our faith tells us, and that is you are in a glorious place called heaven."

Many came by the closed casket and said their goodbyes. They noticed the beautiful crystal dancer, that looked like Amy, and an album of pictures, on another table for display, of Bryan and her on all the trips they took. They also displayed all of Mile's love letters to Amy and how he communicated to her throughout their lives.

Their closest friends, Sheila, Pam, and Pastor Mark, planned the funeral. Sheila knew there was an extra key to get inside Amy's house, under the welcome mat. It was from Amy's house they took the items, along with Bryan

Chapter 26

cam-recorder, to use at the funeral. The videos of the team dancing, and Bryan films of her in their moments together at home, would show on the screen throughout the funeral. The tapes were taken and fused together as one. All the memories Amy and Bryan shared. So, they could be played in one continual flow. They wanted to honor Bryan through his passion for filming.

Amy's brother, Will, flew in from out west and broke down in tears. He collapsed before the casket and regretted he had not been closer to his only sister. He was soon comforted by Pastor Mark and encouraged. He began to realize what Amy had with Bryan, was very special and unique, after hearing their story of love. Will realized he had to make a change in his own life, instead of being too busy pursuing the American Dream of wealth and prosperity. He needed to establish a relationship with God, and start focusing his time and attention on the well being of others and not just the almighty dollar—because life was too short..

The casket was covered with roses and lilies…Amy's favorite flowers.

The passing of them both would be very hard for many, including Pam and Sheila, who were their dear friends. Pastor Mark would eventually train another person for the sound booth, but no one would ever run it as good as Bryan. He also had to decide who would carry Amy's legacy forward and eventually decided that Pam and Sheila would do it.

They were the most mature and faithful. They could train up other dancers to follow in Amy's footsteps, in dance and plays. They were ready to carry the torch forward in Amy's honor. The office would never be the same without Amy's smile and infectious bubbly personality. Mary cried at her desk, recalling the many goofy and lunch date conversations they had together. All she could look at now, was the empty desk where Amy once sat. It was very hard, but time would heal everyone…believers and unbelievers alike. They were so loved by many. People took comfort in their faith, knowing Bryan and Amy were together forever in heaven.

About a month later, Pastor Mark got a certified letter about Bryan's and Amy's will and it stated that everything that Amy and Bryan owned was his—including both houses and the fortune she left behind. He was overwhelmingly surprised, and it came to him right away, what to do with the houses. They would be turned into separate outreaches to help the community. Amy's house would be a dance studio, to hold dance, drama, and art classes. Sheila and Pam could train people of all ages. Bryan house would be turned into assisting and counseling people, recently released from jail, who had nowhere to go. The home would be a place of healing and hope for the broken lives of people, who would be at a place in their lives were Bryan once was.

Pastor Mark would run Bryan former home, with an assistant pastor who was young, but very humble and had the heart for people in jail who needed a fresh start. This young man reminded Pastor Mark of a young Amy, who had that same heart for others. In using their homes in this manner, Pastor Mark would to honor both of their legacies. Both homes would be a help to many up and coming artists in the community, and ex-inmates like Bryan, who just needed a fresh start. He knew there would be many Bryans coming through those doors, and he was ready to help. He would love each one unconditionally, as he had done to Bryan.

It was now early June. A few feet down from the crash site of the plane, two boys, Sid and Russel, were planning to do some hiking and riding around on their bikes. School was out and they were free to enjoy the pleasure summer brings. "Let's go!" Sid said, "I am ready for the day's adventure!" They packed sandwiches and off they went. Russel said, "Hey…I have an idea. Do you remember the place in the field where that plane went down a few months back?"

Chapter 26

"Yes!" said Sid, "I do!! In fact, it's right up the road a few miles. Do you want to go? That's where they found those two bodies fused together…cool! Let's go check it out! Maybe we can find some treasures, like rings and things left over!"

"I have my dad's metal detector!" said Russell.

"Well, let's hurry and get out there!" said Sid. They rode up to the crash site and got off their bikes. The ground was indeed burned black from where the plane crashed, but the new growth of grass was starting to fill in the area, as the boys scouted around, the metal detector did not pick up anything. The boys hiked near the crash site. Russell caught a glimpse of something and took off running to the edge of the woods. He saw something whitish that did not seem to fit in with the nature and shady trees around it. The object was white and under a larger rock.

Russell pulled it out. "Oh, cool, neato! Sid, look what I found!!" Sid caught up to him and was shocked.

Sid said, "Hey Russell, isn't that the mask of that serial killer that was all over the news, that turned from bad to good? I heard Mom talking about him about a five years ago or so. I was only five then, but I remember Mom saying something about it then."

Russell said, "I really think it is! Wow! We did find a treasure!"

Sid said, "Why don't we keep it as our little secret?"

"Deal!" said Russel, as they shook hands. Russell put the mask on and both boys grabbed their bikes and rode off… enjoying the summer day.

Epilogue and Disclaimer

This story is based on fictional characters, and is not affiliated with any franchise, films or stories, but some characters are an inspired from real life happening. The story holds its own as a unique, creative story, that is set to touch hearts and change lives. This is the story of love and redemption without limits and there are echoes of biblical contexts throughout the story. It is a reflection of God's heart towards the best and worst of us. That everyone has value and is worthy of another chance at life. This story relates to many people from different walks of lives, as the characters' lives are laid out without shame before the reader. This is a story of true, raw, unconditional love, that is relentless, passionate, possessive, jealous, transforming and is based on a love that will never die. The highest love in this world, is God's love for His people and the next is the intimate love in marriage, between two people. It also reflects an allegory of God's passionate heart, as each page is penned with passion, in a thriller-suspense allegory and eventually becomes a romantic thriller that reflects times of tension, tenderness, and humor. May this story be a tremendous blessing, to each of you as you read it.

Passages are from the King James Bible version.

Resource Page

To order additional copies of *"Redemption Has No Limits"* find out more about other life changing resources by Zoe Life Publishing visit our website at www.zoelifebooks.com.

If you have a story to tell, a devotionals is comforting, poems that inspire, a message to share or a God-given lesson to teach, call or e-mail Zoë Life Christian Communications' publisher, Sabrina Adams, and let us know, you may be just one step away from achieving your dream of becoming a successfully published author.

Zoë Life Christian Communications
P.O. Box 871066
Canton, MI 48187
(888) 400-4922
sabrina.adams@zoelifepub.com
www.zoelifebooks.com

Zoe Life Christian Communication